YOUR VOICE IS ALL I HEAR

LEAH SCHEIER

sourcebooks
fire

Published by Sourcebooks Fire, an imprint of Sourcebooks, Inc.
P.O. Box 4410, Naperville, Illinois 60567-4410
(630) 961-3900
Fax: (630) 961-2168
www.sourcebooks.com

Library of Congress Cataloging-in-Publication Data

Scheier, Leah.
  Your voice is all I hear / Leah Scheier.
    pages cm
  Summary: "When her only friend transfers to a different high school, April braces for the worst year of her life, until she meets a charismatic boy named Jonah, who is diagnosed with schizophrenia. When his health declines, April must make an impossible choice: stick with the boy she loves or let him go so they can both heal"-- Provided by publisher.
  (13 : alk. paper) [1. Friendship--Fiction. 2. Love--Fiction. 3. Self-acceptance--Fiction. 4. Schizophrenia--Fiction. 5. High schools--Fiction. 6. Schools--Fiction.] I. Title.
  PZ7.S34313Yo 2015
  [Fic]--dc23

2015009886

Printed and bound in the United States of America.
VP 10 9 8 7 6 5 4 3 2

To my parents

PROLOGUE

I KNOW MY WAY AROUND THE MENTAL HOSPITAL.

I doubt most of the girls in my neighborhood could claim that, even though many of us lived just a few minutes from its leafy, sterile grounds, and some of us picnicked on the lawn outside its gate during summer break.

By the end of tenth grade, I knew Shady Grove Hospital better than I knew my school. I knew that the security guard's name was Carla and that she'd worked at her depressing post since the place was built. I knew the quiet path behind the topiary garden where I could wait until visiting hours began and she let me in. I'd memorized the shape and color of his shadow behind the dark-red curtains, and I knew where I had to stand so he could see me from his eleventh-story window. From that distant spot, I could even guess how well the medicine was working for him that day; I could tell what kind of visit it would be by counting the paces of his shadow.

I had the place mapped out, his daily routine memorized, the doctors' names and call schedule, every pointless detail carefully recorded in his special little book. He'd given me those notes as if they were classified secrets, the papers wrapped in strips of hospital linen sealed together with bubble gum, long wads of partially chewed Wrigley's tied into a crisscrossed mesh. That tattered spiral notebook was crammed with data he'd gathered over months: patients' names and histories, nurses' phone numbers, the cleaning crew's shift hours. I would never know how these bits of information came together for him or how he even found them out. But somewhere in these random nothings, he'd put together a story for me, a clue of how to get to him, a coded message that, for some reason, he believed only I could read. I was the one he trusted, the only one who had not betrayed him. I was the one he loved, the only one who believed him, even when his own mother had locked him up and thrown away the key.

And now, nearly three months after they'd taken him away, I was finally ready. I was going to march up to the security window, look into the tired guard's blurry eyes, state my name and the name of the patient I was visiting, and hear the buzz and click of the locked gate sliding open. I was going to walk down the white-tiled hallway, knock on his doctor's office door, slam his secret notebook on her desk, and make her read it, make her understand what he was hiding, make her see what only I had seen.

I was finally going to do it.

I was going to betray him.

CHAPTER 1
SIX MONTHS EARLIER

I'D LOST THE HOMESCHOOLING ARGUMENT AGAIN. ALSO THE SCHOOL TRANSFER argument, the study abroad argument, and finally (in a pathetic, last-ditch effort that stank of desperation), the chronic fatigue syndrome argument.

The truth was that I hadn't really expected to win. I knew what my mother was going to say before she said it. Simplified, her points were: single parent, can't afford it; can't afford that; can't afford that either; you don't have that illness or any other, April, so stop being ridiculous and get your books ready for school and don't forget to set your alarm, please, good night.

"But I can't, I just *can't* go without Kristin," I wailed, unleashing my last and final weapon—honesty. *That has to get through to her*, I thought. She couldn't ignore her only daughter baring her soul. My mom was all about "sharing your emotions," "listening to your primal voice," and "nursing your inner baby"—or whatever. (She reads *a lot* of self-help books.) So maybe if I dumped a buttload of truth and suffering on her, she'd celebrate my personal growth, shed a couple of cleansing tears, and let me stay home. "Mom, *please*, you know how hard it's been for me to make friends at Fallstaff High," I pleaded. "I just can't go back there tomorrow; I need a little bit more time—"

I should have expected the next part, I guess. She'd just gotten through her latest favorite: *Face Your Fear* by some celebrity healer. What did I think was going to happen? Fast-forward half an hour, and we were still in the same position on the living room rug. I was tired. She was just getting started. Somewhere between "fighting back against the darkness" (*you've never been to Fallstaff High, have you, Mom?*) and "knotting the spiritual umbilical cord" (*knotting my spiritual what?*), I humbly admitted defeat. Or exhaustion. Same result.

Bottom line: I was going to start tenth grade tomorrow (Mom's words).

I was going to "connect with others" and "strengthen my inner immunity" (Mom again).

I was going to end up sitting alone at lunch, everyone was going to treat me like I had leprosy, and I was going to be miserable (me—obviously).

CHAPTER 2

IT'S NOT THAT THE OTHER SOPHOMORES AT FALLSTAFF HIGH WANTED ME dead or anything. There were no "I hate April Wesley" clubs that I knew of. I hadn't made any great embarrassing fails (boob-baring wardrobe malfunction, accidental pants-wetting, etc.) or offended the popular kids in any way. But if you mentioned my name, most of that crowd would have to think for a minute, and then they'd probably say, "Oh, yeah. She's in math class with me. Brown hair, right?"

But my relative invisibility hadn't bothered me before. I'd always relied on my best friend, Kristin, so I hadn't really needed them to notice me. Kris and I had been inseparable since the second grade. When I entered high school, Mom started worry-ing about my dependence on my only friend and kept encourag-ing me to "branch out" and meet new people. "What about Briana, your lab partner?" she asked. "Maybe she could come by for a movie sometime?"

So I tried, I really did. It's just that casual small talk somehow got harder and harder for me as I got older. It's not that I had nothing to say. It's that somewhere inside me lived a tiny nag-ging fear that no one really wanted to hear anything I had to say. And new people never gave me a chance to relax and be myself. So, in an effort to appear more natural, I began to jot conversation topics on my hand and rehearse clever jokes in front of the mirror.

Problem was, my reflection was always attentive and happy to see me. Briana, on the other hand, started to fidget before I opened my mouth. She didn't want to talk about English class. Or music. Or *The Big Bang Theory*. I finally gave up when I realized she was searching the hallway for an escape.

"Sorry, I'm really late," she said, glancing at her wrist. (She wasn't wearing a watch. And we were on our way to lunch.)

As she hurried away, I unclenched my fist and looked at the black smear across my palm. The words "Watch a movie together?" had washed away completely, and only the question mark was left.

It was pretty much the same story any time I tried to get to know somebody new. So to keep from torturing my classmates with my blurry banter, I chose not to bother them too much. And they didn't bother me.

But with Kristin by my side, I didn't really care. She was safe; she never gave me a bored or baffled look, and I never felt out of place when she was next to me. I had someone to eat lunch with, to watch movies with, to share secrets with. To be honest, they were mostly her secrets, because Kris always had drama in her life. But I loved listening to her stories, and she loved being listened to. She had accepted my plain, girl-next-door self the day we'd met, and I'd never stopped to wonder why she preferred to hang out with me when she could have easily slipped into the popular crowd with a single flip of her shiny hair. But that was my best friend—easygoing, charming, pretty-as-a-model Kristin, whose loyalty I never questioned until the morning after ninth grade finals when she dropped the bomb.

She was leaving Fallstaff High to attend a fancy private school.

To be fair, the school switch had not been her choice. But her father had recently been promoted at work, so he decided that public school was no longer good enough for his only girl, and their semidetached house on our street was no longer big enough for his family. Kristin was going to be a bus ride away from me instead of my next-door neighbor, and lunch was going to be the longest hour of the day.

I spent the summer banging out whiny chords on my keyboard, composing pages of depressing lyrics, and staring at the incoming tenth grade roster. There were three new students on the list: two girls and a boy. I scribbled down their names and did a little harmless Facebook stalking. Tessa Gilberts was going to be a "popular," I could see that right away. She was from LA, and there were about five hundred pictures of her in a bikini with her arms around blond dudes. She was pursing her lips and pushing out her boobs in all of the shots. I would have to roast my pale skin and torture my brown hair with bleach and lemons to get her look, and I still wouldn't make the cut.

Tori Nadle was an honor student at her old school, president of the debate and drama clubs, and an amateur dog trainer. It was possible that she was friend material, but I would have to find an amazing hidden talent in the next few weeks, or else take on the role of Supergirl's mediocre sidekick. That wasn't going to happen.

I was less interested in the boy, because the guys at Fallstaff High tended to hang out with each other, except when one of them hooked up with one of the popular girls (never me). The new boy's name was Jonah, and he had privacy-protected everything on his wall except his hometown (Boston) and his profile picture, which was a close-up of a cocker spaniel's snout. Nothing to be learned there.

So when the first day of school arrived, I wasn't exactly racing for the door. Naturally, I took more time than usual with my clothes, just in case this Jonah guy turned out to be super hot, but I didn't have very high hopes. Hot guys usually posted their selfies proudly on their profile page for everyone to see; he had put up a picture of a dog, which meant that he probably looked like one. I finally settled on the dark-green tee, which Kristin said brought out the hazel in my eyes, and medium hoop earrings, which made me look like I was trying but not too hard. It didn't matter what I wore or how much mousse weighed down my forest of hair though. Somehow I always wound up looking like the pale, fluffy-haired "before" picture in a makeover ad. Jonah would end up staring at Bikini Tessa, like everybody else.

Five minutes before my bus arrived, my cell phone rang.

"April-I-have-so-much-to-tell-you-I-don't-know-where-to-start!" Kristin's sentences were usually breathless run-on phrases.

"Seriously, have you even gotten to school yet?" I slung my bag over my shoulder and shouted a good-bye to my mom.

"Yeah, my father dropped me off. But, April, you won't believe how awesome this place is. I have to tell you—"

I sighed and balanced the phone against my ear, pulled the door shut behind me, and headed for the bus stop. As I trudged along, Kris chattered on about the clubs and programs at her new school—junior modeling, fashion design, filmmaking. I listened to her bubble happily for the entire bus ride and into homeroom period, when the teacher finally forced me to hang up.

I wasn't all that sorry when I told her I had to go. Her enthusiasm was beginning to grate on me. It was selfish, I know, but it would have been easier if she hadn't been so obviously thrilled by everyone and everything she saw. Three months ago when she first told me about the transfer, we'd shared some days of mutual crying, but her tears dried up when the packet from Fancy Private High arrived. I couldn't blame her, really. It's always easier to be the one who's leaving.

Homeroom period was a confused half hour, during which I (unofficially) met the two new girls. Tessa was everything I'd expected her to be. Cora, Fallstaff High's Miss Popular, took the new recruit under her wing immediately, and Tessa slid into her assistant princess role easily, as if she'd been trained for it. She had a list of phone numbers before the bell rang. Miles, the hottest guy in school, took one look at her and planted himself in a nearby seat, as if staking out his territory.

I stared at my books and tried to ignore the rabid flirting going on across the room. I'd promised myself that I wouldn't think about Miles anymore, despite my lengthy and completely hopeless crush on him. It was totally over between us. I'd ended it (in my head) the day after finals when I stumbled in on him making out with Cora in the girls' bathroom. That had been a really bad day for me. I'd found out that my best friend was switching schools and witnessed my imaginary boyfriend sucking face with Princess Cora on the same morning.

Okay, I'd known that they were going out. But you know how they say that a picture is worth a thousand words? Well, a sound is worth a million, and *that* sound will echo in my ears forever. I heard him *slurp*.

The second girl, Tori, didn't stay long enough for me to form an opinion of her. It was long enough for her though, because she hovered by the door for fifteen minutes with a condescending scowl on her face, like a bored visitor in a zoo, before finally stalking out. No one was sorry to see her go.

Homeroom ended, and the new boy didn't show. As we gathered our stuff, Michael, a tiny nerdy guy who I suspected was the only one in Fallstaff to have ever had a crush on me, sidled up and poked my elbow.

"April, have you heard the news?" he asked, grinning eagerly at me.

I shrugged my shoulders and pretended to be busy with my bag. Michael was always raking up bits of gossip for me. He liked to use his knowledge as an excuse to poke me.

"Ms. Lowry is coming back," he said. "I've heard she's teaching history again."

Okay, *this* was interesting. "Are you sure?" I asked him. "I thought she was still in the ICU."

Ms. Lowry scared us to death last year. Suddenly, without warning, she stopped mid sentence, hand still pointing to the board, and dropped like lead to the ground. It took us a few seconds to realize what was happening. Ms. Lowry was the kookiest teacher in the school, and her unusual lesson plans had sometimes gotten her into trouble. So for a moment, we all thought that she was acting out the fall of the Roman Empire. I'd never seen a seizure before, so I didn't understand what I was witnessing, but later, after the sirens died down and everyone stopped hyperventilating, we learned that Ms. Lowry had some rare heart problem that caused the seizure and that she'd almost died right there in front of us.

I loved Ms. Lowry's history class. She knew how to make wars and dates and dead kings interesting. She'd split the students up into aristocrats and peasants and then stage an uprising. She'd encourage half the class to fast all day, and then she'd make the hungry students watch their "wealthy" classmates eat. Then when we were really pissed and cranky, she'd help us plan the storming of the Bastille and the murder of our enemies.

She got into a bit of trouble for that. Some parents complained that she was encouraging violence and anorexia; she'd almost been suspended. But for us, that only made her that much cooler. So when she'd collapsed so suddenly in front of us, we couldn't believe it. Ms. Lowry was too awesome to get sick like that.

We visited her in the hospital, but she was in and out of the cardiac unit so many times that we'd given up hope that she'd ever stand in front of us again.

And now she was back.

"We have her next period," Michael said, peering over my shoulder and poking at the schedule in my hand. "This should be *very* interesting."

"Why?" I asked him. "She was making jokes even when she had all those tubes and wires sticking out all over her. She'll be the same old Lowry."

She was the same, I saw, as we filed into her classroom. A little thinner and a whole lot paler, but her hennaed hair still stuck out in red-and-purple spikes around her face, she was still draped in spotted scarves and beads, and she'd sneaked in a few more piercings than was strictly allowed. *Good for her*, I thought as I slid into my chair. The principal had probably been too nervous to comment on the onyx nose ring; better to let that slide than risk another heart attack.

Ms. Lowry scanned our faces and smiled at us as we squirmed uncomfortably in our seats. None of us would have admitted it, but I think we were all a little scared. She looked like a shadow of her former self. But when she spoke in that singsong, raspy voice of hers, I felt myself relax. She sounded the same as always, even if she looked a little bit like the undead.

"Most of you probably remember me," she began with a faint smirk, "as the one who pulled the Harry-Potter-meets-Voldemort spastic fit." She threw her head back and flailed her arms out in a mock convulsion. A couple of people moaned, and someone snickered nervously. I smiled to myself. Only Ms. Lowry would make fun of her own near-death experience. "Well, class, I'm happy to report that I've rejoined the land of the living. And after much thought, I've decided to turn my medical scare into a learning opportunity for you."

There was a unanimous groan.

"But you're a history teacher," Michael protested. "Wouldn't that be a biology lesson or something?"

She shook her head. "We're going to start off the year with a special assignment focusing on the history of medicine. Don't worry, the presentation won't be due until after spring break, so you'll all have plenty of time. I want each of you to choose an illness that's affected you or someone in your family. You don't have to go nuts researching neurotransmitters and muscle fibers, because, as Michael pointed out, this is not biology class. Instead, I want you to tell your fellow students the *story* of the disease, famous people who suffered from it, treatments throughout history—all the way to the current day. For example, did you know that during the Middle Ages, children who suffered from seizures were thought to be possessed by demons? The parents would call exorcists and sometimes beat or starve their kid to exorcise Satan from his soul? These are the kinds of details I want to hear from you. Sickness can be a story too, one that we can all learn from."

I stared blankly at Cora, who was furiously scribbling the assignment down in her floral binder. *What would she be writing about*, I wondered. Her miraculous nose job? "In the olden days, people suffered terribly from gigantic schnozzes…"

I raised my hand. "But, Ms. Lowry, my family's pretty healthy. What should I write about?"

She took out a dry-erase marker from her drawer.

"You've never had the flu? Did you know that over forty million people died of Spanish influenza in 1918? Or you can pick something more chronic if you want. Maybe someone in your family had diabetes, for example? Or migraines? Stomach ulcers?"

"Hemorrhoids?" Miles craned his head back and grinned at me. "Or crabs?"

God, what had I ever seen in him? "How about *mono*?" I hissed back. That shut him up briefly. He and Cora had been out for weeks with the "kissing" bug.

I couldn't help feeling a little proud of myself as I watched him sit back stiffly and cross his arms. Over the last year, I'd barely said two words to him—and now I'd managed three. No notes on my hand, no preparation—and I'd even been a bit clever too.

"Too bad they haven't found a cure for ugly," I heard him mutter. "Easy A for you right there."

So much for personal progress, I thought and slumped back in my chair. At least when I kept my mouth shut, I didn't get hurt.

I scrawled out "watch TV medical drama" in my notebook and flipped the page. I didn't want to write about the common cold or pinkeye, and my mom's irritable bowels were not a subject for class discussion.

Ms. Lowry finished writing down suggestions on the board and started to hand out the semester's syllabus packets when the door creaked open and a student entered, pushing a heavy bag of books in front of him. He looked at the board and then turned doubtfully to the teacher. "Is this tenth grade history?" he asked, edging back in the direction of the exit.

Ms. Lowry smiled and reached out her hand. "That's right. And you are?"

He shook her hand awkwardly and hoisted his bag over his shoulder. "I'm Jonah."

She glanced at the class roster on her desk. "Jonah Golden, right? You're new at Fallstaff?"

He looked embarrassed. "Yeah, sorry I'm late—there are no signs on any of the doors here."

"It's fine, Jonah. Why don't you take a seat, and one of your classmates will catch you up."

He turned toward us, and for the first time, I got a good look at him. He was tall and thin but not clumsy or gawky like most teenage boys. His cheekbones were high, black curls framed his face, and thick dark brows arched over large, blue-gray eyes. He was cute, I decided, even though he wasn't magazine-cover gorgeous or football-jock ripped. Still, there was something about him, something that held the entire class's attention as he calmly scanned our faces. We were all judging him, of course, and he knew it. The girls were trying to decide if he was boyfriend material; the guys were sizing up the competition. I held my breath as Jonah's eyes flickered over the quiet class. There were three empty chairs in the room: one in front of me (Kristin's old seat), one behind Cora (Miles sat there until they broke up), and one in the corner in the back (the class slacker used to sit there, but he was repeating ninth grade).

Please, I prayed. *Please, don't sit behind Cora.*

Jonah could have been a total jerk, and I knew that I might regret my prayer later—but I saw Cora sit up and swish her blond hair forward, as if waving him into place behind her. Every guy who sat there last year had fallen for her, and just this once, I wanted her to lose, even if I didn't benefit from her failure. The war would be lost the moment I opened my mouth to speak to him and "ummmmm…ugggggg…uhhhhhh" came out. But I wanted to win the first battle at least. Even if I knew my victory wouldn't last.

I think my feelings must have been written all over my face, because Jonah met my eyes and smiled suddenly, gripped his bag strap, and stepped over to the seat in front of me. As he slid into the chair, I caught a glimpse of Cora's shocked expression, and I turned my face quickly so she wouldn't see the triumph in my eyes.

It was like that awful moment in gym class, when the captains are picking out their teams. You're thinking "Not last, please…" and suddenly you hear your name called—as you try to hide that pathetic exhale of relief. Well, I think I must have exhaled pretty loudly, because no sooner had Jonah settled in his seat than he twisted around to face me. I saw the flash of a grin. "It's okay," he whispered. "You can let the pen go now."

I looked down at my fingers and saw that I was clutching my pen cap with both hands so tightly that my nails had gone white. I relaxed my grip, the pen clattered to the desk, and he turned back to face the front again. His shoulders quivered for a minute, and he put one palm across his lips to hide his smile. *Damn it.* I'd managed to look idiotic, and I hadn't even opened my mouth.

Ms. Lowry began to talk about some topic that obviously excited her, the Irish potato famine or Chinese dictators or something, but I was finding it very difficult to concentrate. *I don't care what Jonah thinks*, I told myself. I'd barely even met him. He had no right to laugh at me! He could go sit anywhere he liked. I wasn't going to think about it anymore.

And then suddenly, without warning, he turned around again.

"I was wondering," he asked me, in a hushed voice, "do you like this school?"

His expression was calm and serious; he was definitely not teasing anymore. But the question was so strange and unexpected. He didn't even know my name. Why was he asking me how I felt about Fallstaff?

"It's not my favorite place, exactly," I replied cautiously. "I've thought of transferring."

He seemed to consider that for a moment, then leaned a little closer. "Where to?"

Uh oh. I hadn't expected a follow-up question. How was I supposed to answer that? I had no idea; I'd never really looked into it. "Uhh…well, I don't know," I admitted after an awkward pause. "Where else would I go? Ballet school?" The last bit was meant to be a joke, but he didn't return my smile and quickly turned away to face the board.

I bit my lip in frustration. Damn damn *damn it.* Why hadn't I just made something up? I could have said Fancy Private High, for example. How would he know that I couldn't afford it? Or—even better—*I was considering a tiny rustic school near a village in Tuscany, Jonah. It would give me a chance to brush up on my Italian and learn how to ferment grapes and churn exotic butter.*

Even a silly answer would have been better than "Uhh… well, I don't know." Now he'd think of me as the dim, pen-squeezing girl. He'd chosen to sit in front of me, dooming himself to constant puffs of stink from Smelly Todd in the front row, when he could have been enjoying raspberry-scented lip gloss and swishes of blond hair from the prettiest sophomore in school.

The rest of history was probably very educational, but I basically studied the back of Jonah's head. He didn't turn around again but spent the period busily scribbling in his spiral notebook.

When the bell rang, Cora jumped from her seat and strode purposefully over to Jonah's desk. She was wearing an emerald sleeveless dress that curved along her body in a perfect *S*. Her hips swayed back and forth as she came forward, her yellow hair floating over her shoulders like a shiny scarf. I watched her, fascinated. She was so comfortable in her own skin. I wished I had that power; she walked as if she expected people to stop and stare. It didn't matter what she said. People like Cora didn't have to be interesting.

Jonah stopped gathering his papers as she slid one green butt cheek onto the corner of his desk.

"You know," she said, pouting sweetly, "they have to fix that chair. We can switch it with another if you want."

He gave her a confused look. "Sorry, what?"

Cora hesitated for a minute; a shade of doubt tugged at her smile, but she soldiered bravely on.

"The chair behind me. The legs are crooked." She sighed and threw a pitying look in my direction. "It's okay, Jonas. You can always move tomorrow."

Most of the students had already filed out, but I didn't move. I saw the flicker of indecision in his eyes, a timid smile, and suddenly I couldn't look away. Cora was trying too hard, but it was hard to blame her. He was really attractive, in a quiet, simple way, and there was something fascinating about the constant shift of color in his cheeks. They were flaming scarlet now. "It's *Jonah*," he said slowly. "And you are?"

"Cora," she responded, ignoring his correction. "If you want, I can show you to your next class." She glanced over her shoulder at me. "So you don't lose your way again."

Jonah zipped up his bag. "Thanks, Cora, you seem *very* nice but—"

She was practically purring, even though his tone had been clearly sarcastic. He inhaled sharply, like a swimmer about to take a dive, and turned back to her. "The truth is, Cora, I sat here because I wanted to," he said, waving a hand in my direction. "I think she's pretty."

Well, okay then.

WHAT?

The same thought seemed to be screaming through Cora's head, because her skin tone suddenly matched her dress. But Jonah hadn't said the words maliciously, jokingly, or even thoughtfully. He'd simply said them as if pointing out the obvious.

I had no idea how to react. It was so awesome—and yet so very strange! He was the new kid in school, and he'd just blown off the princess and complimented the "before" girl. In front of witnesses too! Nobody seemed to know how to respond. Tessa kept opening her mouth and shutting it again, and Smelly Todd looked strangely gleeful.

Jonah didn't wait for a response. He glanced briefly at his watch then at the schedule in his hand, slung his bag over his shoulder, and left the room.

CHAPTER 3

I WAS GOING TO BE LATE TO MATH CLASS BECAUSE I'D FORGOTTEN WHAT I looked like. I'd eventually have to make up a believable excuse, but it would be a while before I tore myself away from the bathroom mirror.

The face that stared back at me was familiar, yet for the first time, I had trouble recognizing it. I studied my thin, V-shaped eyebrows, small nose, and pointy chin. Not perfect, but at least symmetrical. Pale skin with freckles instead of a tan, hazel eyes, which sometimes looked green. Decent smile, if I was careful not to show too many teeth. I was slim, with slight curves, but nothing like Cora's perfect hourglass.

It was my hair that generally ruined the picture. I groaned inwardly and ran wet fingers through the uneven coils. Most days, I'd gather up the mass of brown and twist it into a bun or braid, but that morning, I'd loaded it with gel and let it hang loose over my shoulders. Big mistake. The problem was that it didn't hang, or flow, like good hair. Instead, it rose and tried to take flight, slowly expanding and swelling upward until it appeared to be taking over the world.

I sprinkled more water into the frizz and twisted the strands hard around my fingers. Better, a little better, but not much. I still looked like the "before" girl. I wasn't sure what part of me Jonah thought was pretty, but I really wasn't seeing it. Maybe he'd just felt bad for me and wanted to put Cora in her place.

I frowned into the mirror, grabbed my schoolbag, and pushed the bathroom door open. There was a little shout on the other side.

"Sorry!" I called out as I rushed to catch the handle of the swinging door.

"It's not just the blondes in this school. Even the doors are vicious." It was Jonah, of course. Just my luck.

"I'm sorry," I told him, "I didn't think there would be anyone in the hall—"

"No, it's fine. I'm supposed to be in class now, but I'm actually lost again. I've been wandering the halls hoping someone would take pity on me."

He was grinning at me, and I noticed for the first time how blue his eyes were and that his brows tilted up when he smiled, as if his grin had caught him by surprise.

"I'm also late," I explained. "I was just in the bathroom because—" I stopped in the middle of my excuse and realized, to my horror, that there was really no way to finish that. What was I going to say? *The truth is, Jonah, I was staring at myself in the mirror and wondering how you could possibly find me attractive.*

I should have let it go and moved on. But I was suddenly and unreasonably preoccupied with finishing my sentence. Even if it meant making a complete fool of myself. What had I been doing in the bathroom? Well—

"Stomach trouble," I blurted out. "I ate a bad burrito."

Oh God. *What the hell was wrong with me?*

Jonah blinked once; his smile faded, and his eyebrows descended. A little bubble of panic began to rise up in my throat. This had to be the worst of awkward silences. Was that really the first thing that I'd told him about myself? Indigestion? I opened my mouth to speak, but nothing came out; my mind was racing, grasping blindly for some way to take my last words back. But what was I supposed to say? *Oh, come on, Jonah, everyone at Fallstaff High introduces themselves that way!*

He was staring at me quietly, the faintest hint of laughter in his eyes. Then his lips twitched. "Thank you so much for telling me about it," he murmured with mock gravity. "I feel very close to you now."

I felt the color rising to my cheeks. He was obviously teasing me, and I really couldn't blame him. This was some kind of a personal record for me; I'd managed to strike out in less than one minute flat.

"I have to go—" I began. But even that harmless statement sounded weird now, considering what had just happened. "—to class," I finished miserably. "Just to class. I have to go to class, not to the—" Oh God. *Please just kill me now.*

He started shuffling through his bag as I sputtered to a stop. "It looks like I have math now," he said, pulling out his schedule and smoothing it out against the wall. "Do you have any idea where that would be?"

Did I know where math was? I took a deep breath and felt myself relax a little. An easy question. *Come on, April, you can do this.*

"It depends—which teacher do you have?"

"Roberts."

I glanced down at my own schedule and groaned inwardly. Same period, same teacher. A floor away. A two-minute walk at least.

"You're in my class," I told him. "It's downstairs. Come with me. I'll show you." Somehow my breathing had slowed a little; my heart was no longer drumming in my ears. "I'm April Wesley," I said as we headed down the stairs.

"Jonah. Nice to meet you."

"So, did you just move to Baltimore?" *Good job, April. This is how normal people introduce themselves.*

"Yeah, just a few weeks ago."

"You're from Boston?"

"Uh, yeah, actually. Wait, how did you—?"

Oh. *Oh crap!*

I realized my mistake as the words came out of my mouth. I wasn't supposed to know that. Now he'd guess that I'd tried to Facebook stalk him. How much more pathetic could I be? Who looks up classmates before they meet them? Bad Burrito Stalker Girl, that's who.

I had to say something clever quickly—anything, to distract him…

"April, did you…did you look me up?"

Too late.

Oh well, I thought. I might as well own up to it. Embrace the weirdness and tell the truth. It was over anyway. We were almost at the classroom door.

"Well, no, not just you. I looked up all the new kids," I admitted, my voice quavering a little. "My best friend switched schools this year, and I really didn't want to come back here without her."

It wasn't much of an explanation, but it was the best I could come up with. Besides, it didn't really matter what I said. All he had to do now was push the door open, step into the classroom, and pick a chair somewhere far away from me.

Why wasn't he moving then? Why was he looking at me like that? There was a strange flicker of a smile in his eyes, but his face was sober, quiet. One hand was on the doorknob, and the other played with his bag strap.

"You're missing your best friend," he said finally. It was more of a statement than a question.

I nodded. "Attached at the hip since second grade," I replied, mimicking Kristin's expression, then paused, suddenly self-conscious again. Why had I just told him that? Why would he care?

His eyes were still on me, but they were darker now, and the laughter in them had drained away. "Two friends against the world," he murmured, almost inaudibly.

"Something like that." I smiled. "I've got nothing against the world or anything. But things were perfect when it was just the two of us. We didn't need anybody else."

He nodded. "I know exactly what you mean." And with a quick shove, he pushed the classroom door open.

CHAPTER 4

JONAH DIDN'T PICK A SEAT FAR AWAY FROM ME. IN FACT, HE SAT DOWN right next to me. Of course, by the time we got to class, there were only three seats left—two empty ones by the door and one by the opposite wall near the window. So he hadn't felt the need to sprint the length of the room to get away from me. That was something. I thought the occasion deserved a text to Kris.

Cute new guy sitting next to me in math. Details to follow.

My phone flashed. FLIRT WITH HIM

Easy for her to say. That was Kris's default mode when talking to guys.

I glanced over at Jonah and saw that he was scribbling in a thick spiral notebook. It was hard to see past his arm and hunched shoulders, but from what I could make out, the cramped writing didn't have anything to do with the subject on the board. In fact, it didn't look like math at all. I looked up at the teacher and then back at the crowded margins of Jonah's notes. What on earth was he writing? Today's lesson was just an introductory review of last year's material. Most of us were barely paying attention. But Jonah was working with the concentration of a student at a killer final exam. He appeared to be completely oblivious to the fact that I was staring at him; even as the class bell rang, he didn't change position. Only when I reached out and nudged him on the shoulder did he finally spring up as if I'd startled him awake. His hand came swiftly down over the notebook.

"What were you doing back there?" I asked him as we filed out the door. "You seemed really wrapped up in your schoolwork."

He looked confused for a moment; his bright eyes, distracted, shifted quickly between my perplexed face and the notebook clutched firmly to his chest. "It's just something I've been working on," he said in a low voice. "A project."

"Oh, like independent study?"

"Something like that."

I was hoping he'd elaborate, but his phone buzzed in his pocket before he had a chance to explain. Then my cell vibrated while he was answering his text.

Well, how did the flirting go?

I looked up from Kris's message to find that Jonah had disappeared. Not sure, I wrote. Does talking about indigestion count?

Her response was very prompt: Please tell me you're joking.

And then five minutes later: OMG, you weren't joking, were you? Sorry. Maybe you should try again at lunch?

I sighed and slipped my phone back into my pocket.

I wasn't looking forward to next period. With my best friend by my side, lunch hour had been easy and simple. Kris had friends in most of the cliques and I'd gotten used to slipping in beside her, unnoticed. But with Kris gone, I had no idea if I'd be welcome anywhere.

As the hour ticked by, I glanced anxiously from my Spanish teacher to the clock. Could I sit next to Jonah at his table? Would he think I was being too bold? He wasn't in my Spanish class, so maybe he'd made a bunch of friends during the last period—and maybe those kids wouldn't want me to sit with them.

If Kris had been there, she'd have rolled her eyes and pushed me toward him. Or better yet, walked up to him and declared, "My friend there thinks you're hot. You want to ask her out?"

I was overthinking the whole situation, and I knew it, but I didn't want to ruin our chances at a friendship by acting like I assumed that Jonah and I were friends. So it was a bit of a relief when Jonah stopped me on the way into the cafeteria and asked me where I was sitting.

"I don't know yet," I answered cautiously, "Where did you want to sit?"

He shrugged. "Don't care. Just far away from those two." He pointed at Cora and Tessa, who'd arranged themselves in the center of the sophomores' table. "Is it okay if I sit with you?"

"Yeah, no problem! Of course!" My voice echoed through the hall.

Wow. Too loud and very eager. I had to tone it down. "Sure. I mean, you know, if you want, whatever."

Perfect.

He went off to get a tray, and I used the opportunity to update Kris. (It wasn't as if I felt the need to compulsively text her every time I burped or anything. There was just something calming and encouraging about her replies as I was trying to start this new friendship. It was like she was cheering me on.)

Cute guy sitting next to me at lunch, I typed.

Well, great, came her reply. THEN WHY ARE YOU TEXTING ME?

Fair point. Still, it was better than scribbling conversation notes on my hand. I was making progress, and it was only the first day. As I tore open my crumpled lunch bag, Jonah returned, carrying his tray, and slipped onto the bench across from me. His plate was piled high with noodles and meatballs, and somehow he'd scored two extra slices of cake. "Do you want some of my food?" he asked me, glancing at my Melba toast and probiotic yogurt. My mom had packed me a weird lunch again. She has a thing against normal food.

"Oh, no," I told him. "This is supposed to be good for me."

He wrinkled his nose and twisted his fork into his pasta mountain. "Stomach still bothering you a bit?"

I felt my face grow hot. Oh, for the love of God. We were *not* going back to that topic. "No, all better now, thanks," I muttered into my toast.

His lips curled down a little at the edges, and his dark brows came together. "So, I've been wondering about what you told me earlier." He tapped one finger slowly on his cup rim and swirled the liquid around the glass. "I can see that you don't like it here, and not just because you miss your friend. But come on—there must be something good about this school. No place is completely awful, right? Maybe you can cheer me up? I'd love to have something to look forward to."

I smiled and felt the tension drain from me. He was actually trying to start a conversation; I didn't have to scramble for a topic or reveal my inability to make small talk. He'd asked me for my opinion and actually seemed to care about the answer. I was secretly grateful. "The teachers are really dedicated," I replied. "Like Ms. Lowry, for example. She's amazing. Everyone loves her."

Jonah shrugged and took a sip of juice. "Yeah, that's why I'm here. My mom heard about Fallstaff's reputation—or the great staff or something. Anyway, she told me that I had to give it a chance, so here I am."

"But you'd rather be somewhere else?"

He nodded vigorously. "Well, I'd rather be back in Boston, for one thing." He hesitated for a minute and glanced up at me. "But my mom thought Baltimore would be a healthy change for us—for me," he concluded in a bitter tone. "So I have to give it one whole year. And then maybe I can transfer—if I'm miserable enough."

Only a year, I thought unhappily. What chance did we have if he was so set on leaving? "Where would you go?" I asked him, trying to keep the disappointment from my voice. "Back to Boston?"

He shook his head and poked a meatball irritably with his fork. "No, that's never going to happen. My mom has a new job here. So I think that's pretty final." He stopped eating and was staring sadly at the muddled pasta on his plate.

Was he missing his hometown so much? I wondered. Or was it something more? He hadn't mentioned his dad at all. Had his parents recently divorced? Is that what was behind the sudden mood shift? It was probably too soon to ask about that.

"Is it just the two of you?" I inquired.

"Yeah, and my little sister, Katie."

I was right about the father then. Probably the reason that they'd moved, I guessed. "My parents are divorced too," I told him after a brief silence. "I never see my dad."

There was a flicker of protest in his eyes, a blush of color; a muscle in his jaw tensed for a moment. "Yes, well, neither do I," he muttered.

I'd clearly touched on a sore topic. I shifted uncomfortably on the hard bench and cast about for another subject, a safe and easy one.

"Where do you live?" I asked him finally.

"Berkley Road. Near some apartment complex."

"Berkley! You're just around the corner from me. Why didn't I see you on the bus?"

"My mom drove me this morning—and she's planning to pick me up this afternoon." His voice was warm now, like the rumble of a bass string. He paused thoughtfully and took a long sip of his juice. "So, you know," he concluded hesitantly, "if you want, we can give you a lift home after school."

I stared at him. Was he serious? It was one thing to sit next to me at lunch. He was new in school, and maybe he'd latched on to the first person who'd spoken to him. But he didn't need to offer me a ride! I could hear Kris's voice squeaking at me, *Stop overanalyzing and just answer him already!*

"That would be great, thanks!" I said, snapping out of my trance. "I'll have to think of a way to pay you back though—"

He grinned and his eyebrows shot up. "Well," he suggested playfully, "in return for the ride, maybe you can help me unpack my room?"

His *room?* He was inviting me to his house?

That was good, right? Better than good?

But wait, a little annoying voice cautioned me. Wasn't he being strangely forward? We'd only just met. Was unpacking his room a code for something else? Was he the kind of guy who invited girls up to his room to "unpack" and then dumped them?

I couldn't accept just yet, I decided. I needed to talk to Kris. She'd ask all the right questions and get to the bottom of this. Kris had been with enough jerks to know a user when she saw one.

"I forgot, I can't today," I told him regretfully. "On Tuesday afternoons, I take the bus to my piano teacher's house."

He didn't seem upset by my refusal. "You play the piano?" he asked eagerly. "What kind of music?"

"Some jazz and blues when I'm at home. But mostly classical at my teacher's. I've been playing since I was little."

"Then you must be pretty good."

I wasn't anything special, really. I could play well enough to enjoy myself, and it was my favorite thing to do when I was stressed or sad. Once a month, I uploaded a recording to YouTube. So far I'd gotten a total of twenty views, mostly from my mother. Still, with Jonah looking at me like that, his eyes fixed on mine, I felt a sudden surge of confidence.

"I write lyrics too," I blurted out. "I've written pages of lyrics."

"You're a songwriter?"

He looked so pleased that I was sorry to admit the truth.

"Not songs, exactly. Just the words. I don't have the music yet."

It sounded a bit pathetic to me, but he didn't seem disappointed by my admission.

"That's pretty cool."

"Really? Well, I'm glad you think so. Except for my friend Kris, no one even knows I play."

"Why not?"

The bell rang, and everyone started gathering up their trays and tossing their leftovers into the trash. I glanced over my shoulder at the crowd of students pushing their way out of the cafeteria.

"Isn't it obvious?" I shouted over the roar of the rushing crowd. "Being artistic doesn't get you cool points at this school."

CHAPTER 5

When you're walking through a sea of normals
And nobody knows your name
When you keep on nudging shoulders
With words that no one claims
You'll write and you'll erase
From a safe and secret place
Sheltered in a forest
Where trees fall but never make a sound.

MY CELL RANG AS I WAS WALKING HOME. "PLEASE COME OVER," I begged Kristin. "I don't think we can talk about this day over the phone."

Less than an hour later, she was sitting on my sofa, balancing a Coke in one hand and my laptop on her knee. "Try again," she urged me for the millionth time that evening. "He should be home by now."

I logged in again, and a new screen popped into view. "He accepted my friend request!" I announced.

Kris leaned close to peek over my shoulder. "Oh, you're right, April. He's really hot," she breathed into my ear.

"He's just a friend," I replied cautiously, trying to keep the excitement from my voice and failing. *It's too soon to get all squealy*, I told myself.

But still, I finally had a little drama of my own.

The soap opera life was Kristin's, not mine. It was no wonder romance and heartbreak followed her everywhere she went. She looked like a teen movie star: blond, tall, and leggy, with long-lashed green eyes and impossibly full lips. I'd spent years listening to the ups and downs of her love troubles, the idiots, the jocks, the losers who paraded through her life. I'd been more than happy to look on from the outside and comfort her as best I could when, inevitably, her relationships ended in tubs of chocolate ice cream. But sometimes, after she'd gone home, I wondered how she'd react when I finally had my own adventure.

"This is a gold mine!" she exclaimed, clicking across his page. "He has a dog—aw, what a cute puppy. Likes to listen to indie bands. And he draws and paints! Wow, very artsy. Ooh, here are some great pics. Wait, why does he look so shocked in all of these?"

I laughed. "That's how he smiles," I told her. "His eyebrows go up. I think it's kind of cute."

"Hmm. Looks like he's surprised that a girl he's never met is stalking him on Facebook. Can't say I blame him." She opened up a folder titled "Boston summer" and scrolled through shots of Jonah bicycling, swimming, and climbing rocks. A freckled, red-haired boy appeared in most of the photos, but his image wasn't tagged. There was one album titled "Broadway!!!!" that showed Jonah with his arm around Neil Patrick Harris. The red-haired boy was standing behind them and pointing at the famous actor.

The boy's mouth was open in a brilliant smile, and his eyes were shining with excitement.

"There are girls in some of the school pics," Kristin remarked after we'd browsed through his page, "but none of them seem too important to him. That's good—I think."

I looked at her suspiciously. "What's that supposed to mean? His relationship status says 'single.'"

"Oh, I know. It's just—well, never mind."

"*What*, Kristin?"

She sighed and plucked nervously at her sleeve. "Don't get mad—I was just thinking—well, he's into *art* and stuff, and you said that he seemed so sensitive—"

All right, so I did get a little mad then. I couldn't help it. I realized that she meant well, but it bothered me that she thought I was so naive that I would crush on a gay guy.

"Next to 'Interested in' he's written 'women,'" I pointed out.

She shrugged. "That doesn't mean anything. No one comes out in high school. Not at Fallstaff, anyway. It's suicide."

She was right, of course. And even the bravest boy wouldn't come out on his first day in a new school. Maybe he'd just been interested in me as a friend. Maybe he'd called me pretty because he thought that it would make me happy, not because he was actually attracted to me. That made him sweet, as I guessed before, but hardly boyfriend material.

I thought back to the timid smile he'd given me, the way he'd leaned in to listen to me at lunchtime when we'd chatted for a precious half hour. It felt so perfect.

"I don't care," I declared. "I don't care if he's gay or straight."

She wrinkled her nose at me. "Come again?"

"I mean it shouldn't matter to me, right? I've only just met him. I'm not in love with him or anything. And if it turns out that he's gay, then we'll just be friends."

She didn't look convinced. "That's very mature of you."

I snorted and rolled my eyes. "Yeah, Kris, I'm really growing. Look, let's stop talking about this, okay? Why don't you tell me about your school?"

Her face lit up. "Well, it's just the first day, of course, but I've got some pictures to show you too." She scooted closer to me and placed the computer on our laps. "Some of these friend requests are totally drool-worthy. Want to go through them together and do pros and cons?"

I nodded eagerly, and she clicked on her "friend" icon. "First bachelor is Marty Price," I read out.

"Pro," she announced, skimming over his photos. "Boy is tall and *hot*. And not afraid to pose without a shirt, apparently."

I frowned. "Yeah...but in *all* of his pictures?"

"Huh. Okay, so maybe that's a con. Marty, my dear, you like to be naked too often." She smacked her lips. "But he's so shiny. Check out those biceps."

"Kris, look at his birth date. Has he been held back a year?"

"Umm, two."

"So basically he's kind of a sparkly mimbo?"

"Pretty much." We stared at him for a few seconds, Kris's manicured fingers tapping thoughtfully against the keyboard. "Okay then, next! Danny Gorman." Her expression grew serious. "I don't know. What do you think?"

I clicked back and forth across his time line. "There isn't a single photo of him here. Just links to metal bands and pictures of guitars."

"Yeah. He's probably not my type. But I'm not sure. You can decide for me."

I stared at her and shook my head. "You do realize I've never met him, don't you? We go to different schools, remember?"

"Right. I know." She blinked at me in surprise, like I'd just shaken her awake. "But you know what's funny?" she remarked after a pause. "Every time I met a new kid or teacher, I could hear your snarky little voice commenting about them in my head."

I slipped my arm around her shoulder and gave her a quick hug. "I missed you too."

"April, this isn't going to be easy," she told me glumly.

"No, it isn't."

"But you have to promise me that we're not going to grow apart. I don't want to be like those friends who swear they'll keep in touch and then never do."

I nodded. "So let's make a deal. From now on, Saturday afternoons will be sacred Kris and April time. No matter how busy we are during the week, we'll always get together. No excuses. What do you think?"

"It still won't be the same."

I smiled. "Kris, you just made me very happy."

She rolled her eyes and gave me a playful shove. "My misery makes you happy?"

"A little," I said, turning back to the computer on my lap. "Come on, let's get back to the important stuff or I'll just get depressed again. Don't you want to hear my opinions about Mr. Piercings and Hair Cream here? Now *he* looks like a real winner."

CHAPTER 6

WHEN I CAME DOWN TO BREAKFAST THE NEXT MORNING, I FOUND MY MOM toasting multigrain bread and pureeing a mess of fruit in the blender. She'd gotten home from work very late the night before, and Kris had ordered greasy pizza for our dinner. My mother was going to be overcompensating for my unhealthy meal for the remainder of the week.

Mom has actually been overcompensating for most of my life. She suffers from a mutated form of Jewish mother's guilt, which she directs at herself, not at me.

When my father moved out ten years ago, my mother found herself completely alone. She'd been disowned by her religious family for marrying outside the faith. Her clan of siblings and cousins had all turned their backs on her. So, with no one else to love, she channeled all of her energy in my direction. She memorized *The Whole-Brain Child*, quoting liberally from it when I misbehaved. She participated in three different parenting groups. Even though she worked as a secretary in a pediatrician's office, she took me to an herbalist when I was ill. She engineered my meals, constructing them out of organic, preservative-free whole grains, flavorless tofu strips, homemade barley bread, wheatgrass, and every kind of seed. As a child, I had the healthiest colon in all of Baltimore.

She worked hard, but lately, between her job and trying to be an entire family to her only daughter, she was starting to look a little frazzled.

"Don't worry about making me anything," I told her as I stuffed my notebooks into my bag. "I'll just grab lunch at school."

She looked horrified. "You know what they put in those deep-frying vats, don't you?"

"Animal fat, I know. It's okay, Mom. I could use a little lard."

I was baiting her a little, mostly to keep her from asking me about my first day. I didn't feel like talking about it yet.

"That's disgusting, April," she huffed.

"Why?" I demanded. "We aren't vegans. And we don't keep kosher."

She stared grimly at me and then hit the pulse button on the blender one more time. "So, how was your first day?" she asked, ignoring my challenge. "Did you meet any new people?"

Despite the granola crunchiness, my mom is surprisingly in tune with what's going on in my life. If it wasn't for the incessant worrying, I would actually consider her a good friend.

"A couple, yeah. A girl named Tessa and a guy."

She looked up from her fruit mountain. "Tessa, huh? Does she seem nice?"

I shook my head. "No, definitely not."

"Oh. Well, okay then. I'm sorry to hear that." She was suddenly very busy peeling things.

Oh, for God's sake, I thought. I had to give her something. I took a deep breath and leaned a little deeper into my cereal bowl. "The new boy seems pretty decent. For a guy."

The peeler clattered to the counter. Damn it. Why did I think this would be a good idea? *Why?*

"A boy!" she exclaimed. "What kind of boy?"

Why do parents ask questions like that? And how do they expect us to answer them? The kind of boy, Mom, who will treat me with respect and let me make my own decisions, never pressure me to have sex, be responsible with motor vehicles, always drug and alcohol free, and who eventually will propose marriage when we are old enough. Is that what she wanted to hear?

"I think he's a regular human boy, Mom, but I'll have to wait until the next full moon to be absolutely sure."

"Very funny, April."

"Look, I'm going to be late for school, so I'll get going now, okay?"

She swept a few apple peels into a plastic bag and tied off the ends for me. She packed me apple peels, not the actual apple. A while back, she'd read that the peel was the healthiest part of fruit, so I'd been eating compost lunches for a few months now.

"You look very nice this morning," she told me. "Are you wearing makeup?"

All right, so I'd spent a little time on my appearance. "Just some eye shadow," I admitted, scraping the remainder of my cereal into the trash.

She sniffed the air and smiled knowingly. "And perfume?"

"Mom! It's scented soap!" Okay, so I'd spent *a lot* of time. I'd gotten up at dawn. I'd scrubbed and buffed and shined myself like a new Porsche. But she didn't need to stare at me as if she was used to seeing Jabba the Hutt at the breakfast table.

"Well," she said after a short silence, "I'll be home in time for dinner tonight, so if you like, maybe you can bring over your new friend? I'd love to meet him." She was trying her best to sound cool and casual. I wasn't buying it.

"Mom, I met him yesterday. Please don't make a bigger deal of this than it is."

"Of course, I know, I know. But I'm here for you if you have any questions—"

"What questions could I possibly have at this point?"

She paused uncertainly and gave me a terrified look, as if she'd suddenly decided that her entire parenting career hinged on giving me the correct answer. I was actually sorry for her. She couldn't use her own experiences to guide her. I knew she'd never had talks about boys with her mother when she was growing up. As I understand it, the first long conversation she'd had with her mom had also been her last. I had to give her credit for trying.

"Don't worry, Mom," I told her as I headed for the door. "I learned the basics in sex ed years ago."

CHAPTER 7

I HAD OVERANALYZED EVERYTHING, I TOLD MYSELF AS I ENTERED THE school building. I should never have spent so much time thinking about Jonah. How could I act naturally around him now? Why couldn't I be more like other teens, who wandered in and out of friendships easily and traded boyfriends like playing cards? Why was I looking for him around every corner? *This isn't healthy*, I decided. I was going to stop caring.

Except then I saw Jonah by the lockers, chatting with some junior boys. His hair was still damp from his morning shower, his arms were folded across his chest, and he was laughing at something one of the other guys was saying. And suddenly I cared so much I almost fled in the opposite direction.

He turned around and saw me, then waved me over with a smile. "April, you have to help me. Robby wants me to join the basketball team. And I'm trying to explain to them that I can't play. What do you think? Should I sign up and make a fool of myself?"

"You just need a little practice," Robby suggested. "You're taller than most of us—and we really need more players."

"Yeah, and you couldn't possibly make them any worse," I chimed in. "Last season wasn't exactly Fallstaff's best."

(They'd actually lost each and every single game. There had been jokes about pitting them against the girls' team.)

Jonah shrugged and shook his head. "All right, but you'll be sorry when I trip over the ball."

"Oh, come on," Robby exclaimed. "You can't be that bad. You must have played something at your old school."

Jonah laughed shortly and slammed his locker shut. "I went to an art school. I mostly sketched and painted."

They took a step back, as if he'd just admitted to having Ebola.

"You're, like, some sort of artist then?"

"Well, I try to be."

Robby's eyes narrowed suspiciously. "So, what are you—some kind of fag?"

A sick knot of anger turned over in my stomach, and I felt my fists clench. But Jonah barely moved. There was a bored and patient expression on his face, as if he was used to answering this question. "No, Robby, I usually draw naked chicks," he responded coldly. "It keeps the gay off."

One of the guys snickered. "Yeah, sure. Whatever, man."

Jonah smiled stiffly at him, shoved his hands into his pockets, and stalked off down the hall. I hurried after him and caught up to him by the classroom entrance. "Why weren't you angry at that jerk?" I asked him. "Most guys would have punched him."

"Most guys care what people like Robby think. I don't."

"I don't care about Robby either," I said. "But what about the rest of the school? What if they start spreading rumors?"

"So what if they do? It wouldn't be the first time." He smiled and leaned closer to me, then reached out for my hand and shaped my fingers into a ball. "But next time you're thinking of punching someone, make sure you make a decent fist, okay? Thumb goes on the outside. Unless you want to break your knuckles."

I glanced down at our hands, and suddenly I was ready to be the female Evander Holyfield if it meant that Jonah would hold my hand forever. He was warm and close; he smelled faintly of chocolate mint and aftershave. I was beginning to feel a little dizzy.

He held my fingers for a few seconds longer—maybe a shade longer than he really needed to. "Look, it's really sweet of you to care so much," he said. "But honestly, I checked out the minute I walked into this place." He swallowed hard and seemed about to speak again, but then a group of students began to push past us, and he dropped my hand and hurried into the classroom after them.

I inhaled deeply, tugged my sleeve back into place, and slowly floated into history class.

The first thing Ms. Lowry talked about that morning was the composition of history essays; she said that our goal was proving our main hypothesis. Then she said a lot of other things, but I wasn't really listening after that. I had an important hypothesis of my own to prove—namely, that Jonah wasn't gay.

I constructed a simple chart and jotted down the currently known facts about my new friend.

The page was split into two columns and read something like this:

Jonah

Not Gay	Gay
Fistfights?	Artsy stuff (admits this openly)
His clothes are nothing special	Apparently not attracted to Cora
Held my hand for a few seconds	Smells really good
Complimented me twice	Complimented me twice
Says he's straight	Says he's straight

I needed to show my chart to Kristin and ask her for help. But I'd recently pulled a mature and progressive attitude and declared that I didn't care one way or the other. I couldn't show up at her door with my neurotic notes. Asking my mom's opinion was out of the question. She'd probably faint and then check out twenty books on teen sexuality from the library and make me read them. I needed more data, I decided. I'd try to take things as they came.

Still, I probably shouldn't have written Jonah's name at the top of my chart. That was truly an advanced level of stupid. Or I should have at least hidden the paper.

Oops.

We were gathering up our books after the bell rang when Jonah leaned back to say something to me. I realized suddenly that my gay analysis chart was sitting in plain view on top of my open binder. With a quick motion, I slammed the cover down to hide the page. My movement was too sudden; the loose sheets fluttered out onto the floor. I made a mad dive for them and caught one just in time—only to realize that I was holding the first page of my history syllabus. And Jonah had kindly picked up the other sheet—and was now staring at it quietly. I made a futile grab for it, but he stepped quickly aside, his eyes still fixed on the paper in front of him.

Then he raised his eyes to look at me, and I felt the blood rush to my face. *How bad was it?* I wondered, trying desperately to remember what I'd written. I hadn't said anything negative about him. He might think it funny and maybe even complimentary—I had, after all, mentioned that he smelled nice. Maybe we would laugh at this over lunch.

And maybe not.

The room got slowly quieter as the other students filed out. I stared at him, hoping for him to speak and dreading it at the same time. I couldn't interpret his expression; it seemed absolutely blank. Was it shock? Disappointment? Why wouldn't he say something? Get mad, like a normal guy, tear up the sheet, call me a moron? Was he waiting for me to talk? What did he want me to say? I'd ruined our friendship before it had even started. If he was gay, I realized, then that page would look like I was judging him. If he was straight and he'd actually been attracted to me—well, he wouldn't be anymore.

I cleared my throat and tried to say his name, but I only managed a strangled raspy noise. Without a word, Jonah held the sheet out to me, dropped it at my feet, then turned and walked slowly out of the classroom. The door shut behind him softly, and his retreating footsteps faded into the rumble of the students in the hall. I picked up the page, crumpled it in my hand, and crept miserably to the girls' bathroom.

CHAPTER 8

I MISSED MATH COMPLETELY; I DID BATHROOM INDEPENDENT STUDY INSTEAD. To the outside eye, I was looking at my reflection and trying not to cry. But a lot actually happened on the inside. After forty minutes of intense mirror-staring, I made an important decision. I wasn't going to give this friendship up, not without a fight. I wasn't going to feel sorry for myself. I was going to admit my feelings openly, and if that wasn't enough, then screw it. Things couldn't get any worse anyway.

Spanish was a total blur, and English was miserable because Jonah sat next to me and didn't look at me once. *It doesn't matter*, I thought as I watched the clock and chewed my pen. I was going to do this. During lunch. Even if it killed me.

I was shaking by the time the bell rang. My hands were numb, and there was a strange metallic flavor in my mouth. Jonah fled the classroom before I had a chance to speak. *It doesn't matter*, I told myself again. I would find him in the cafeteria whether he liked it or not.

He was standing by the salad bar when I came in. Cora was hovering behind him, whispering and pointing at her table. I pushed through the room toward them. My knees were weak, my skin felt cold, and my stomach was churning. But I was going to go through with it, no matter what. When I reached them, I put my hand out and touched Jonah's sleeve. They both turned around and stared at me.

"Jonah, can I speak to you—alone?"

He nodded dumbly and, ignoring Cora's malicious smile, led me to the corner of the room. I glanced around us to make sure that nobody was listening and swallowed slowly. I would need a drink when this was over; I didn't know that fear could taste so bitter.

"I wanted to tell you," I began, playing back the speech that I'd rehearsed all morning in my head, "that I'm sorry. You see, the thing is, it's always been hard for me to make new friends, and I've never had a boyfriend—or anything even close to that. The truth is—" Here came the impossible part. "The truth is, I think you're…cute. Hot, I mean. I should have written that down, instead of that stupid chart. And so, well, that's it, actually. I'm sorry."

Wow, that had sounded *so* much better in my head. It came out in little ragged gasps and swallows, and in the middle, my tongue started sticking to my gums. And what in God's name was that taste? Why was he looking at me like that, like he was trying not to laugh? Maybe I hadn't been so eloquent, but at least I'd spoken from the heart! *This was a big deal for me*, I wanted to yell at him. Do you have any idea how hard it was to say those things? *Say something*, why don't you? Put me out of my misery already!

"April," he whispered finally, his voice vibrating with suppressed laughter. "You're *drooling blue*."

Well, that was the last thing I'd expected him to say. "*What?*"

He reached out and touched a finger to my lip and then held it out in front of me. His skin was stained with navy ink. I glanced down in horror at my hands. How had I missed those streaks? And was *that* what I was tasting? I remembered chewing on my pen in English, but I never imagined that I'd bitten through it. My God, had I been spitting blue the whole time I was pouring out my heart?

"I think I'm going to be sick," I muttered into my hand.

I made it to the bathroom and puked up a navy-colored breakfast. For the next few minutes, I was too busy washing out my mouth and scrubbing my fingers to think about my humiliation and what Jonah (and probably the rest of the sophomore class) was saying about me. But as the last of the blue ink ran into the drain and my lips lost their dead Smurf hue, I realized that no one would ever forget this. Cora had seen me with the pen all over my face and had probably spread the story already. But what made the whole episode truly mortifying was that I'd told the new boy in school that he was hot—while spitting blue drool. If Jonah shared that last detail with the class, then I might as well pack up my books and leave Fallstaff High—no, leave Baltimore forever. It would take about five minutes for that story to go viral.

I was too absorbed in my misery to pay attention to the faint scratching sound at the bathroom door.

"April, are you in there?"

"Don't come in!" I called out automatically and then realized that I'd just unintentionally announced myself.

"I wasn't planning on barging into the girls' bathroom," he said. "But I was hoping you'd come out."

I didn't really have much choice. Even though Jonah was the last person I wanted to see, at some point, I would have to leave the bathroom. I took a deep breath, pushed the door open, and stepped into the hallway. He was hovering nervously by the entrance, and before I had a chance to speak, he thrust out his hand abruptly. He was holding a plastic cup and a small plate covered in foil. His smile was apologetic, and his eyebrows shot up to his hairline.

"I brought you some water," he blurted out. "And a brownie."

"Oh." I took them from him and slowly unwrapped the plate. "Thank you."

"Come with me to the cafeteria?"

I laughed shortly. "There's no way I'm going back in there," I declared. "I'm not facing those people—not after that."

"Why not?"

"Are you serious? After Cora saw me—"

"She saw that you had ink on your face," he interrupted. "So what? Big deal."

"It doesn't take that much to get them started! Last year, a girl spilled some lemonade on her pants—right in the crotch area—and they teased her so badly that she transferred to another school."

He exhaled impatiently and crossed his arms. "Look, I know all about bullies and teasing. All you have to do is pretend that they don't bother you. That's the only way they'll stop."

"That's your advice?" I exclaimed hotly. "Really? 'Just pretend it doesn't bother you.' Yeah, sure, I'll try to remember that."

"I didn't mean it like that!"

"Then what *do* you mean?"

"Walk back with me to the cafeteria and I'll show you," he said, placing a gentle hand on my elbow. "Relax, April. I know what I'm doing."

I didn't know why he was being so nice to me or what he had in mind, but I let him lead me down the hall.

As we approached the lunch room, I slowed my pace and pulled him back. "Wait, can I have a second to think about it?"

"No. You've thought enough." He gave me a little shove and whispered dramatically, "Smile for your audience—it's show-time," and we were in the cafeteria.

Almost nobody in the room looked up at us. If this had been a TV movie, the entire student body would have swung about in unison and a hush would have fallen over the crowd. That's what I'd been expecting. But what actually happened was everybody kept chattering and shoveling food into their mouths, and only a few kids at the sophomore table turned to stare at us. Cora pointed at me, and Tessa giggled.

"Now let's sit down," Jonah suggested, indicating an empty table in the corner. "And when I finish talking, I want you to throw your head back and laugh, like I'm the funniest guy in the world."

"What?"

"Laugh!" he commanded. I let out a forced chuckle, and he groaned under his breath. "God, that's awful. You're a terrible actress."

I scowled at him, jerked my chin back, then howled with laughter, giving him a playful shove that almost knocked him over.

He stumbled forward, his shoulders shaking with suppressed laughter, and quickly pulled me down next to him on the bench.

"Don't look up yet," he whispered, "but Cora looks like she's just swallowed a roach. I told you I knew what I was doing. Not bad for the second day of school, huh?" he continued slyly as I sneaked a peek at the whispering group of girls. "It seems that I've got two admirers." He leaned forward and gave me a wicked smile. "Although Cora's declaration will probably never be as original as yours."

"That isn't funny! It was really hard for me to say those things."

His smile faded and he nodded humbly. "I know it was." A hint of teasing crept back into his voice. "But April, did I really make you so nervous that you actually ate your pen? Seriously?"

"You could have said something in English class! I must have been covered in ink."

"Well, I didn't see you then, I swear. I was too busy trying to ignore you."

"Yeah, I noticed that." I paused for a moment and shook my head. "Look, I'm really sorry about the chart. I don't know what I was thinking."

He took a piece of brownie and tossed it in his mouth. "It's okay. I'll get over it. Honestly, I'm really sick of the topic. And it's kind of a sensitive subject for me."

Okay, here it comes, I thought, my heart sinking. Kristin was right. *Well, I won't be disappointed*, I decided quickly. I will be mature and supportive.

"I told you I knew all about bullies, right?" he began, leaning closer to me. "Well, it's because my best friend was gay. Ricky and I grew up together in the same neighborhood, went to the same school. He came out to me first—even before he came out to his family. Ricky was actually scared to tell anyone because he thought it would make *my* life more difficult." He smiled bitterly. "The kids in our class had been teasing him for months. But when he came out, they backed off for a bit. And then they started in on me."

"That must have been so hard for him," I said. "For both of you."

He nodded. "When people found out that Ricky was gay, they naturally assumed that he and I were a couple. Even my own parents. The ironic thing was that the only person who accepted that I was straight was my gay best friend. But I didn't care what they thought. They were going to say what they were going to say; I wasn't going to abandon him. School sucked, but Ricky and I had each other, so it didn't matter. He used to say that it was the two of us 'against the world.' When the teasing got really bad, our parents finally switched us to the public art school."

"And things got better after that?"

"Yeah, I couldn't believe it. It was the best year of our lives."

He was quiet for a moment.

"Ricky must be sad now that you've left Boston," I remarked after a short pause. "Is he a painter, like you?"

Jonah gave me a startled, defensive look, as if I'd said something out of place. "No, he was in drama and musical theater."

"Oh!" I said, remembering the photos in his "Broadway!!!!" album. "Is that how you two met Neil Patrick Harris?"

He grinned at me. "Ah," he teased. "The stalker strikes again!"

I shrugged. "I have a best friend too. And Kris has to know all."

"Well, if she asks," he said, "you can tell her that Ricky and I met Neil Patrick Harris after a Broadway show."

"Really? That's so cool!"

"Yeah, my friend talked about that day for months! The guy was his hero." Jonah's lips tensed and his brow furrowed. "Ricky's dream was to be in a musical with him one day."

"Ricky's a singer?"

Jonah pushed his plate away and looked down at his lap. "Yeah. Best voice you ever heard. There was a ton of talent in our art school. But he was always the star."

I smiled uncomfortably and played with the brownie crumbs on my plate. Something about Jonah's expression made me nervous; it was sad and distracted, and his blue eyes seemed a shade darker. *Why did he keep referring to his friend in the past tense?* I wondered.

I was trying to figure out how to ask him about it when the bell rang, and the crash of feet and clatter of trays interrupted our conversation. I stayed seated and waited for Jonah to rise. I didn't want to rush off in the middle of our talk, not if he had something else to tell me.

But then Michael skidded past and poked me on the shoulder. "Hey, you're my lab partner," he called out. "You can't be late to biology."

I couldn't ignore the emptying cafeteria anymore. "I think I have to go now," I told Jonah softly.

He started slightly and rose from the bench. The dark light had vanished from his eyes, and he was smiling again, as if the memory of his story had disappeared as suddenly as it had come. "The offer is still open, you know," he said as we left the lunchroom.

"Okay." I hesitated and cast my mind back over our conversation. "Wait, what offer?"

"Do you want a ride home after school today? My mom starts her new job soon, so next week I'll be taking the bus. But in the meantime, she's picking me up, so—"

"Oh, yeah, of course—thank you!"

He grinned at me and hurried off to his classroom. I walked around in happy, aimless circles for a couple of minutes and then, smiling stupidly, sprinted off to lab.

CHAPTER 9

I WAS HALFWAY OUT OF THE SCHOOL BUILDING WHEN I REALIZED THAT I'D be meeting Jonah's mom that day. I don't know why it hadn't occurred to me sooner, but I suddenly panicked and scurried anxiously into the bathroom to check my hair.

A few minutes later, I found Jonah in the parking lot. As we slipped into the backseat of his mother's van, Mrs. Golden turned around to greet me. She was a sweet, round, smiling person, all curls and curves, with a towering mass of black hair, large, dark eyes, and dimpled cherry cheeks. As I introduced myself, she nodded cheerily. She seemed a little *too* pleased to see me, I thought.

I shifted in my seat uncomfortably, partly because I was unsure how to start a conversation with her and partly because whatever I was sitting on had suddenly begun to move.

"Hey, you're on my Harry Potter wand!" a little voice declared, and I jumped aside to reveal a buzzing baton that was lying across my seat. The declaration had come from the back of the van, and I turned around to find a pair of large blue eyes peeping shyly at me from behind the seat cushion.

"Katie, come sit next to us and say hello," Jonah ordered playfully.

"Only if you read to me," she replied. "You haven't read to me all week. And you promised."

"And you promised to knock before you come into my room," he retorted. "I might actually agree to read to you if I could get dressed just once without you bursting in on me."

I laughed and patted the space next to me. "Katie, if you sit here and put on your seat belt, maybe I can read to you a bit."

A moment later, a large book landed on my lap, and the little girl scrambled over the seat and plopped down beside me. She was adorable, with a mass of sandy curls and a freckled button nose.

"We're on chapter four," she informed me gravely. "If you don't finish, you can read to me after dinner too."

"What she means to say is we'd love to have you for dinner, April," Mrs. Golden chimed in apologetically.

"I'll check with my mom," I said. "But that sounds great."

"And don't worry, you're not obligated to do bedtime story hour. That's actually Jonah's job."

"Yeah, and he does all the voices," Katie informed me. "So you have to do them too."

When we pulled into their driveway, Katie jumped out of the car and raced to the house. An old cocker spaniel was snoring peacefully beneath a swing on the porch; she opened one eye and gazed dully at us for a moment, then shut it again.

"That's Lady," Katie explained. "I want to get a Tramp too, but they won't let me."

"Katie is a Disney princess," Jonah told me. "You should see her room; it's terrifying. Come on. Let's go before she decides she owns you."

His mom unlocked the door, and I followed them inside.

The Goldens' living room belonged on the cover of *Better Homes and Gardens*. It was better than *my* home, at any rate. It seemed unbelievable to me that they'd moved in just a month ago. There wasn't a box anywhere, and in their short stay, they'd somehow managed to color-coordinate the wallpaper to their furniture. Everything was floral, in shades of coral, pink, and orange, with seashells and plush throw rugs, lacy lampshades, and overstuffed accent pillows. The cherry striped sofa looked like no one had ever sat on it; even the giant fireplace hearth was sparkling white as if the fire had been taught how to clean up after itself. I was beginning to suspect that Jonah's request to help him unpack was just a joke when he touched my shoulder and said, "Let's go upstairs. I don't really live in this part."

His mom frowned at him as we headed for the staircase. "Your room is a danger zone. Are you sure you want to show it to your friend?"

"It isn't that bad, Mom," he answered and bounded up the stairs. I caught up to him by his bedroom door. He pushed it open with a little shrug, and a pile of underwear tumbled out into the hallway. "Oh," he said, wrinkling his nose. "Don't look down. Also, no deep breaths."

I stuck my head in after him. "Wow, Jonah. I'm going to need a shovel."

It was like a storage closet after an earthquake. There were half-open boxes everywhere, piles of magazines and rolled-up laundry on each surface. The floor was covered with socks; a shadeless lamp and a pair of boxing gloves hung on the bedpost. The only clear area in the place was by a corner near the window; a five-foot square had been left bare, and in the center of the open space was a large punching bag, suspended from an iron hook nailed into the ceiling.

"So," Jonah declared. "Where do we start?"

"It smells like cheese in here," I said, shaking my head.

"Oh, that isn't me," Jonah assured me. "I lost a plate of wacky mac last week. If you find it, it's yours."

I laughed. "You'll have to give me rides home for the rest of the year to pay me back for cleaning up this mess. How does your mom let you keep it like this?"

"She doesn't come in here. And she comforts herself with that cotton-candy-explosion living room."

"Well, if you want me to come over again," I teased, "you'll have to clear a place for us to sit down."

Jonah turned around to grin at me, and I ducked my head over a stack of papers. Had I just flirted with him? I couldn't tell. Judging by his smile, he seemed to be enjoying my accidental flirting, and I was pretty proud of myself. I glanced around the room, looking for something else to talk about, and my eyes fell on the punching bag.

I picked up one of his boxing gloves and slipped it on my hand. "Is this another of your hobbies?" I asked, prodding the heavy bag with my fist.

"It's more of a skill than a hobby."

"What's the difference?"

"Well, a hobby is something you do because you love it, and a skill is something you develop because it's useful. Or necessary."

I poked the bag with playful little punches and jumped around in a goofy imitation of a boxer. Jonah laughed shortly and walked up behind me. "Hit square and flat, between the knuckles, here." He demonstrated with his left hand, a straight cut to the middle of his target, a sudden slice, and the bag swayed backward from the power of his swing. "Now you try," he prompted, indicating the spot he'd hit.

I stepped back and swung with all my strength, but my fist glanced off with a soft pop. It was a pretty bad effort; I knew it before I saw his shaking head.

"No, look," he said with a smile. "You're hitting from the arm only. Here, let me show you—" He placed his left hand on my shoulder and his other hand on my elbow. "Relax for a minute," he instructed, and I timidly rested my back against his chest. "Now let me move your arms for you."

I nodded and swallowed hard, concentrating on the target in front of me. It took all my effort to breathe normally. I felt his hair brush lightly against my skin, his warm breath on my cheek. *Stay still*, I told myself. *Stay still and let him lead.*

With a swift movement, he brought my right elbow back and pivoted my left shoulder forward. "Now follow through the motion with your hips," he instructed, guiding my arm. There was a satisfying thump, and the bag quivered in place. "Not bad!" he said, releasing me. "A little practice and you can try to knock me out."

"Awesome. Is that how you start all your friendships?" I retorted, aiming a few more jabs at the trembling bag.

He laughed. "No. I only let cute girls punch me."

I stopped smacking the bag and twisted around to look at him.

"Wow. Sorry. That line sounded *a lot* better in my head," he muttered. He was smiling broadly, but his cheeks were flaming crimson. It was sweet that he blushed so easily. It made my own shyness feel normal.

"So are you a good fighter then?" I asked him.

"I'm okay. I can defend myself if I have to."

"Really?" I laughed. "Why? Is someone after you?"

He hesitated for a moment. "I just can, that's all," he said. There was a ring of defiance in his voice. I wondered if I'd accidentally stepped into forbidden territory again.

"I was only joking." I pointed to his clutter of papers. "So where are you hiding your sketches? Somewhere under this mess?"

His face brightened. "Don't worry about the mess," he told me. "I can clean that up later." He bounded across the room. "If you want, I can show you where I keep them."

He led me out into the hallway, then down the corridor past a purple play area to a narrow door at the far end of the hall. I didn't ask him where we were going. His unpredictability was exciting and mysterious to me; I was actually enjoying his little mood swings.

Without a word, Jonah pushed the door open and I followed him inside.

"Oh!" I said, taking it all in. "Is this your studio?"

The floor was dark, bare hardwood; there was a single metal stool standing near the window and a small desk piled high with paint bottles and brushes. The rest of the room was filled with easels, each holding a canvas draped in a clean, white sheet. The sunlight from the open window hit the corner of one easel and made it glow; I reached out to touch the edges of the cloth and brushed the warm fabric with my fingers.

"Are there finished paintings behind these?"

He nodded. "You can look underneath it if you want."

Carefully, I lifted the corner of the sheet and pulled it back.

Grinning back at us, winking from behind a speckled mushroom, was Jonah's sister, Katie. He'd drawn her as an elf, a miniature woodland sprite surrounded by fireflies and stardust, peeking at us from her tiny toadstool home. Jonah had captured her perfectly—the expression in her eyes, the little tilt of her blond head, the teasing, knowing smile.

"It's a surprise," he whispered. "Promise you won't tell her."

"I promise." I dropped the cloth back into place. "Is that why you keep them hidden behind sheets? Are they all presents for people?"

He looked confused. "No, I just—I don't know. I always cover my paintings."

"So the sunlight doesn't damage them?" I asked, putting up a hand to block the rays streaming through the window. "That makes sense. Can I see another one?"

He gave me a pleased nod, and I stepped over to an easel in the corner. "How about this one?" I'd picked it at random, but I saw him tense slightly before he answered me.

"All right, I guess. Why not?"

I flipped the cover over and stepped back to look. This one wasn't magical at all. It was hard to believe that the artist who'd captured Katie's fairyland had also painted this. I was looking at a study of sharp angles. There was a shiny metal desk, a pile of heavy textbooks, pointed pencils in a mesh cup, a silver calculator, and a razor-sharp letter opener, slicing through a stack of blank white paper. Behind the desk, a dark-haired, handsome man was sitting, leaning slightly forward, his arms crossed, his clear gray eyes concentrating on some point directly in front of him. His expression was faraway, severe, determined.

"Who *is* that?" I asked.

"That's my father."

"Oh. Is your father an accountant?"

"No, he's a cardiac surgeon. But I've never seen him in the operating room. That's how I imagine him—when I think of him." Jonah's tone was strangely dull—emotionless, just like the painting.

"Can I look at another one?" I asked him after an uncomfortable silence.

"Be my guest."

I wanted to uncover all of the easels, but I sensed that he'd view that as an intrusion. I scanned the room for a moment and spotted a canvas hidden in a corner behind some empty cans. Something told me to choose a different one; as I approached it, I saw him bite his lip and look away. A moment later, I wished I'd listened to my instinct.

I only stared for a few seconds before I threw the sheet back down, but I will never forget it. The painting showed a red-haired, fair-skinned boy who was holding on to a balcony railing with an outstretched arm. He'd slipped and fallen, and his body was dangling over a steep drop, his muddied clothing wet and clinging to him. The fingers around the metal bar were bleeding; he was just a second away from falling. And yet, it wasn't the pose that shocked me—it was the look in the boy's eyes. He was staring directly at me, with an expression of indescribable fear.

"There are more than twenty portraits in this room, but you had to pick *that* one," Jonah muttered.

"I'm really sorry. I was just curious—" I paused, remembering the boy from Jonah's Facebook photos. "That was Ricky, wasn't it?"

He nodded. "I finished that one before we moved here. My parents haven't seen it yet. Actually, come to think of it, you're the first one to see it."

I hesitated and glanced back at the covered canvas. "Ricky hasn't…I mean, he—" I stopped, unsure how to finish the question.

"No, I did that one from memory. He never saw it." He studied me quietly for a minute. "Ricky died before I painted it."

"*Oh.*" I reached my hand out to him, but he didn't notice the gesture, so I let it drop to my side. "I'm so sorry. I shouldn't have brought it up."

He nodded and sank slowly onto the wood floor. I sat down next to him and leaned back against the wall. "I'm not trying to be mysterious or anything," he said after a moment. "I'm just tired of talking about it, tired of watching other people trying to get me to talk about it—as if that would solve anything. I've been through my share of counselors, believe me. But what could they possibly tell me? That it wasn't my fault? That I'd been a good friend to him? I was *so sick* of hearing that. Ricky's father said that at his funeral, went on and on about how much I'd meant to his son. I knew what he was thinking though—what they were all thinking. And they were right. When it mattered most, I wasn't there."

I didn't understand; I was still missing a big part of the story. "But if it was an accident," I began, carefully picking my words, "you couldn't have known—"

He was glaring at me now, not in anger, but in protest, as if he couldn't stand that I was trying to defend him.

"It *wasn't* an accident. He didn't fall, there was no balcony, and it wasn't raining either. But I couldn't paint what actually happened. That wouldn't be fair to anyone."

I felt terrible for bringing it up. He seemed miserable and exhausted, like I'd just added to the weight that he was carrying. He'd recently lost his childhood friend, and I was making him relive the trauma now. When Kris had left my school and neighborhood, I'd felt so alone. I couldn't imagine how I'd feel if I had to say good-bye to her forever. "Jonah, you don't have to explain. I'm sorry. I shouldn't have asked. We could talk about other things—"

"That would be nice, thanks." He rubbed his hands over his eyes and smoothed his dark curls back from his forehead. We sat quietly for a few minutes, and when he turned to me, his face was pale and calm.

"There are, like, fifteen other portraits in here," he said. "I promise none of the others will freak you out." He got up and walked over to the nearest one. "Look, here's one I did last year of my old math teacher." He uncovered a picture of a heavy, elderly woman with white curls and ruddy cheeks. She was standing in an empty garden, reaching out to touch a wilted ivy stem. "What do you feel when you look at her?" Jonah prompted. "Don't think—just say the first thing that comes to mind."

"She's waiting for someone," I said quickly. "She misses them. She's been waiting a long time."

His face glowed with pride. "That's what I was going for!" he told me. "She was always talking about her grandchildren—

knitting for them, baking for them—but then she'd bring whole plates of cookies into class, untouched. And her office—wall to wall photos, stacks of them in every corner. I asked her once—she told me that her kids moved to England a long time ago. She lived alone, and she spent all year waiting for them to visit."

I looked away. "How awful. Not the painting, of course—that's fantastic. Are there any happy pictures in here? Besides the one of Katie?"

He considered for a minute. "I don't know. I've never thought of it like that. I don't paint them happy or sad. They are who they are."

"Well, you have to show these to people. Maybe put together an exhibit? They're beautiful."

There was a soft knock at the door, and Katie entered, dragging a purple feather boa behind her. "Mom says to come down to dinner," she began, and then stopped mid-thought. "Oh, I don't like the lonely teacher painting, Jonah!" she exclaimed. "Show her a good one."

Jonah threw the cover down. "My favorite eight-year-old critic. Katie, you know you're not allowed in here; I've told you about a hundred times."

"I knocked. Anyway, Mom wants you downstairs. She can't open a jar."

Katie and I followed Jonah out of the room. Halfway down the stairs she grabbed me by the hand and gestured for me to lean down. "I've been in his studio before," she whispered confidentially. "I sneak in when he's at school. Have you seen the picture he did of me?"

I nodded, smiling. "It's supposed to be a surprise."

She wrinkled her nose. "Don't tell, okay?"

I thought about the other paintings that I'd seen—about Ricky's terrifying final portrait. "Katie," I began, trying to sound stern, "have you looked at all the paintings in there?"

She gave me a tired look, as if I'd just insulted her young intelligence. "You mean the one of Ricky on the balcony? Yeah, sure. Jonah did that a couple of months after Ricky was killed."

"Wait a minute—you know what happened to Ricky?"

She sat down on the bottom step and stared gravely up at me. "They didn't realize I was awake. But I overheard Jonah screaming at Daddy."

I wasn't sure what to say to her. I couldn't ask an eight-year-old to explain what she should never have heard. And she clearly assumed I knew the details, like everybody else. "Katie, I don't think we should talk about this anymore."

She shrugged. "I don't want to anyway. I just wish they'd start speaking to each other again."

"Jonah doesn't talk to your dad?"

She shook her head and sighed. "It was bad enough before Ricky died. But at least we were all talking to each other then."

"I'm sorry, Katie. I'm sure it'll get better soon."

She looked doubtfully at me. "It's been like this for a long time."

I was about to answer her when Jonah called to us from the dining room. Katie sprang up from the bottom step. "Don't tell him what I said!" she whispered and then danced off to the kitchen.

Jonah was setting the table when I came in, and his mother was carrying a huge tossed salad and a bowl of dumplings on a server. The dining room looked like it had been decorated for a special guest; there were three large pots of food stewing on the stove.

Jonah smiled at my embarrassed expression and handed me the tray of silverware. "Don't worry," he said. "My mom cooks like this every night. She didn't even know that you were coming."

"Well, enjoy it while it lasts," she remarked. "I go back to work next week."

"Where will you work, Mrs. Golden?" I asked her as we settled ourselves around the table.

"I'll be joining Reisterstown Decorators. I'm an interior design consultant."

Of course, I thought. Why hadn't I guessed that? No normal person could match a real seashell with a light fixture.

"You have lovely taste," I told her, because that seemed to be the only polite thing to say.

Jonah grinned wickedly into his chicken stew. "As you can see, April, art runs in the family." His mom beamed at him and spooned another helping of potatoes onto his plate. I had the urge to kick him under the table.

We spent the next few minutes intently cutting up our food and chewing. I knew that Jonah's mom was dying to ask me something about myself. I could tell by the bashful glances she kept shooting at me and the way she kept opening her mouth to speak and then shutting it again.

It was Katie who finally broke the silence. "So, Mommy," she said. "Did you know that April plays the piano?"

A look of relief washed over her face. "Really?" she cooed, a little too enthusiastically. "What a wonderful hobby! Have you been taking lessons long?"

"Since I was seven." Music seemed like a harmless topic. But then I realized that I'd never mentioned my hobby to anyone except for Jonah. "Katie, how did you know I played?"

Katie gave Jonah a sly smile. "I saw the videos you posted on YouTube," she told me proudly and shoved a giant meatball in her mouth with a flourish of triumph.

"You heard me—?" I paused and turned sharply to her brother. He was concentrating on his food and flipping his potatoes back and forth across his plate. "Wait a minute—which recording did you see?"

"The moon sonata!" Katie called out, spitting beef in all directions.

"'Moonlight Sonata,'" Jonah growled, still glaring at his fork. "And I'm locking my door from now on."

"He watched the other ones too," she whispered to me. "But he liked the moon one best. You had your hair up. And you were wearing a yellow dress with no sleeves. He watched that one, like, a hundred times—"

"*Katie!*"

I picked up my napkin and pretended to wipe the pleased smile off my face. "Thank you, Katie," I said cheerfully. "You've just made my day."

CHAPTER 10

MY MOM FOUND ME IN MY ROOM THAT EVENING. I'D BEEN PLAYING ON MY keyboard for an hour, rehearsing a piece that my teacher had assigned. It was the most difficult thing he'd ever given me, and I'd struggled over it for months without success. But now I was brimming with new confidence, and for the first time, I found that I could actually make it through. I was determined to post a new recording on YouTube before the end of the week. Wearing the sleeveless yellow dress, of course.

I stopped playing when I heard my mom knock. She entered, glanced around the room nervously, and then sank down on my bed. "That sounded really good," she told me proudly. "I was listening at the door."

"Thanks, Mom."

She plucked at her sleeve and sighed; a few minutes of weird, pregnant silence passed and nothing happened. It was obvious that I was going to have to start this conversation.

"I went over to Jonah's house today," I told her innocently, as if she hadn't known that. As if she wasn't sitting there waiting for this information.

She nodded slowly. I could see her mind working furiously. *What can I ask without seeming too nosy?* she was thinking. *What can I say that won't make her shut down and tell me nothing?*

"He seems really nice, Mom," I said when she didn't speak.

She made a brave effort. I could see her making it. There was an exhaled breath, a lip quiver, an eyebrow twitch. And then the frame collapsed.

"Oh God, Mom. Are you *crying*?"

She wasn't exactly, but her eyes were very red. I heard a squeak from her and nothing more.

"Mom, I'm going to stop telling you things if you keep overreacting."

She swallowed and cleared her throat. "I know. I know. I'm sorry. I'm fine. Give me a second."

"Mom. I met him yesterday. *Please.*"

"Yes. You're right. I'm just—"

"Do you want to talk about something else while you get yourself together?"

"I'm together. Totally together," she insisted.

"Sure, Mom. You know, most girls my age have already been through half a dozen boyfriends. Some of them are on birth control." What the hell was I doing? She looked like she was going to faint. "You know if Kristin's parents acted like this every time she met someone, they'd both be in a coma. She's been in and out of relationships since she was twelve."

"I know, April. But you're not Kristin." She took a deep breath. "You're not like a lot of your classmates," she continued in a steadier voice. "Friendships mean more to you. And so will your relationships."

"I'll be careful. I'm taking things slow."

She shook her head at me. "I'm not worried about the speed. I'm worried about the intensity. Honestly, I see a lot of myself in you. Now don't roll your eyes, I actually know you, believe it or not. We're the type that can get completely swept away. And we'll stay loyal to the people we love, no matter what."

She was talking about her own history now, not mine. Mom was raised in the ultra-Orthodox Jewish section of New Square, and her parents were the strictest of the strict, religious role models for their community. All their children followed their example—all except my mom, whose unexpected teenage rebellion shook her family to the core. At eighteen, she declared that she was going to stop "arranged" dating for a while and travel out of state to study psychology.

Near the end of her junior year, her parents' worst fears came true. My mother met Mark Wesley: fellow psych major, handsome flirt, and lapsed Catholic. When they married the following summer, my grandparents mourned their daughter as if she'd died. My mom sent baby pictures after I was born and continued mailing photos of me and letters about my progress for several years. She never heard another word from her parents, and eventually she stopped trying.

"Loyalty isn't a bad thing, Mom."

"It is when you're fifteen and you have no experience. The truth is I wouldn't be worried about Kristin if I were her mother. Kris will drop a guy because he didn't like a movie she liked." She paused a moment to let her words sink in. *Well, she got that right*, I thought. Kris would drop a guy over a movie. Or a sports team. Or a flavor of ice cream.

"So what? Do you want me to be like Kris?"

"No. But I don't want you to marry yourself to this boy after a week of dating either."

"We're not—we're not even dating!" I was sure of that, at least. Well, pretty sure. Hold on a minute. *Were* we dating?

My mom shot me a doubtful look. "You're not?"

I was supposed to know the answer to that. "I'm not sure," I admitted in a low voice. "I was going to call Kris later and ask her what she thought."

She laughed and leaned back against the wall. "Okay. Kris will tell you if you're dating a guy that she's never met?"

"Fine, *you* can meet him if you want, if you think you know so much about it," I shot back irritably and then immediately regretted it. *Don't take me up on it, don't take me up on it, please don't take me up on it.*

"Great!" she responded, brightening. "Bring him by tomorrow after school."

Damn.

"Oh—but—but you have work…"

"It's okay! I'll take off early and fix dinner for us."

"Oh, no. No, I really don't think that's a good idea."

She looked offended. "Why not? What's going on with you? Are you doing that 'my mom is so embarrassing' thing? Because I've never actually given you a reason—"

"I know you haven't." *Because I've never given you the chance to,* I thought grimly. Kris is used to the fruitiness, and how often do I bring over new people?

"So what is it then? Just ask him if he's free."

He would be free, and just my luck, my mother would serve stewed tofu niblets and quinoa cakes. I could already picture it.

"Okay, fine," I mumbled.

"Good, that's settled," she said, clapping her hands together. "I can't wait to meet him. I'll make my watercress omelet."

I closed my eyes and leaned back against my pillow. "Could we just order pizza tomorrow? *Please?*"

There was a short silence; I could hear her fighting the urge to argue. "Okay," she agreed after a moment. "I suppose that'll be all right."

She hung around for a while longer, as if she expected me to speak again, but when I didn't open my eyes, she slid off the bed and slipped out of the room, shutting the door quietly behind her. It was a relief that she was gone. I didn't want to answer any more questions about Jonah.

Normally I don't mind my mother's company. She's a patient listener, and she's so anxious to be a good parent that she rarely actually parents me. She usually alternates between the role of supportive older sister and timid roommate. I wished now that she had stayed that way. Her newfound maternal confidence and sage advice were getting on my nerves.

I needed time alone to think. If Jonah really was my boyfriend, then I had some serious texting and obsessing to do. Then, after I finished messaging Kris, I planned to devote the rest of the night to hard core daydreaming. I couldn't wait. It would be the best fantasy ever, because now my dreams came with a tiny ray of hope.

CHAPTER 11

JONAH AND I WERE DEFINITELY DATING. UNLESS FRIENDS NORMALLY LEAN back in history class and whisper, "I was thinking last night how much fun it would be to paint you," I think it was fair at that point to call our relationship official.

I took my cell phone out and texted Kris the news. He says he wants to paint me.

Her answer came back ten seconds later. Nice. But does he want to kiss you?

Oh. Well. I didn't expect him to think about that yet. And as for my own daydreams—

I met him three days ago, Kris. Give it some time.

My phone blinked. When can I meet him?

I tapped Jonah on the shoulder. He turned around to me, glanced at the cell phone in my hand, and grinned. "I'm free this evening if she is," he whispered.

He couldn't possibly have seen her message; the screen was hidden behind my textbook. "How did you know what I was going to ask?"

"What else could it be?"

Come by after school I wrote and slipped the phone back into my pocket.

And then, just a few periods later, it was lunchtime, my favorite hour in the day. We sat together at the corner bench and talked about everything. He told me more about his old school, about some of his teachers, about Boston. I told him about Kristin, about my anxious mother and her strange family whom I'd never met. I couldn't believe how easy it was to talk to Jonah. It never once occurred to me to jot conversation topics down on my palm. Only a couple of days ago, I'd been so panicked about the idea of being alone. Those fears seemed so far away now with him sitting next to me. He actually leaned forward when I spoke to him, his eyes alive with interest, his smile reacting to my words. I felt bold when I talked to him. Bold enough to actually comment on his new relaxed smile, and laugh when he blushed at my observation. "When we first met, you had this shocked 'deer in the headlights' grin," I remarked. "But now, it's different."

He shook his head and made a "facepalm" gesture. "Half of my photos!" he groaned. "I look like I sat on a pinecone. It's my nervous 'smile for the camera.' It goes away when I calm down."

"You mean your eyebrows come down when you relax?"

He nodded. "But when I meet new people or get into tense situations, it can get pretty ugly."

"So this evening when you meet my mother, they'll probably fly straight off your forehead?"

His shoulders shook with laughter.

I couldn't believe I was making him laugh. I felt like I had stepped into another girl's life. He actually thought I was funny! He'd admitted to being nervous around *me*. He was worried about meeting my mom. His awkwardness made me feel normal, and the coming evening seemed a little less terrifying.

Still, there's nothing quite like bringing over a prospective boyfriend to make you see your home in a different light. I had taken our small semidetached rancher for granted, but now for the first time, I wondered what it would look like to a stranger. As we entered my house, I saw Jonah glance around curiously, and I was suddenly aware of the mismatched weirdness of the place. It was like several different cultures had burst into our living room and made war with one another. Wooden African sculptures faced off with a giant Chinese screen; a replica of an eighteenth-century French painting hung opposite a Mata Ortiz pot. Even the furniture appeared to be having an identity crisis. The place was cluttered with battered antiques from different eras: a stiff pink armchair from the sixties, a coffee table from the baroque period. I knew the story behind every one of the eclectic pieces, how my mom had picked each treasure up for pennies at some flea market and how she'd researched the history of every one of her unusual finds. But the sum total of the collection was pretty overwhelming.

I watched him stare for a little bit and then suggested we go off to my room. I wasn't embarrassed by that at least. I too had chosen every item in the place, but I'd done it carefully and tastefully (I thought). My walls were covered with posters of my favorite musicians: Evanescence, Linkin Park, Dido, Billie Holiday, Mozart. My throw rug and bedspread were striped navy corduroy, plain but warm, with no silly lace or puffs. My keyboard was propped up in the center of the room beneath my open window; I'd draped the corners of its stand with an embroidered tapestry from an old Druze village. The Druze thing might have been my mother's influence, but I liked it, and everything else in there was mine.

Jonah didn't look impressed. He walked over to my keyboard, ran his fingers over the edge, and then turned to me with a disappointed expression. "Oh," he said. "I pictured an actual piano."

"Seriously? What, a baby grand?" I retorted. "Where would I put one? There isn't even room in here for a small upright. And besides, I can record myself on a keyboard."

He didn't look convinced. There was a bothered expression on his face, like he was trying to work out a complicated problem that he didn't know how to explain.

"I just don't think electronics and art are a good combination," he declared finally.

I laughed and sat back on my bed. "The majority of the music world would probably disagree with you."

He had paused beside my keyboard and was staring at it now with a strange intensity, as if he'd seen something on the keys that upset him. "You don't *understand*," he told me, his voice rising slightly. "Recordings can be taken away from you. Someone could take them."

I frowned at him and shook my head. "What are you talking about? Who would take my practice tracks? Why would anybody want them?"

Again, the furrowed brow. He wasn't looking at me anymore but was concentrating on something far away, something that was frightening him. I saw his body tense, and he turned his head quickly to the door. "Did your mom just come inside?" he asked me hesitantly.

I got up and peered out the window. "No, not yet. I don't see her car. Why? Did you hear something?"

He leaned back against the wall and rubbed his forehead. "I just thought I heard someone call out. Never mind. I must be tired."

I was about to answer him when I heard a rhythmic tapping on the front door. Jonah started violently at the sound and then shot me a questioning look, as if waiting for an explanation for the unexpected noise.

"Oh, you have better ears than me," I said. "You must have heard Kristin coming up the street. That's her at the door. She always taps out 'Hail the Conquering Hero' when she comes over."

He relaxed a little and smiled back at me, but the smile didn't make it to his eyes.

"Don't be anxious," I told him as I went to answer the door. "Kristin can be a little blunt sometimes, but she's really sweet. You'll like her, I promise."

He followed me into the living room and hovered a few feet behind me. I was watching his expression as Kris stepped into the light, and for the briefest moment, I felt a stab of envy as she smiled at him. I hadn't realized until that moment just how pretty Kristin was. I'd always taken her looks for granted, ever since we were little. But now, in the same way that I was seeing my own home with fresh eyes, I was meeting my best friend again through Jonah. And though his greeting was casual and

deliberately polite, I couldn't help noticing the flash of appreciation in his eyes, that quiet acknowledgment of beauty that I'd
seen so many times in others when they met her. It had never
bothered me before. Even though Jonah never leered or stared,
and though I saw his gaze shift immediately to me, that second
of admiration awoke the voice of a thousand insecurities. In the
moment that it took Kristin to say hello, I'd already counted all
the differences between us and come up short on every point.
Sleek, blond ponytail vs. Mount St. Hair, *Teen Vogue* smile vs.
"lost her retainer after a month," tanning cream commercial vs.
connect-the-dots freckles and pores.

I never meant to show what I was feeling; my expression was
carefully pleasant, and I'm certain that my smile never changed. So
I have no idea how he sensed what I was thinking. But before my
self-examination could progress southward into a hopeless cata-
loging of my body's imperfections, I felt Jonah's arm steal quickly
around my shoulder, and I was pulled gently but firmly to his side.
It was the smallest gesture, outwardly casual and totally natural,
but to me, it was as if he'd dipped me back and kissed me in front
of the entire world. He noticed me—even with Kris standing
there, all blond and unconsciously beautiful, it was me he wanted.

We settled down on the living room sofas, Kristin opposite
us and Jonah still solidly by my side, his arm wrapped securely
around me. Our happy couple demonstration wasn't lost on
Kristin. She gave him a grudging nod. "Very sweet, Jonah," she
said, waving her finger over us. "I see what you're doing with that
arm there. Now put it back down at your side unless you want to
lose it. April's mom is at the door."

We all sprang up in unison, and I scurried forward as the knob turned and my mother entered. Her eyes went immediately to Jonah. Smiling sweetly, she stepped over to him and extended her hand.

"I'm so glad you could come by this evening," she began, and I held my breath and waited for the rest. But no, it actually looked like she was done. Jonah murmured a polite response, and now we were all sitting in a circle in the living room again and talking—about something.

It was actually going well, I realized as I listened to them chatter. Incredibly, I was the only anxious one in the room. Whatever had bothered Jonah earlier had disappeared, and he seemed completely at ease now, lounging next to me (at a respectable distance) on the sofa. Kris was ordering a couple of large pizzas (with my mom's permission), Jonah was doing an impression of Ms. Lowry and making them both laugh, and my mother was telling us a funny story that had happened at the office. It was unbelievable. I'd been worried about nothing.

The pizzas arrived, and we all dug in. I got tomato sauce on my shirt and had to change, and when I returned, Jonah was complimenting my mom on one of her unusual paintings, and she was beaming at him. She was so *together*, as if she'd stowed away all of her nervous energy for the occasion. And she looked good too; the outfit she'd chosen highlighted her small, slim form, her straight black hair was wound around her head in a spiral bun, and she was actually wearing makeup. I was proud of her and grateful at the same time.

After Jonah went home, my mom walked over to me and hugged me silently, then shuffled off to the kitchen, smiling happily to herself. I didn't need to ask her what she thought of Jonah. It was obvious. I helped her carry the glasses to the sink, and then Kris took my arm, and we walked together to her bus stop.

"Well?" I nudged my friend as she waited for her ride. "What did you think?"

"Definitely not gay," she declared. "Very intense though. His eyes especially."

"Yeah, I know. But I love that about him."

"I can see that."

We were quiet for a moment; she was staring intently down my empty street as if silently willing the bus to appear and rescue her.

"Okay. What is it, Kris?"

"Nothing. *Nothing.* He's very sweet. And really cute."

"But?"

"But nothing. I'm happy for you. I honestly hope it works out."

Her bus rounded the corner, and she stepped quickly, eagerly, over to the curb. Something was still bothering me though, and as the doors slid open, I put my hand out and stopped her.

"Kris, I meant to ask you something."

She turned around, one foot suspended over the first step. "Yeah?"

"When you came over this afternoon, did you call out to us before you knocked?"

She looked strangely at me and shook her head. "No, I rapped the knocker like I always do. Why would I have called out?"

"Oh, never mind then. It's not important," I told her as I turned away. "I guess he must have imagined it."

CHAPTER 12

NO ONE BELIEVES ME WHEN I TELL THEM THAT JONAH WAS THE BEST boyfriend in the world. They think I'm painting too rosy of a picture, considering what happened later. They insist that there must have been some signs, something wrong, some clue where this was headed. They want to hear symptoms. But I can only tell them how I felt with him.

We became best friends by the end of the first week. Jonah seemed to need me as much as I needed him, even if he hid his social anxiety better than I did. And I was so relieved that I wouldn't have to spend sophomore year alone that I never stopped to count the hours we spent together.

We were rarely apart. After school, we hung out in my room or his until our moms separated us for the night. We took the train down to DC and roamed the National Gallery of Art, and Jonah showed me details about the great masters' paintings that I could never have imagined. I learned about light sources and shadows. I learned how to critique art, what to look for in a portrait, how to interpret an artist's choice of color and palette.

We listened to music, studied for tests, watched movies on his laptop. He learned that I cried at happy endings and became angry at sad ones. I found out that he liked action-adventure flicks and oddball comedies. And I discovered that I didn't care what we watched as long as I was sitting close to him and I could feel the tremble of his body when he laughed.

Most of all, I enjoyed watching him when he wasn't looking. I'd never had a boyfriend before, so I don't know if this was normal, but everything he did fascinated me. I loved the way he bit his lip when he was concentrating on an assignment and then rubbed his eyes when he was frustrated. I loved it when he'd ask for help with a math problem and then make fish faces when I tried to explain the answer. I loved the sound of my name when he whispered good night to me. I even loved it when he fell asleep in the middle of a movie, because then I could just watch him. I'd brush the black curls from his forehead and trace his dark brows with my eyes, memorize the dimple over his open lips, the curve and hollow of his cheeks. I'd touch the dark hairs on his arms and follow them to his wrists, then slip my fingers into his hands. I'd study the open button at his neck, run my eyes over the dip beneath his collarbone and then imagine the rest, the hidden I couldn't see. I'd wonder how his lips would feel against mine when he finally kissed me. I'd count the days we'd been together and worry that maybe he didn't want to. But when he woke, I was always careful to look away, because I couldn't let him know what I'd been thinking. I was embarrassed to let him see how much I cared.

Kris felt the whole kiss situation was very concerning. Jonah and I were into the second week when her texts starting getting embarrassing.

Are we there yet?

No.

How about now?

Get a hobby, Kris.

During the second weekend of our relationship, Jonah's mother called mine and invited us to a family picnic near Quarry Lake. I was totally against the idea at first, but my mom had already made a giant quinoa pudding, so I didn't have much choice. As it turned out, Mrs. Golden was a quinoa *fanatic*, so their friendship was instant (and very wholesome). After ten minutes of listening to "Really? Quinoa meatloaf?" Jonah suggested a private stroll across the playground. Katie was swinging on the jungle gym, and our mothers were walking Lady. It was the perfect time to sneak away. Halfway up the garden path, we paused and looked over the green. It was a beautiful spot—quiet, secluded, with a gorgeous outlook. There was a cluster of trees close to the path, and we settled beneath them for a rest. It was a cool and hazy evening, and the setting sun had stained the clouds a wild indigo against the darkening sky. We didn't have much longer, I realized. Our family would be looking for us soon, but I wanted to savor this moment before we had to go.

Jonah pulled me close to him when we sat down, and his arms tightened around my shoulders; I felt him lay his cheek against my forehead. I turned around to look at him, and he ran his fingers through my hair, pulled me close, and kissed me, timidly at first, then slightly bolder, and then with an intensity that took my breath away.

I'd waited forever for that perfect moment. I'd dreamed of it every night since I'd met him and practiced it over and over in my imagination. But no dream could have come close to the reality. In my fantasy, I hadn't heard him catch his breath before he bent his head toward me. I hadn't imagined the feel of his firm hands against my cheeks. I hadn't felt the thrill of warmth as his lips brushed mine. I could never have guessed that I'd be shaking by the end.

He looked worried when I pulled away. "Is something wrong?" he whispered hoarsely. "Moving too fast?"

"Not at all." My voice caught on the words.

"You sure?"

I smiled. "If you didn't make a move today, I was prepared to tackle you."

He laughed and pulled me roughly onto his lap. "Damn it. I knew I should have waited longer." With one finger, he traced the outline of my lips, then parted them and kissed me again.

And that's where my daydream ends when I think about that day. I'm curled up in his arms. He's smiling at me and brushing his hand against my cheek.

But if I have to, when they force me to remember everything and describe when I first sensed something was wrong, I have to end that scene the way it really happened. I have to remember past our kiss. He was holding me as I described. I glanced up at him and was about to speak when I saw that he wasn't looking at me anymore. His body was tense, his eyes narrowed in concentration. I slid off his lap and stared out into the darkness, trying to see what he was staring at. "What's wrong, Jonah?" I asked him as he scrambled to his feet.

He shook his head distractedly and started back across the path. "I heard Katie scream. She must have fallen and hurt herself."

I hadn't heard anything, but of course I hadn't been paying attention to anyone but him. I hurried down the hill and caught up to him by the playground.

Katie was there just where we'd left her, swinging happily from the jungle gym. Our mothers were sitting on a nearby bench and watching her. Lady was snoring peacefully near the sandbox. Mrs. Golden looked up at us and waved.

"There you are, guys," she called. "We were about to go looking for you."

Jonah appeared not to have heard her. He was staring at his sister with a frightened expression on his face. "Are you okay, Katie? Did something happen to you?"

She dropped down from the bars and skipped over to him. "No, I'm good. But I'm glad you came. I want to show you a trick I learned." She tripped back to the slide. "Watch me, Jonah! Watch me!"

But he wasn't looking at her anymore. He wasn't looking at any of us. He dropped heavily onto a nearby bench and put his head in his hands. His mom rushed over and sat down next to him. "Are you okay, sweetheart?" she asked him quietly. "Is it another migraine?" He shook his head and placed his hands over his ears. Mrs. Golden reached out to touch him, and her fingers brushed against his neck. "Oh God, Jonah, you've broken out into a sweat," she fretted. "That's it. We're going back to Dr. Rosen and asking her to look at you again. I'm calling her office now."

Jonah pulled away and grabbed the phone from her hand. "I'm not sick, Mom," he insisted sharply. "I'm just a little tired. And I had this—this ringing in my ears. I'm fine now. I just want to go to bed."

Mrs. Golden didn't look convinced, but she took the phone from him and dropped it in her purse. As we headed for the car, I overheard her whispering to my mother. "He gets these sudden headaches," she murmured in a worried voice. "But he doesn't want to talk about them with the doctor."

"Why don't you take him to Dr. Steiner?" my mom suggested. "I've worked as his secretary for years, and he's great with teenagers."

Jonah muttered something under his breath and slumped down in the backseat next to me. Katie slid in on the other side and rested her head against my shoulder. It was a short ride home, but as soon as the car left the parking lot, Jonah appeared to doze off. As we rounded the corner onto our street, the car swayed and I accidentally bumped his arm. He shifted over without speaking, and I realized that he hadn't actually been sleeping. The muscles in his shoulders were clenched tight, his arms rigid at the elbows; he was gripping the fabric of his jeans, his knuckles white over his knotted fists.

He was suffering, but it was obvious that he didn't want us to notice, so I said nothing and waited for it to pass. When my mother pulled our car into their driveway, he sprang out without a word and rushed into the house. His mom gave us an apologetic shrug. "Maybe I'll call later for that doctor's number," she said and hurried after her son.

CHAPTER 13

IT WASN'T WHY I WAS WITH HIM, OF COURSE, BUT I COULDN'T HELP WON-dering if dating a cute guy might boost my reputation at Fallstaff. And maybe it would have done that—if Cora hadn't been in the picture. But the rumor that Jonah had rejected the Princess of Fallstaff High was the hottest gossip of the year. So when he and I began to date, the wrath of the princess boiled over and consumed her.

If it had just been Cora's anger, I would have been fine with it. It might even have been fun to be the object of her envy. But Cora had the sworn allegiance of at least half the girls in our class and almost all the guys. So when she decided to make my life miserable, she had lots of help. She may have been an awful student, but she had an advanced degree in classmate torture.

It began quietly enough. Name-calling, a missing notebook from my bag, gum stuck to my chair. But one morning after phys ed, as I was changing out of my gym uniform, I reached down to grab my shirt and discovered that my schoolbag had vanished. Not only that but the gym clothes that I'd just taken off had also disappeared. I found myself standing nearly naked, shaking and mortified in my underwear, with no way to call for help. The two girls who had been changing in the room with me had fled with all my things. I searched the bathroom frantically, but the lockers were all empty or closed; there was nothing in the entire place with which to cover myself. I couldn't even call anyone—my cell phone was in my missing bag.

I sat down and waited, hoping that someone would eventually rescue me. More than half an hour passed as I shivered in misery. Finally, near the end of English class, I heard a gentle tapping and the sound of Jonah's voice. "April, are you in there?"

I scrambled over to the door and opened it a crack. "Oh, thank God! How did you know?"

"You didn't show up to English, and then I saw Cora whispering to Tessa and pointing to your empty seat. What happened?" He tried to push the door in, but I jammed it with my foot.

"They took my schoolbag and my clothes. Can you hand me your sweater? I'm freezing."

He pulled it off and passed it through the crack. "You have to tell the principal."

It was hopeless though, and we both knew it. By the time the principal came back with us to investigate, my schoolbag and clothing had magically reappeared. I wasn't physically hurt and none of my property had been stolen, so of course she told us to go back to class; there was nothing she could do.

I changed into my school clothes and met Jonah in the cafeteria. "I can't do this anymore," I told him. "It's getting worse each day. Did you hear they've started spreading rumors about me now?"

He nodded. "I think everyone has."

"Oh, great. So then you've heard the latest one?"

"About you cornering Miles in the library and asking him to—"

I put my hands over my ears. "You don't have to say it!"

He looked embarrassed. "I've been thinking about this, and if you'll let me, I can try to make them stop."

"How exactly?"

He tapped his fingers on the lunchroom table and glanced at the group of girls around Cora. "Just follow my lead, okay?" he whispered. "No matter what I do, just trust me."

"Hold on, Jonah, can you at least tell me what—"

But I never got to finish my question. He got up abruptly and backed away from me, his face a picture of disgust. "I *trusted* you!" he shouted at me suddenly. "You *bitch*!"

There was a sudden clatter of trays, and a hush settled over the lunchroom. Everyone turned to look at us, and I felt my stomach knot up. What the hell was going on? How was this going to make anything better?

"Jonah—" I began. But he stopped me with a gesture.

"No, *screw* you, April! Just leave me alone!"

And before I could say anything, he slammed his drink into the trash and stalked out of the cafeteria. I stayed long enough to see Cora scurrying out into the hallway after him. Then I gathered up my things, ran down to the bathroom, and called my mom to beg her to take me home.

As soon as the school day was over, I marched over to Jonah's house. His mom said he was up in his room, but I would have known that without her telling me. The floor was vibrating with a deep bass beat, and as I climbed the stairs, I recognized Linkin Park's song "New Divide" echoing through the hallway. He was blasting it, and the words hit me like a crash of waves when I pushed open his door.

Jonah was pounding at the punching bag with all his strength. His fists were flying in rhythm to the music, and he was panting from the effort; his cheeks were flushed and damp, his curls clinging to his forehead. He didn't see me at first—his eyes were closed, and the beat was so loud that I had to shout his name a few times before he heard me. He wheeled around suddenly, and his eyes flew open. There was a startled, confused expression on his face, as if he hadn't recognized me or couldn't understand why I was there. Then he switched the music off, pulled me inside, and shut the door.

"Jonah, what the hell is going on? How could you scream at me like that in front of the entire school? Do you have any idea what that was like for me?"

"I know, I know—I'm sorry." His words came out in little bursts and gasps. "Look—I was going to come over—and explain later. I just had to—I needed to clear my head first."

"Good," I said sarcastically. "Do you need more time? Because I'll go home if you're too busy murdering your punching bag to speak to me."

He exhaled sharply. "I know exactly what I'm doing."

"Well, do you mind letting me in on your little secret then?"

He reached out and took my hand. "Just calm down and give me a chance, okay? Please, April, I need you to trust me."

I moved away from him, but he stepped forward quickly and drew me into his arms. I was crying now; I started to push him back, but I was so miserable that I couldn't find the strength to fight. Then he kissed me quietly and brushed the tears off of my cheeks, and suddenly I didn't want to fight at all. I was almost ready to forget that I was angry. I stopped crying and relaxed against him, and he kissed me again, harder than he'd ever kissed me before, and then I nearly forgot why I'd come there in the first place. Slowly, purposefully, his mouth traveled across my cheek and behind my ear. I felt his hands move gently up my back. "There," he whispered into my hair. "Do you still want to punch me? You can if you want." I burbled something into his shirt, and he laughed softly. "Don't get mad, okay? Just listen. The plan is simple. I'm going to break up with you for a few days. We won't talk to one another or be seen together anywhere, even outside of school. Are you with me?"

I nodded mutely, my face still buried in his shoulder.

"Okay, good. Also, I'm asking Cora out tomorrow."

I jerked back and tried to push him away. But he'd anticipated that, and I found myself wrapped tighter in his arms.

"Come on now," he murmured impatiently as I struggled to free myself. "Stop it! Do you really think I'd betray you like that? Seriously?"

He relaxed his hold, and I slipped out of his arms. "Dating Cora is part of your plan?"

He nodded. "Just give me the next four days. I promise that this will all be over before the weekend, and the bullying will stop for good. Please. Let me do this for you."

I frowned and crossed my arms. "Okay, but what if it doesn't work?"

"Then we'll be gone by next year anyway."

"Gone? What do you mean?"

"I'm planning to transfer to the Baltimore School for the Arts. I want you to come with me."

"To an art school?"

"Why not?"

"Because I'm not an artist. I write lyrics without music and I mess around on the keyboard. There's no way they'll ever take me."

"Oh please! You don't have to be a child prodigy! I've heard you play. You're better than most of the musicians at my old school."

"You're exaggerating."

"No, I'm not. You just need more confidence. Look, it's up to you. I promised my mom a year at Fallstaff, but that's it. I can't take it anymore. I've had enough of their advanced academics and brain control."

"Brain control? What are you talking about?"

"I'm just asking you to think about it. I won't go without you. I don't even want to spend the next four days without you. But I can't stay at Fallstaff much longer. It's not…"

He hesitated for a moment.

"It's not *what*, Jonah?"

He looked down at his hands. "I can't say right now. Just promise me you'll think about it."

CHAPTER 14

Before I'd even raised the phone to my ear, Kris's voice boomed out, hissing outrage into the air.

"He called you a *bitch* in front of the entire school? What the *hell*, April?"

I groaned and considered hanging up. I didn't want to have to justify Jonah's behavior, especially since I didn't exactly understand what he'd been thinking either.

"Look. He had his reasons, okay? Please don't judge. You weren't there."

She snorted. "It's a good thing that I wasn't there. I would have kicked his ass."

I couldn't help smiling. "I would have loved to see that. You know, for an ex-student, you are super tuned into Fallstaff gossip."

"I'm not tuned in. I've barely heard from you over the last few weeks. Then I log in to see half a dozen Facebook updates and comments about Jonah's tantrum. It's all spelled out on Cora's wall. And so I think, 'ohhhh, that's why April hasn't been calling me. She's embarrassed because her new boyfriend is a douche.'"

I gripped the phone close to my mouth. "Don't. You. Talk. About. Him. That. Way."

"He called you a bitch!"

"You don't know the whole story!"

She exhaled and mumbled something inaudible.

"Look, I don't want to discuss this on the phone," I told her. "Can you come over later?"

"Yeah, I'm already on the bus to your house."

We arrived at the same time. Kris marched into my living room without a word and flopped down on the sofa. "Okay. What's going on with you two?"

"It's complicated."

"Well, maybe it wouldn't be so complicated if you kept me updated. What happened to 'April and Kris Saturdays'? *You* were the one who suggested the idea in the first place. But so far, all I've gotten is a month of excuses."

"I know. I'm sorry. It's just that it was the beginning of our relationship. And I thought that you and I could just catch up later. I didn't mean to ignore you, I promise."

She shrugged. "I've had news to tell you too, you know. I was going to call you tonight. And then I read all that stuff online and I thought…"

"Yeah, I know. You thought 'what the hell?'" I interrupted. "You said that already. Kris, you have to believe me. Everything's fine between Jonah and me." I hesitated for a moment and leaned forward confidentially. "Actually, it's *better* than fine. I've been meaning to tell you about it. I was saving it for this Saturday, in fact."

"Okay, so what happened?"

I hesitated. "It's what's going to happen. Our relationship has gotten pretty serious."

"And?"

"I think—I think he's going to tell me he loves me."

I'd been hoping for a squeak, a smile, some sign of encouragement. But she just crossed her arms. "Does he normally yell at his girlfriend before telling her he loves her?"

"That was nothing!" I exclaimed. "He was just trying to help me. Cora and her gang have been torturing me, and he has this plan to make her stop. So he's pretending to break up with me. Just for a few days."

Her expression softened a little. "Oh. So you were in on it, then?"

"Not at the beginning," I admitted. "He explained the plan to me…afterward. I *was* a little upset at first. But I'm fine now. We straightened it out."

"How sweet."

This was not the reaction I'd hoped for at all. "I'm really *happy*, Kris." There was a defensive edge to my voice. "I wish you'd believe me."

"I do," she replied after a pause. "I'm just a little worried."

"About *what?*"

"I'm worried he's going to hurt you."

"He would never do that!"

"So why didn't he tell you what he was planning to do until afterward?" she demanded. "You must have been so embarrassed when he yelled at you in front of everyone."

"I was. But like I said—"

"I know you think you're in love. But I'm just telling you to be careful," she persisted.

"You're not exactly the expert on guys, you know," I countered angrily. "Since when have *you* ever been careful?"

"I didn't need to be. I've never been in love with any of them."

"So what are you saying? That it's a bad thing to care about someone?"

"I'm just telling you to be careful. Look, this is all happening pretty quickly, right? So I'm just saying, take it a little slower."

I shook my head. "Whatever. I have to do my homework."

She got up off the sofa. "Fine. Just think about it, okay?"

CHAPTER 15

The vague tapping on my door
Is enough to wake the dead
The birds chirping by the window
Is like screaming in my head.

I HAD PLENTY OF TIME TO THINK ABOUT IT, BECAUSE THE NEXT FOUR DAYS were the loneliest and most miserable of my life. Jonah played his part without a fault. Not once did he even look in my direction. I had to watch as he flirted shamelessly with Cora. It didn't help that I trusted him. When Cora sidled up beside him and snaked her arm around his waist, acid burned my throat. I'd like to say that I channeled some of my pain into my music, but I'm not sure how anyone actually does that. I mostly just wet my keyboard with my tears and wrote tuneless lyrics about birds.

But then, on Friday afternoon, just as he had promised, the game was over. Jonah met me at the lockers and wrapped his arms around my shoulders. "I missed you, baby," he murmured into my ear. Cora was standing in a corner glaring at us, and Jonah turned me around to face her. "Cora has something to say to you, April."

She swallowed and glanced around the hallway miserably. A crowd had begun to gather. Teenagers can sense a brewing scandal like sharks sense blood in water.

Cora's apology was barely audible at first.

"Louder, so we can all hear you," Jonah ordered between his teeth.

"I'm sorry, April," she moaned weakly.

"Okay, good. Now tell her what you're sorry for," he prompted.

She was trembling, her face crimson with shame. I felt bad for her. All the cruelty and pride had drained away, leaving behind a miserable, desperate little girl.

"It's fine, Jonah," I said. "That's good enough."

He looked vaguely disappointed but shrugged his shoulders at the crowd, as if signaling the end of the show. They melted away as quickly as they'd come, whispering excitedly to one another. I smiled, linked my arm through Jonah's, and walked with him to the bus stop. Everything seemed suddenly bright again, and I slid in beside him and leaned my head against his shoulder as the bus pulled out of the parking lot.

"Well, Mr. Mysterious?" I asked him when we got to his house. "Are you going to tell me how you managed that?"

He pulled his cell phone from his jacket pocket. "Nothing magical. Just used a little old-fashioned blackmail."

"What do you mean? What's on the phone?"

He flipped to his "video" folder and clicked Play. Cora's voice rose from it, shrill, whiny, and abusive. She was complaining about Tessa and calling her a traitor and a whore for flirting with Miles. Then she moved on to Miles, and then Robby, and then half a dozen of her closest friends. There was an hour of trash and gossip on his phone, but we only listened to the beginning before turning it off.

"How did you get her to say all that?"

He chuckled to himself. "I have *a lot* of boyish charm apparently."

"Jonah!"

"*What?* I'm serious. I can be very persuasive. Poor thing just needed someone to talk to."

"That's all you did? You listened to her?"

"I *swear*. Come on, stop glaring at me like that. Okay, maybe we should talk about something else. How about this: I have a surprise for you. A special present. Do you want to see it?"

I wavered for a moment; I didn't want to prolong the argument, because I really did believe him, but I didn't want him to think that he could get away with anything just by dangling a present in front of me.

"Okay," I agreed grudgingly. "But we're going to come back to this later."

"Nope. I think we're finished with this subject. Come on. Your present is hidden in my studio."

"Your studio?" My pout evaporated. "It's finally ready then?"

I'd been waiting for this all month. Of course I knew what he was going to show me. He'd hinted for weeks about a new painting. I hadn't been allowed in his studio since that first time, even though I begged repeatedly to see it. "No one watches me paint," he explained. "It isn't safe to show until it's done."

There was a new canvas standing in the corner by the window. It was covered with a sheet like all the others, but he'd cleared a space around the bottom, and some of his supplies still lay on a little rumpled mat beneath. I hurried over to the easel, lifted up the cover, and threw it back.

The painting was absolutely stunning. I'd tried to imagine how it would look. I'd even guessed the background from the streaks of blue under his fingernails. But I wasn't prepared for this.

He'd painted me, of course. I'd been expecting that. Over the last few weeks, I'd noticed him staring at my features, as if he meant to memorize everything about me. But seeing my face now lit up in color was not what took my breath away. It was how he'd drawn me.

I was *beautiful* in his portrait. It was the first thing I noticed when the sheet fell back—the vision of a pretty girl standing on a hilltop. But then I stepped back in disbelief. I recognized myself: pale face, hazel eyes, thick brown hair. But I was also seeing myself for the first time, seeing myself as he saw me. And I loved the girl he'd captured in the painting, not just because she was pretty, but because she looked hopeful and at peace. I'd never seen that expression on my face before. When my reflection stared back at me in the mirror, there was usually a wrinkled forehead and critical, narrowed eyes. I'd never really liked the April in the mirror. But he'd washed all my insecurities and doubts away.

He'd drawn me standing on a grassy hill, surrounded by a stormy ocean. Near the horizon, palm tree branches poked their leaves up between the waves, but I was dry and warm, untouched and unaware of the flood around me. I wore a simple navy dress, and my hair was loose around my shoulders; there was a delicate golden necklace around my neck. Nestled in the bend above my elbow, a small white bird peeped out from the wrinkles of my sleeve. I didn't really see the little bird at first, because its body was mostly hidden by my dress and I was too excited by the beauty of the portrait to wonder at the tiny creature in my arms. It was much later, in the privacy of my room, that I noticed that its wings were torn and its little body was crushed and soaked in mud. But at that moment, I wasn't thinking about birds or symbolism; I couldn't take my eyes off the beautiful girl in the painting.

Jonah was watching my reaction closely. He must have heard me catch my breath, but I'd been completely speechless for a few moments. I didn't know what to say. Finally, I turned to him and threw my arms around his neck. "Can I take it home with me?" I asked him. "Please, please, can I keep it?"

I felt his body stiffen in protest. "No, April, I'm sorry."

I begged and pleaded. I held onto him like a little girl. I kissed and teased him. He was obviously pleased with my persistence, but there was something bothering him that he couldn't share with me. We bargained and argued for a long time until he finally gave in to me. There was one condition, he insisted, as I danced around in victory. I had to promise him that I'd hide the portrait in my room and make sure that no one saw it, not even my mom.

"I don't understand," I said as he wrapped the canvas in paper. "You must show your drawings to other people. What about the teachers at your art school? They must have seen your work."

"They did," he told me simply. "But everything is different now. Things have changed for me. I can't explain it. I'm sorry, I just can't."

I shrugged as I tucked my prize under my arm. "You'd better get over this shyness soon. I've been working really hard to get ready to audition at your art school. But there's no way I'm going without you. It was your idea. *You* were the one who lectured me about self-confidence."

"You've really decided to go for it? Because of what I said?"

"Well, if you can spend hours painting me, then I can spend a little time practicing on my keyboard for you. Not that I think it will make any difference. But I promise you I'll try."

CHAPTER 16

I REALLY DID TRY—I WENT FROM PLAYING SEVERAL MINUTES ON THE PIANO to banging away for hours every day. My music teacher noticed the difference right away and complimented me on my progress. My mother hovered near my door, listening and dropping little whispers of encouragement. "I'm proud of you. You're so focused now."

And I was, for the first time in my life. The truth was that I was working hard for Jonah, to make him proud of me. I was scared that he would pass on to his gilded path without me and that I'd be left behind. I saw it as my only chance to follow him, and I was determined to do it, no matter what it took. I would play better, be more confident. I'd mold myself into a real artist. I would change for him.

But, as Jonah had hinted, something else was changing at the same time. It was before Christmas break that it became obvious to everyone, but I think I started feeling it right before Thanksgiving.

When was the first real warning sign? The first instance of unusual behavior? That's what everyone wants to know, it seems. When did it all begin to come undone? I don't tell them about the episode after our first kiss, of course. There's no reason to tear that memory apart. The first warning sign, I tell them, was in history class, sometime near the beginning of November.

Ms. Lowry was talking about the Chinese Cultural Revolution. We'd opened up our books and were copying out the relevant facts and dates—Mao Zedong, 1966, Red Guards—when Jonah's hand shot up.

"Yes, Jonah?" Ms. Lowry paused, one finger still pointing to the time line on the board.

"So you're saying that the government arrested teachers and artists? Destroyed books and paintings? They threw professors in jail?" There was a note of fear in his voice.

"That's right, Jonah. The revolutionaries were suspicious of anyone who was educated or creative—if they didn't use their creativity to further the socialist agenda."

"And what did they do to them?"

She hesitated for a moment. "Well, some were sent to rural labor camps. Many intellectuals were tortured and killed—"

"So now you're talking about a kind of brain control." Jonah's voice rose, tense and sharp, cutting off her explanation. "You're talking about *national* mind control." Everyone turned to look at him; Cora raised her eyebrows, Miles was chuckling and shaking his head. Even Ms. Lowry appeared confused. She loved when her students got excited and passionate about history. But this wasn't normal interest. Jonah was clearly scared, as if he thought the Red Guards were waiting for us outside our classroom door.

Ms. Lowry cleared her throat and slowly laid her eraser down. "Jonah, I don't know exactly what you mean by brain control. Yes, independent thought was definitely discouraged. But that was hardly the first time that a government tried to snuff out art and science when it felt they threatened its authority."

"No, you're right—and it wasn't the last time either," Jonah declared. "They're doing it all the time."

There was an uncomfortable silence; several people giggled nervously. Jonah pulled out his navy spiral notebook and began scribbling furiously in the margins. Ms. Lowry gave him a long, bewildered look and quietly resumed her lesson.

When the class bell rang, Ms. Lowry caught me on the way out and motioned for me to come to the office with her. I didn't want to go, but I could see by her expression that I didn't have much choice. She closed the door and motioned for me to sit down.

"April, I'm sorry to bring you in here like this, but I feel that I have to ask for your input. Jonah's little explosion today—"

"I realize it looked strange," I interrupted. "And I was going to talk to him about it. I'm sure he's just stressed out about something."

"What I was going to say, actually, was that his outburst didn't really surprise me. The fact is, I've been worried about Jonah for some time now. I've been planning to call his mother in for a conference. But I know that you and Jonah are dating, and I was wondering if you'd noticed any other changes in him recently."

I couldn't answer that question directly. I didn't want to think about what she was implying. "I don't know what you mean, Ms. Lowry," I replied in a defensive voice. "He's always been a little moody. Is that what you're worried about?"

She sighed and settled back into her chair. "No, April. Moodiness is normal in teenagers. It's his school performance that I'm concerned about. Take this paper I assigned last week about the Confucian influence on Chinese culture. He told me that you worked on it together."

That was technically true. We sat next to each other in his room and looked up the sources together. But Jonah spent many more hours on it than I had. He was still typing madly on his laptop after I wrapped up and went home.

"But I know that he did the assignment. I watched him do it. Didn't he hand it in?"

"Yes, he handed it in. But my goodness, it was more than twenty pages long! And I'd only asked for three."

"Oh. Is that a problem?"

"Well, the paper started off okay, but somewhere on the fourth page, I lost track of his train of thought. He began to ramble about conspiracies and religions trying to destroy our culture, government plots…"

"Oh, he just reads a lot about that kind of thing!" I said. "Spy novels, mysteries—he can't get enough. He really needs to cut back."

I don't know why I lied to her. Jonah didn't read novels, and if he did, he wouldn't have chosen thrillers. But I was trying desperately to protect him, without really understanding why.

Ms. Lowry stood up slowly and walked over to my chair. "April, this wasn't just a disorganized paper. I'm worried because Jonah stopped making sense. It was a twenty-page paranoid rant. He's one of the brightest students in my class. I was wondering if you're aware of any stress at home, anything I should know about before I call his mom…"

"No, there's nothing!" I shot back. "Everything's fine. And really, I think that you're overreacting. I mean, if you normally call in every mother when their child writes a bad assignment or has a bad day, well, then that's up to you. But I don't think there's anything to worry about. And I'm late to class now, so I'm going to go."

She stepped aside to let me pass, and I fled the room as if she was about to tackle me to the ground and torture the truth out of me. Somehow I was convinced that if I stayed any longer in that office, Ms. Lowry might actually persuade me that something was wrong with the boy I loved. I would rather have faced the Red Guards and all their interrogation equipment than risk that.

CHAPTER 17

I DON'T KNOW IF MS. LOWRY EVER CALLED JONAH'S MOM IN THE END. MRS. Golden had been acting so nervous recently that a little more worry wouldn't have been noticeable to me. She did her best to hide her fears in front of Jonah. But no matter how phony she was or how cheerful she pretended to be, it was clear that she was becoming more and more frightened for her son. And for some reason, the only thing that seemed to calm her down was having me around. I didn't realize this at first, but after the tenth invitation to come for dinner, I began to get the picture. So when school let out, I frequently went straight to his house and stayed there until my mother called me home.

The Monday before Thanksgiving break, I came over as usual to spend the evening at Jonah's. I waved hello to Mrs. Golden and then followed Jonah upstairs to his room. We curled up on his bed together, and I pulled out our notebooks and spread them across his blanket. He was falling behind in math, and I'd promised to help him with his homework. It was rough going for a while, but we plowed through half of the chapter before I realized that he'd stopped listening to me and was just copying down my work.

"Jonah, you can't do that," I said, shoving my textbook aside. "You actually have to understand how to solve these questions yourself, or you'll just fail the test next week."

He stared at me for a moment and then shut his book. "I know. I just can't—it's hard to concentrate today."

I sighed and leaned back against the wall. "You haven't been able to concentrate for a while. Everyone's been noticing that you're distracted. Even your teachers have commented about it."

I regretted the words as soon as they were out of my mouth. Jonah sat up straighter; I saw the muscles in his neck go taut. "Hold on, which teachers do you mean? Have they been talking to you about me?"

"It was just one teacher, and seriously, you need to relax!" I exclaimed. "Ms. Lowry was concerned about you, and I—"

"Ms. Lowry!" he shouted, pushing himself off the bed and swinging around to face me. "I should have known that she would rat me out!"

"What are you talking about? Since when do history teachers rat their students out?"

He looked confused for a moment. "Just stop, please," he muttered finally, turning his face away from me. "I need you to stop. I just can't—I can't listen to you right now."

"What do you mean you can't listen to me—"

"Damn it, April!" he interrupted furiously. "I'm *begging* you! I need a break from the noise!"

Before I could speak again, he bent down and clutched his head, covering his ears with white, clenched fists.

"Jonah?" I whispered, drawing closer him. "Why are you doing that?"

He didn't answer me. His breathing was deep and ragged; a cold sweat spread over his forehead. "I need to be alone," he whimpered. "Please, just go help my mom or something. Five minutes, that's all I'm asking."

"Jonah—"

"*Please*, April!"

I backed away and slipped out of his room without another word, then wavered for a few seconds outside his door, trying to decide which way to go. There was no way that I was going to leave him alone in pain. I couldn't just run down to the dining room and fold napkins like nothing was wrong. But he didn't want me anywhere near him either.

I crouched down on the stairs outside his room and waited, silently listening for some sign that he was going to be okay. A few minutes passed like that; I didn't move, just sat there on the top step, my chin resting on my knees. The clock on the landing ticked. Lady waddled by and sniffed me, then passed on to more interesting things.

Mrs. Golden's voice drifted up to us, calling us down for dinner. I heard Katie shout out, "April! Meatloaf!" and still I didn't move. For the first time since this all began, I was really frightened for Jonah. Ms. Lowry's words echoed in my mind: "*Jonah stopped making sense.*"

It was true, I realized. He'd sounded really strange. But maybe if I waited, maybe if he would just explain himself…

I was knocked out of my daydream by a muffled shout and a soft kick from behind. "God, April! I didn't see you."

I scrambled to my feet and turned around to face him; Jonah was staring at me like I'd just lost my mind. "What are you doing here?" he asked. "I almost tripped on you!"

"I was waiting for you. I had to make sure you were okay."

He laughed and put his arms around me. "I'm fine. I was just a little stressed out. Thanks for waiting for me." He looked down at me and smiled, and I felt my throat contract. *Ms. Lowry is crazy*, I told myself. There was nothing wrong with him. How had I doubted that?

But even as I hugged him, something still felt off to me. He seemed different now. His smile didn't reach his eyes; they were frightened and far away, like a child's after a nightmare. His face had changed too. He was a lot paler, and there were dark hollows in his cheeks.

"I'm having trouble sleeping," he'd told me earlier in the week. If I hadn't been so blind, if I hadn't been so busy pretending everything was fine, I would have seen it sooner. It was time to pay attention.

So when he sat down across from me at the dining room table, I began to watch him, really watch him, for the first time. I watched him nod pleasantly at his mother and scoop out a large helping of potatoes. I watched him joke with Katie and throw a green bean at her. I watched him duck when his mother smacked him playfully and laugh when she scolded him for throwing food.

"Stop messing around and eat," she chided. The pinched, worried look in her eyes had faded a little. "You're getting thinner every day, Jonah."

"I'm eating," he mumbled through mouthfuls of potato. "I just don't like the school cafeteria food, that's all." He swallowed and poked at the beef at the edge of his plate. "Mom, what's in this meatloaf?"

"Oh, I was trying something new. I didn't expect you'd notice. Your school newsletter has a recipe section on the back page. I got the idea from there. Do you like it?"

I didn't need to be watching him carefully to see the change that came over his face. We could all see it. He paled as if she'd punched him in the stomach. Then slowly, deliberately, he wiped off his fork and placed it on the table. "Why would you do that?" he asked her, his voice sinking into an accusatory whisper. "What are you trying to do?"

She looked confused. "I—I just like making new things, that's all. The potatoes are also a new recipe. I got a few ideas from the newsletter…"

She never finished her thought. Jonah froze in place and glared at his food as if he'd just seen something nasty crawling about inside his mashed potatoes. He swallowed, and his face convulsed; he seemed to be choking back the urge to gag.

"Jonah," she ventured, her voice cracking like a child's. "I can make you something else. If you don't like that, I have some frozen stuff that I can thaw…"

He shook his head and pushed himself back from the table. "No, I'm fine." He sounded like he was trying to keep his voice steady. "I'm not hungry anymore."

Katie was watching her brother as closely as I was. While his mother and I stared helplessly at him, she slipped quietly off her chair and, before he could protest, climbed onto his lap and laid her curly head against his cheek. "I'm not hungry either,

Jonah," she whispered confidentially. "It tastes pretty weird to me too."

He looked down at her and smiled, but it was a vacant smile, like a ceramic doll's grin. "Thank you, Katie," he murmured and closed his eyes.

A few minutes later, when Mrs. Golden and I began to scrape our plates, Jonah lifted his head suddenly, glanced around as if he'd just woken up, and gently nudged his sister off his lap. "I'm going to go upstairs for a little while," he told us. "There's a book that I need to finish for school, and I'm sort of..."

No one interrupted him. We were all quiet, anticipating the end of his thought. But his sentence stopped there, as if he'd been shut off, like a tape recorder that someone suddenly disconnected.

CHAPTER 18

Why must all these people
Make you believe what they believe
The water's closing over your head
And it's hard for you to breathe

I DECIDED NOT TO FOLLOW JONAH UPSTAIRS; HE OBVIOUSLY NEEDED TO BE alone. So I went home and waited for the fog to lift. And sure enough, the next day, he seemed to be okay again. Not a hundred percent or anything. His face seemed even thinner than before, and his hands were bruised and bandaged, but his eyes had regained a little of their former glow. Maybe a night of pummeling his punching bag had cleared his head a little. Maybe we were all overreacting.

But then, two days later, he didn't show up to school. My phone calls went to voice mail. That evening when I came by, his mother informed me that he wouldn't leave his room. He let me sit by him though; he listened to me patiently as I talked about my day. But he refused to speak a word. I pretended to ignore his silence at first; I even tried to trick him into talking by dropping innocent little questions. After the tenth failed attempt, he finally scribbled two words on a piece of paper and handed it to me.

I'm sorry.

So I went home again and waited. I was sure that this would pass, just like last week's episode. He was still my Jonah. Despite the hollow eyes and terrifying silences, he hadn't vanished completely; he was just hiding, temporarily out of sight.

One afternoon in mid-December, we went shopping for Hanukkah presents with our families. The afternoon went well; we browsed for a little while, and then Jonah whispered something to my mom and bolted off into the crowd. In normal circumstances, I would have blown it off. But I couldn't help it; I was scared now, always on my guard. My mother watched me quietly for a moment and then drew me aside.

"What's the matter, April? You've been craning your neck since Jonah walked off. Tell me what's going on."

"What did he say to you?" I asked her miserably. "Did he tell you where he was going?"

She shook her head. "He told me he wanted to buy you a present and that he'd join us in a little while." Her voice sunk into a whisper. "What on earth did you think he was doing?"

The truth was I didn't know. I had no idea what was happening to him, and so I was imagining the worst—without having an idea of what the worst could be. And of course my mother thought that I was being paranoid and silly, because Jonah joined us a few minutes later, clutching a wrapped package in his hand and smiling happily to himself.

Later that afternoon, we all went back to our house, and Jonah followed me to my room. We were talking normally again; it wasn't perfect, but I felt him with me. His eyes had lost some of the blankness and were almost alive again. So I was happy; my mood was so entwined with his that every shift carried me along, both to darkness and to light. He settled on my bed and waved a hand in the direction of my keyboard. "Your mom keeps bragging about your playing. She says you've become a little star."

I laughed and sat down beside him. "My mom likes to exaggerate. I am practicing though. I think I've gotten better."

"Can I hear?" he asked me hesitantly. "It doesn't have to be anything long. I'm just curious."

I protested at first. I wasn't ready yet; my fingers were too cold—I brought out all the excuses. But he convinced me with one sentence: "April, I painted you."

There was no way to argue with that. So I sat down and played, a slow composition first, just to get myself warmed up. Then I moved on to something lighthearted and fun and much more difficult. When I was done, I turned around to look at him. He was lying on my bed, his head propped up on my pillow, his eyes closed. I climbed up beside him, and he wrapped his arm around me.

"Thank you," he whispered simply.

"I'm glad I played for you," I told him. "If I'm going to audition for your art school, I have to get used to performing."

He shook his head. "No, I mean thank you for everything. I know that you've been working hard for me. And not just on the piano either."

He shifted over onto his side and rested his head against his wrist. I turned around to face him and reached my hand out to brush the curls from his forehead. It was painful to see the dark shadows beneath his eyes, the paleness of his lips, the hollows in his cheeks. He was still beautiful—he would always be beautiful—but it was a starving beauty now.

"I'll practice as hard as I have to," I vowed. "But you have to promise me that you'll come with me. I can't do this alone."

He smiled and reached out to me; his eyes were peaceful, his touch soft against my cheek. "I love you, April," he said.

It was all I'd waited for. I put my arms around him and kissed him. He pulled me close, ran his hands over my back, and brushed his lips over my neck and chin. We hadn't been alone together for days, and I'd longed for him whenever we were apart. And yet, the harder I kissed him now, the stranger his touch felt. He seemed suddenly unsure; his confidence had vanished, his pent-up desire frozen. I tried to reassure him. I moved closer to him and kissed him harder. But he pulled back suddenly and drew his hands away.

"I'm sorry," he told me. "Can we stop for a minute?"

"Okay." I moved to the edge of the bed. "Did I do something?"

"No! It isn't you. Come on, please don't look at me like that. There's really nothing to worry about—"

"I'm not the only one who's worried, Jonah."

He let out a frustrated sigh. "You think I don't know that? My mom watches me like a hawk all day. Even Katie keeps asking me if I'm all right."

"So couldn't you try to talk to someone? It doesn't have to be me. But if you're in pain, you have to get help."

"I'm *not* in pain. It isn't migraines, for the millionth time. And you can tell my mom to stop looking for drugs; she keeps searching my room while I'm at school."

"So then what—"

"I just can't talk about it," he said, pausing before each word as if considering its meaning. "I'm really sorry. But I know what will happen to me if I do. I have to deal with this on my own. And April, I'll understand if you want to take a break from this, if you want to take a break from me—"

"Don't you *dare*!" I protested, my voice rising. "Don't you even think like that. I'll wait, as long as it takes, and I won't ask again, I promise. I won't say anything until you're ready. Just don't ask me to leave you. I won't, I *won't*—"

He looked alarmed and raised a finger to his lips.

I exhaled and moved closer to him. "I'll be more patient," I whispered. "I love you. Please don't ask me to leave you again."

He was silent for a few minutes. I watched him anxiously and listened to him breathe.

"Jonah, are you being honest with me?" I pleaded finally. "Do you *want* me to leave you? Is that what this is about? Because if that's it, just tell me now…"

He gathered me close to him and stopped my question with a kiss. "Do you really think I want to break up with you? I know I haven't been good to you, but I never meant for you to think that."

I rested my cheek against his. "Good. Then I'm not going anywhere."

He sighed and buried his lips in my hair. "Thank God," he murmured. "I can't do this alone."

In my room later that night, I realized that he'd echoed my words exactly. *I can't do this alone.* But when he'd said them, he wasn't talking about the art school audition. And though I'd asked him—twice—he'd never actually promised to come with me.

CHAPTER 19

THE FOLLOWING FRIDAY EVENING, I FOUND MY MOM IN THE LIVING ROOM.
She was staring vacantly out the window and cracking pistachio
nuts into a bowl.

"Jonah wasn't in school today," I told her. "And he's not
answering his phone. I'm going over there to drop off his
homework, okay?"

"Mmm—" she replied. Her eyes never left the window.

I peered over her shoulder into the street. "Why are you staring
at the neighbor's house?"

"The Greenwalds have such a big family," she said, a touch of
envy coloring her voice. "Eight kids, I think. When I walk past
their home, it's never quiet. Except on Friday evenings."

"Oh. That's nice. Have you met them?"

"No." For some reason, she seemed sad when she answered me.

"Is it okay if I head out now?" I asked after a pause. "I want to
get there before dark."

She turned away from the window, and her distracted eyes
focused on me. "That's fine. But I thought you should know that
I've been talking to Jonah's mother," she told me. "She's trying to
convince him to see Dr. Steiner this week."

I shook my head. "You realize he'll say no, right?"

"I know he will. But Rachel was hoping you can get him used to the idea. So far, he's refused every time she's brought it up. We thought that if you talked to him, maybe he would listen."

I began to back away. "I'm sorry, I won't do that. I have to be on his side. I'm not going to nag him like his mom."

"But something's obviously wrong. If we ignore Jonah's symptoms, they'll only get worse. Rachel's worried because her brother suffered from bipolar disorder for years before he was finally diagnosed. And how would you feel if Jonah totally lost control, if he tried to hurt himself…"

I couldn't listen to her. I'd promised Jonah to give him room, to let him deal with it on his own. How could I begin pestering him without completely losing his trust?

"*No*, Mom, I'm sorry. I'm not going to help his mom drag him to a bunch of doctors. I won't betray him like that."

"It's *not* a betrayal!" she said, her voice rising. "You have an obligation to your boyfriend. Don't you understand that? If the positions were reversed and you were suffering, wouldn't you want him to help you?"

"Yes, I would. But not like that." I turned my back to her. "Everyone just needs to leave us alone."

"Where are you going? I'm not finished talking to you."

"Well, I'm finished talking to you!"

"April, stop this stupid tantrum and listen to me. I've been quiet long enough. But I have to tell you when you're making a mistake. Look, I understand what you're going through…"

"Oh, I *bet* you do!" I wheeled about to face her again. "Remind me, when your family was pressuring you to turn against my father, what did *you* do?"

She gasped as if I'd punched her. We'd always had an unspoken agreement that I would never mention the family she'd lost. I'd never broken that silence, because I didn't want to hurt her. But in that moment, I didn't care.

I fled the house before she could speak again. She called me as I was nearing Jonah's house. I stared at the phone, then pressed reject, and walked up to the door.

There was no answer to my knock. I peeked in through the open shades. The main level was quiet, but a faint sound of music drifted down from the upstairs window. I put my hand on the doorknob and turned; it was unlocked, and the door creaked open. I laid Jonah's math assignment on the dining room table and shouted his name. He didn't reply, but as I climbed the stairs, the beat of a U2 song echoed in the hallway.

I'd lifted my hand to knock when Jonah's voice came booming out from behind the bedroom door. He was screaming at someone inside. "I won't listen to you anymore!" he yelled. "*Please*, just leave me alone!"

There was a short pause, the familiar, rhythmic drum of his boxing glove slamming into the punching bag, and then another cry. "I won't do it! I won't! *Just burn in hell!* I don't believe you!"

More thumping sounds and then a string of curses—ugly, hateful words, a wailing torrent of abuse. I'd never heard him swear like that. Who could he be cursing at? I didn't hear anyone else in the room. Was he on his phone? And if he was, how was he holding up the cell and beating the bag so frantically at the same time?

Then the screaming faded; there was a pitiful sobbing, the dull thud of a body collapsing to the ground. I wavered uncertainly in the hall for a minute and then placed my ear against the door. "Please, God, I can't," he pleaded. "I can't, I can't. *Please*, make them go away. Please just make them stop."

This last sound was much worse than the frantic screaming; I couldn't stand to listen anymore. I tapped softly on the door and called his name.

There was a brief silence and then the shuffle of footsteps. Jonah threw open the door and stared blankly at me. He looked awful; his hair was mussed and damp, his face was streaked with sweat, and his knuckles were torn and bleeding. His eyes were bloodshot, as if he hadn't slept in days.

"Jonah," I began hesitantly. "I came by to bring you your homework—"

He didn't let me finish. With a rough gesture, he took my arm and pulled me into the room, then grabbed his cell phone off the desk and pressed it into my hand. "Take it away," he begged. "Take the damn thing away. I don't want to see it anymore."

Without a word, I slipped his phone into my pocket and took his swollen fingers in mine. He allowed me to lead him to his bed, and without protest, he lay back limply on the pillow that I placed beneath his head. I picked up a towel from the floor and moistened it with water from the bathroom sink, then carefully wrapped his bleeding hand. He shivered when I tried to wash the crusted blood away. I suddenly realized how cold it was; he'd left the window open, and the frosty December air had chilled the room. He was only wearing a light T-shirt and boxers, even though his hands were icy and his fingernails were blue. I shut the window, pulled an extra comforter from the closet, and covered him, then ran the wet washcloth over his forehead and smoothed his tangled curls. He turned to face the wall and closed his eyes.

I watched him for a little while and thought about what I'd heard. Could that have been his father on the phone? Katie had mentioned an awful scene between her father and brother and complained that they hadn't spoken to each other since. But besides the brief discussion about his dad's portrait, Jonah had never spoken about his dad, and I'd never pressed him for an explanation. What could Dr. Golden have done to make him scream that way? I'd never even heard Jonah raise his voice before. And I couldn't imagine talking like that to my parents, no matter how furious I was. It wasn't just an average yelling match; Jonah had been violently abusive, in a way that actually frightened me.

There was a distant rumble of a car engine and the sound of the front door opening below. Lady barked, and Katie's chirping voice echoed through the house. I was strangely relieved that they were home; for the first time in our relationship, I was actually afraid to be alone with Jonah. He'd never been anything but gentle with me, but the person I'd heard swearing into the phone was a stranger. I needed to understand this better. I had to ask his mom about Jonah's history with his father.

But then I realized there was an easier way. I held the answer in my pocket; Jonah had handed me his phone. I crept out into the hallway, closed the door behind me, pulled out his cell, and clicked on "call history."

I expected to find a call from his father. I was actually hoping for it, because at least that would have made some sense. A screaming match with his dad, some bully from his past, even a call from an old girlfriend would have been okay. Anything would have been better than what I found.

The phone's log showed nothing. He had not dialed a number or received a call from anyone that day.

CHAPTER 20

HOW COULD I TALK TO JONAH'S MOM NOW? HOW COULD I REVEAL WHAT I'D just discovered without worrying her even more? And wouldn't that be the worst betrayal of all—to poke around his phone list and then report my findings to his mom? And yet, what else could I do? Was I really protecting him by watching silently while he suffered? Was my mother right? Could he really get worse? I remembered seeing a movie where a kid collapsed and died of a bleeding brain tumor in front of his family. Before he died, he'd gone through a strange personality change. What if we were ignoring something serious that could really hurt Jonah in the end?

I'd made up my mind by the time I walked down the stairs. Jonah's mom was putting away some groceries when I came into the kitchen. She looked up and waved at me, but her smile faded when she saw the expression on my face.

"Mrs. Golden," I told her. "I think Jonah needs to see a doctor."

She bowed her head and leaned against the breakfast counter. "I've been trying to convince him. But I can't drag him kicking and screaming to the pediatrician."

"Let me talk to him. I'll do my best to make him understand."

She hesitated briefly and took my hand. "April, I know that you care about him and that you're only trying to protect him, but you would tell me, wouldn't you? You would tell me if he was doing something—if he was into something—unhealthy…"

"It isn't drugs," I assured her quickly.

She nodded. "I just don't know what else to think. He's never acted like this before. I used to brag to all my friends about what an easy kid he was. Even when that tragedy with Ricky happened, he was still my sweet and thoughtful boy. But he took it so hard. I thought that moving away from Boston would be best for him. To put some distance—"

She paused uncertainly and looked up at the stairs. A door slammed above us, and there was the sound of footsteps. Jonah came into the kitchen and glanced up at the clock, then gave me a bewildered look.

"What—what day is it?" he asked.

"It's Friday. You've only been asleep for a few minutes."

He looked relieved. "Well, I feel better anyway. Is there something to eat? I'm starving."

His mother grabbed her purse from the counter. "I was thinking of getting takeout. I'll go to the Chinese place you like around the corner. How does a plate of lo mein sound?"

She took our orders and bustled purposefully out of the house, throwing me a grateful smile as she went. She was obviously hoping that I'd talk to Jonah right away. But I was dreading our conversation. I didn't know how long Mrs. Golden would be out though, so I couldn't waste any time.

"Jonah, can we talk?" I asked him.

He gave me a frightened look and sank down into a chair beside me. I hesitated for a moment, unsure about how to begin, but after a minute of silence, Jonah spoke up first. "I know what you're going to say," he said in a resigned voice. "And I understand. You don't have to spell it out for me." He was sitting with his head down, like a guilty convict about to receive his sentence, and his hands were shaking in his lap. "Just go, okay?" he begged me. "I can't listen to the speech about staying friends right now. Please, just spare me that."

Of course he'd jumped to that conclusion, I thought miserably. I hadn't even begun, and already I'd managed to screw this up. "How can you think that I was going to break up with you?" I asked him. "I just want to ask you for a favor. Really, I promise."

He looked up at me, his eyes red-rimmed and full, and my throat contracted painfully. Oh God, how could I go through with this? How could I go on when he already looked so hurt?

"I love you," I told him. "But the truth is that I'm scared to be with you sometimes. I'm scared of what might happen."

He stared silently at me for a moment. Then he shook his head and his eyes grew dark. "Hold on, what do you mean?" he asked me. "Do you really think that I could ever hurt you? I've been going through a rough time, but I have never, *I would never…*"

"No, no, that isn't what I meant!" I paused, speechless with frustration. With each sentence, I seemed to be making it worse. I had to change course quickly or I'd lose my chance. Acting on instinct, without a real plan in mind, I went over and put my arms around him. "Jonah," I began in a low voice. "I *am* scared, just like I told you. I've been reading about depression, and I've been finding some terrible things online. There was this case of a guy who ignored his symptoms until it was too late, and they found that he had a tumor and it made him have a seizure, and he got really sick…" I swallowed and felt the tears start in my eyes. I no longer knew what I was saying. I was making this stuff up as I went along, but somehow it was affecting me anyway. "Last year, I saw Ms. Lowry have a seizure," I continued. "No one in the class knew what to do, and she almost died in front of us. I'm worried that something like that will happen to you too, that I'll be standing there helpless while you—" I broke off again and dropped my head. He was looking at me with such pained concern that I felt guilty for my dramatic lying.

"Okay, I'll go," he told me before I could speak again. "I'll tell my mom to call for an appointment."

I stared at him. "You will? Really?"

He nodded. "If it will make you feel better."

I couldn't believe it. I'd gotten exactly what I wanted, and it hadn't even been that hard. So why didn't I feel relieved? Why did I suddenly regret what I had done?

"But, April, would you come with me?" he asked timidly. "I really don't want to go alone. I don't trust them. I don't trust their pills and brain probes and magnetic scans. I don't know what they'll try to do to me, but if I know that you're on my side, that you'll stand by me, then I can go through with it."

And so I promised him, of course, and the next day, my mom set up an appointment with Dr. Steiner.

CHAPTER 21

TEXTING KRIS HAD BECOME A CHORE. SHE SENT ME MESSAGES ALMOST EVERY day, but I was finding it harder and harder to come up with things to tell her. I wanted so much to brag about my gorgeous, talented boyfriend. But I found myself deleting most of the messages I started. It would have been easy enough to gush about the painting Jonah had done of me. But what would I say when she asked to see it? *Sorry, Kris, I promised him I wouldn't show it to anyone, not even my mom.*

I couldn't say that—so I didn't mention the portrait hidden in my closet.

Falling in love with Jonah meant protecting him from everybody's judgment. So I automatically filtered out the strange and scary whenever I spoke of our relationship, even to Kris. Recently though, every day with Jonah had needed "sanitizing" before I could talk about it.

And that evening when Kris told me that someone named Danny had asked her out, I responded with eating dinner at the Goldens' tonight. Can't wait to hear about your date! And the next day, going to the doctor tomorrow, Jonah isn't feeling well.

When she asked me why I was going with him, I snapped back, Because that's what a girlfriend does when her boyfriend is sick.

She replied, Why? Can't his mom take him?

That's when I stopped texting her.

On the day of the doctor's visit, I came by as soon as school was out. "I'm glad you're early," Jonah told me when I walked into his room. "I want to give you your Hanukkah present before we go."

It was a sweet gesture, even though Hanukkah was actually several days away, and I hadn't bought his present yet. He reached behind his pillow and pulled out a small thin package, wrapped in colorful menorah paper. I tore it open, and a dark wool beret fell into my lap.

"A hat?" I asked with a bemused smile. "It's very pretty, thank you."

"I need you to wear it to the doctor's office," he told me seriously.

I should have asked him what he meant, I guess. But he looked so grave and firm that I didn't question the request. As I slipped the beret over my hair, there was a sound like rustling paper, and a smooth, cool strip brushed against my forehead.

"Hold on, there's something stuck in here," I said and pulled it off my head. Inside the beret, several sheets of tinfoil had been taped together to cover up the cloth; as I looked closer, I saw that the edges of the foil had been stapled to the beret's rim.

"I've reinforced it," he explained simply. "They can't get their magnetic scans through that. So you'll be safe."

Why didn't I react then? I think that I would have laughed at Jonah's suggestion if it had come completely out of the blue. I would have tossed the ridiculous helmet back at him. But this was just the last in a string of actions that I couldn't explain. And I was completely focused on getting him to the doctor. My job was to bring Jonah to the pediatrician so he could run a few tests and come up with a diagnosis. Then he could give him an antibiotic, an antidepressant, an antisomething, and we could get back to our normal lives.

So I just did what Jonah asked. I nodded quietly and pulled the tinfoil beret over my hair without a comment. And I wore it as if it was the most normal thing in the world.

When we got to the pediatrician's, my mother waved the three of us into his office. She'd scheduled Jonah for the last appointment of the day, so the waiting room was empty.

Dr. Steiner had been my mother's boss for several years; he recognized me and greeted me pleasantly as we entered. He was a middle-aged man, and he looked and talked like a doctor from a movie: gray-haired, clean-shaven, big glasses.

Jonah had started getting anxious from the moment we entered the building, but when Dr. Steiner smiled and asked him to be seated, he appeared absolutely terrified. He shook his head and slowly backed away, one hand gripping the door handle, as if getting ready to flee.

"Jonah, we're only going to talk," the pediatrician assured him. "There's really nothing to worry about."

"Oh, sure," Jonah snapped back. "That's what you all say. And then you hold your patients down and shoot them up with tranquilizers."

Mrs. Golden got up and walked quickly over to her son. Her face was flushed with shame, and her voice was hoarse with desperation. "Jonah, *please*, I need you to stop this now! No one's going to do anything to you. I just want to listen to the doctor."

But he was vibrating with hostility; his fists were clenched, his pupils were dilated, and the veins were standing out on his neck. "You just want to *listen* to him? Well, good luck with that! How the hell can you hear anything he's saying? How can anyone hear *anything* above those screaming babies?"

We all looked blankly at one another. The office was completely quiet; Jonah was the only patient there.

"What…what babies, Jonah?" his mother asked.

"Out there!" he cried. "Someone's *torturing* them out there—" He paused uncertainly and glared at the doctor. "Why are you *staring* at me like that?" he hissed. "What are you trying to do to me?"

The doctor half rose from his chair and studied Jonah intently; there was a concentrated, troubled look in his eyes. "Jonah, what are you hearing now?" he asked him quietly.

"Nothing!" he shot back. "Just your stupid asshole voice."

"Jonah!" Mrs. Golden grabbed him by the arm and tried to pull him into a chair, but he threw her off and backed up against the wall.

"Mom, we have to leave here *now*! That man is in on it, just like I knew he'd be." He threw open the door and motioned to me. "Let's go, April."

"One minute, Jonah," the doctor called out. "Your mother came all the way here to see me. I understand if you don't want to talk to me, and that's fine. I'm not going to try to force you. So why don't you sit outside in the waiting room for a little while? April's mom is out there. You know her—you can trust her. I'll just talk with your mother for a minute, and then you can all go home."

Jonah hesitated and glanced at me. He looked ready to protest again but then appeared to change his mind. "Okay. But April, you stay in here with her. You can tell me afterward what he says." His eyes flickered over my hat, and he gave me a meaningful look. "Don't worry. He can't hurt you."

And before I could say anything, he touched his head and then shut the door behind him.

Jonah's mom sank weakly into her chair. "I'm so sorry, Doctor," she said. "He's not normally like this. He's usually kind and quiet and so, *so* bright. I don't know what's going on with him, but that person you just saw, I promise you that wasn't Jonah."

"I believe you, Mrs. Golden," Dr. Steiner replied. He paused thoughtfully and put his hands together. "Can you tell me when you noticed a change in him?"

She hesitated. "Well, I'm not sure if this has anything to do with it, but before we moved to Baltimore, his best friend was killed in a fight. Jonah was depressed for a long time after that, but after a few months, things started to get better. He began painting again, and he was dating April. He was *excited* about the future. And then this came on, maybe a few weeks ago, and I just don't know what to think."

"Can you tell me what you noticed?" Dr. Steiner asked.

Jonah's mom shrugged and shook her head. "I'm not even sure how to describe it. I thought at first that it was migraines. He'd close his eyes and place his hands over his ears. But whenever I asked him, he'd tell me that he was fine. And he seemed scared of something; he'd break into a cold sweat for no reason at all. That's what surprised me the most. He's never been frightened of anything before. That boy can knock down a bully twice his size! But now he seems terrified of his own shadow. Do you think—do you think it could be that post-traumatic stress thing? PTSD? Because of what happened to his friend?"

The doctor seemed to consider for a while. "Was your son present when his friend was killed?"

She shook her head. "No, Jonah was at home."

"Well, I suppose it's possible—maybe the loss aggravated his condition—but I don't think that's it."

"Then what could this be? I've thought about drugs, but I've searched his room a dozen times."

"We'll have to check for that, of course," replied the doctor. "And there are a few other tests to run before we come to a diagnosis."

"But are you suspecting something, Doctor?"

Dr. Steiner sighed and leaned forward across the desk. "Mrs. Golden, is there a history of mental illness in your family?"

She seemed to have been anticipating the question. "Yes, actually, my brother has bipolar disorder. But he's been doing well on medication. Do you think that's what it is?"

"It's possible. Has Jonah been experiencing severe mood swings, going from depressed to manic suddenly? Extremely energetic, acting impulsively?"

She shook her head. "No, he's mostly just frightened and withdrawn. Maybe a little depressed. I grew up with a manic brother, so I'd recognize those symptoms if I saw them."

Dr. Steiner turned to me for the first time. "What about you, April? Have you noticed anything unusual in Jonah's behavior?"

I didn't know how to answer him. Telling him what I'd seen seemed like the worst possible betrayal. How can you tell a stranger that your boyfriend just gave you a tinfoil hat to protect you from magnetic brain waves? That you're actually wearing that hat in his office? That you'd overheard your boyfriend screaming at nobody in his room? What would Dr. Steiner do to Jonah if I told him what I knew? How would Jonah feel about me if I betrayed him like that? No, I couldn't risk it.

"I don't know," I replied. "He's been boxing too much. His hands are swollen from it. And he blasts his music really loud."

It seemed harmless to tell him that. Dr. Steiner stared at me for a moment and shook his head. He looked frustrated and tired, and I wondered if he was about to ask me to leave. *Sorry, April, I've got no time to waste on liars.*

But a moment later, I was actually wishing that he'd thrown me out, because his next question made my heart stop. "Have either of you noticed Jonah talking to somebody when there's no one in the room?"

How could he have guessed that? And how could he look so confident, as if he already knew the answer to his question?

"No, Jonah doesn't do that!" I snapped.

Dr. Steiner ignored me and turned to Mrs. Golden. She shook her head and swallowed hard. "What are you trying to say, Doctor?"

He sighed and crossed his arms. "I'm saying that in the five minutes that I observed your son, he appeared to me to be—how do I put it? The medical phrase is 'responding to internal stimuli.' Basically, it's a fancy way of saying that I think that Jonah is hearing voices. I believe that he's hallucinating."

I hated the doctor suddenly, hated him with an intensity that shocked me. How *dare* he say something like that about my Jonah; how could he throw out a phrase like "hearing voices" as casually as if he were describing an ear infection? What gave him the right? He'd met Jonah for a few minutes, had barely even approached him, and he was telling us now that the boy I loved was so sick that he had a fancy *medical phrase* for it?

Jonah's mom was gripping the handle of her purse so hard that the veins were standing out against her knuckles. "What—what does that mean, exactly?"

"I really can't give you a definite diagnosis," he responded. "He would need to be evaluated by a psychiatrist, probably in an inpatient setting—"

"You want to put him in a hospital?" she cried.

"As I said, Mrs. Golden, I'm not a psychiatrist. We would have to run some tests first, eliminate medical causes of psychosis—"

"*Psychosis?* You think that he's psychotic?" She was weeping openly now, her cheeks shining with tears, black mascara running down in streaks over her face.

"I'm sorry, Mrs. Golden. I believe in being honest with my patients. And the truth is, from what I've seen, Jonah appears to be suffering from some psychotic disorder. He's hearing sounds that aren't there, he's paranoid, maybe even delusional. He needs to see someone—and quickly, before this escalates any further."

"Hold on!" I protested. "When you say psychosis, you mean, like, *psycho*? Like the movie? Like that crazy guy who dressed up in his dead mother's clothes and stabbed people to death? Are *you* insane, Doctor? Because Jonah would never hurt anybody. He's the sweetest, most loving—"

"No, April, that isn't what I meant at all," he interrupted. "Psychosis is usually only dangerous to the people who suffer from it. They're so wrapped up in their delusions that they often hurt themselves. But they don't normally hurt other people. At least, they almost never do."

"Almost never?" Mrs. Golden echoed. She'd stopped crying, and my anger was reflected in her flashing eyes. "So Jonah's a lunatic who'll *probably* never hurt me? That is what you're telling me? Dr. Steiner, *you don't know my son.* Jonah came here today because he knew that I was worried about him. He came because he *loves* me."

"I didn't say he didn't love—"

But she was no longer listening to him. "Jonah is the most talented young man *you* have ever met. Did you know that he won art competitions back in Boston? Won *first prize.* Can a psychotic person do that, Doctor? Would a delusional boy stand by his friend, even if it means getting picked on by bullies every day? Would he learn to fight so that he can defend his friend? Would he stick to what he believes is right—even when his own father is pressuring him to give up? Psychotic people don't know right from wrong, isn't that true? But my son is the only person that I know who has *always* held on to his principles, even when it hurt. So maybe the rest of the world is psychotic, I'm not sure, but *my son* is the sanest person I know."

I loved her in that moment; she'd defended Jonah when I hadn't been able to. She was on our side. We were united in our love for Jonah, and so, in that moment, we were also united in hate.

Dr. Steiner looked momentarily chastened; he stared at his desk for several minutes and then finally got up from his chair.

"I understand your feelings, Mrs. Golden," he told her sympathetically. "I never questioned your son's character or his love for you. But good people can also get sick. And Jonah is sick, without a doubt. We aren't talking about right or wrong. We're talking about what's real and what isn't, what's normal and what isn't. And it isn't normal to be terrified of a doctor's visit. Not at his age anyway. It isn't normal to hear babies screaming when the room is quiet."

She flinched and got up from her chair. "Jonah was just stressed today—he didn't want to come. I wish I'd left him alone."

Dr. Steiner gave her an exasperated look and shook his head. "If you leave him alone, this will probably get worse. And the longer he's sick, the harder it will be to treat him."

Mrs. Golden's eyes went cold. "Let's go, April," she said quietly.

We left the office without saying good-bye to the doctor. My mother was talking to Jonah in the waiting room. He looked up as we came in and hurried over to me.

"What did he say to you in there?" he demanded.

His mother took a hand mirror out of her purse and wiped the streaks of makeup off her cheeks. "Nothing worth hearing. Let's go home."

My mom walked over to her and put her hand out in sympathy, but Mrs. Golden shook her head. "I appreciate your help," she said. "But I think we can deal with this on our own."

There was a brief discussion about who would give me a ride back, but I settled that one pretty quickly. Riding with my mom would have meant a long talk about everything, and that just wasn't happening today. I was going in the Goldens' car. Everyone seemed too distracted and tired to argue. As I climbed into their van, my phone buzzed in my pocket.

Is Jonah feeling better? How was the doctor's visit?

It was sweet of Kris to remember. Jonah's fine. He gave me a really nice beret for Hanukkah! I replied before I turned my phone off.

We drove back in silence. Jonah kept stealing nervous glances at both of us. Anyone could sense that something unpleasant had happened in the doctor's office, but for the moment, Jonah seemed relieved that the experience was over and nothing much had changed. But when we were alone again in his room, he turned to me with a troubled, searching look.

"Are you going to tell me why my mother was crying?" he asked. "What actually happened in there?"

Would I ever be able to tell anyone the truth again?

"Dr. Steiner thought you were depressed and he wanted to put you on a bunch of pills," I replied cautiously. "But your mother told him off. She was amazing, actually. You'd have been really proud."

He didn't believe me; I could see in his eyes that he knew I was lying. Without a word, he plucked the hat off my head and laid it on his lap. He ran his fingers over the tinfoil lining and examined the edges, then flipped it inside out and held it up against the light. "It looks okay, I guess," he told me with a little exhale of relief. "Anyway, I'm glad that's done."

He settled back on his bed and waved me over. I climbed up next to him and laid my head against his shoulder. "Jonah, would you like me to stay here with you tonight?" I asked him. "Would it help you if I did?"

He laughed shortly. "Overnight? Are you serious? Your mom won't let you."

"I'll talk to her. If you want me to, I'll try to convince her."

He nodded silently and closed his eyes.

I didn't even have to argue with my mother. She agreed to let me sleep over—as long as the bedroom door stayed open, of course.

My first night with Jonah! It should have been a milestone in our romance. There should have been twenty wild texts to Kris announcing the occasion.

And I should have had to fight for it. Mom should have freaked out and demanded I come home.

But I wasn't staying as Jonah's girlfriend. I was staying as his nurse.

And Mom already knew that.

CHAPTER 22

Hold me while you have the strength
Or fall down to your knees
Turn your blind eyes to the sun
A lost boy on the run
Run away with me.

NOTHING HAPPENED THAT NIGHT. AND I'M NOT EVEN TALKING ABOUT romance. I mean *nothing* happened. Jonah tossed and turned, and I watched him mutter to himself for hours. When the sun rose, he finally dozed off, and I trudged back home exhausted, collapsed on my bed, and immediately fell asleep.

I woke up a couple of hours later to a white and perfect morning. A light snow had begun to fall, and the lawn was bathed in sunlit stillness. The air smelled sweet and pure, and the far-off crunch of footsteps and tinkle of icicles melting at my window was just the background music I needed after the previous week.

School would be closed today. I didn't even have to check. Baltimore city schools closed for days at even a hint of bad weather. I was safe in my bed for now. My mom had gone to work, so I didn't have to worry about talking to anyone for a while. I knew we would eventually have *an important conversation* though. It had been brewing for weeks, and after Jonah's behavior in the doctor's office, I was sure she would sit me down and worry at me. But I wasn't ready for that lecture yet.

A little after noon, the doorbell rang, and there was a familiar, rhythmic tapping at the door. I slipped out of bed and padded over to answer it. Kris was shaking the snow off her jacket and stomping the slush off her boots. I welcomed her inside and put a glass of hot chocolate in the microwave.

"I have something to tell you," she said after she'd warmed her hands. "But before I do, I want to hear your news."

I sat down next to her and wrapped a flannel blanket around my shoulders. "My news?"

She gave me a knowing look. "Well, I called here last night when you didn't pick up your cell. Your mom said that you were at Jonah's house. She said you were *staying over* there all night. So you know—I *assumed* that you might have *something important to tell me* today."

The naive curiosity in her smile stung me. Until then, no matter what was going on, through all of Jonah's moods and silences and unexplained rages, I never once felt sorry for myself. I loved him and accepted what was happening as a sort of test, a stage in our relationship. But now, with Kris staring at me expectantly, I realized that what I was going through wasn't a normal teenage relationship at all. Kris was expecting a hot and steamy tale. The best I could offer was a story about a weird tinfoil beret.

"Nothing *happened*, Kris. Jonah wasn't feeling well. So I stayed over. I don't have news."

"Oh." She looked disappointed. "I was hoping that we could swap stories. Compare experiences. Because I have something to tell you."

I was too tired for this. Normally I would have loved to hear about her life, I would have encouraged her to share the details, but now, after everything that had happened, I didn't want to listen. I didn't want to hear about Kris's perfect, magical, new boyfriend.

"You've met someone?" I asked her, pushing my lips up into what I hoped was a supportive smile.

"Better than that! I've wanted to tell you about Danny for a long time. But every time we talked, it was always about Jonah. And I just can't wait another minute." She smiled brightly. "I've finally decided to go for it. I think I've met the one."

At first, I didn't know what she was talking about. The one what?

And then the penny dropped, and my stomach knotted up. I definitely didn't want to hear any more.

"Wait a minute—do you mean…?"

"Yes, what else did you think? He's just *amazing*. I'm dying for you to meet him. Don't get me wrong though. I'm glad I waited all this time. But I just know it's going to be *unbelievable*."

All this time? I thought. None of her previous relationships had lasted over two weeks. "Wow, Kris. That *is* news. What makes this guy so special?"

"Oh, I knew you'd ask that. You just have to meet Danny. Then you'll understand."

"Danny?" I searched my memory and came up blank. Had she mentioned him before?

"We looked at his profile a while ago," she prompted. "You don't remember?"

"Oh, right. The guitar guy. So have you guys actually…"

"No, not yet," she answered quickly. "I was going to wait for our two-month anniversary. But I knew from the beginning that he was the one. I just kept him waiting so he wouldn't think I was, you know…"

"Slutty?"

Her mouth fell open and her cheeks flushed red. I swallowed hard and looked away. That nasty word was hanging between us, harsh, embarrassing, and wrong. I'd just been horrible to her, the opposite of a best friend. But I wasn't feeling like anybody's friend that morning. And I was afraid to continue talking to her, because I knew that eventually she would ask about Jonah, and I would have nothing good to tell her. What was I supposed to say about him? The doctor thinks that my boyfriend is hallucinating, but I'm trying really hard not to believe it? There's nothing sexy about that.

"I'm so sorry," I said finally. "I should never have said that—"

"April." There was a volume of hurt confusion in my name.

"I swear I didn't mean it, Kris."

"What's going on with you?" There was no anger in her voice. I couldn't believe how calm she sounded. She had every right to scream at me, to walk away from me…

But then she said it.

"It's Jonah, isn't it?"

My silence answered her.

"April, you're really worried about him."

It wasn't a question. The answer was in front of her, in my bowed head and drooping shoulders, in the new quiet between us.

I wasn't ready to admit it though. She still thought of Jonah as my sweet, amazing boyfriend. I couldn't break that illusion.

But a moment later, it was shattered anyway. There was a loud hammering at the door. We both started at the sound, and I ran to answer it, Kris following behind me.

Katie was shivering on our doorstep, her little hands blue and chapped, her thin sneakers caked with snow. She was crying into her sleeve, and as I knelt down, she flung her arms around me and buried her face in my sweater.

"Something's wrong," she gasped. "Please come back with me. I'm really, really scared."

"Katie, where's your mom?" I asked as I led her inside. "Where's Jonah? How did you get here by yourself?"

"Mommy's out grocery shopping," she explained. "I was play-ing at my neighbor's house. But I forgot my wand back in my room, so I ran home to get it. When I got upstairs, I heard Jonah yelling at someone in his studio. So I got scared. I remembered where you lived so I walked over here. I didn't want to call the neighbor. She doesn't know Jonah like you do. Please, April? I don't want to go home by myself."

We helped Katie peel off her wet socks, and Kris wrapped a comforter around her shoulders. Katie let out a feeble sigh and burrowed into the blanket. "I should have called my mom," she said. "But I was so scared I just ran out of the house."

"Don't worry, Katie. I'll go check on Jonah right now," I told her. "You stay here with my friend, okay? She'll put on some movies for you in the basement."

Kris pulled me aside as I was zipping up my boots. "Where are you going?" she whispered anxiously. "What if there's a robbery going on at his house? You can't go back there alone!"

"I can't explain right now," I said. "Please call Jonah's mom when I'm gone and tell her to meet me at her house. Katie knows the number."

I didn't pause to wait for her response. I pulled on my coat and was out the door before she could speak. There was nothing she could have said to stop me, even if I felt deep down that maybe she was right. There were plenty of reasons to be scared. I had no idea what I would find when I got to Jonah's house. But I trusted Katie's instinct, and I knew that she wouldn't have begged for help without good cause.

As I rounded the corner onto his street, I stopped to catch my breath and gazed out at the row of clean, white lawns that stretched into the horizon. Everything was pure and still, the snow gleaming untouched and new over the manicured lane. Only one house marred the perfect view; the Goldens' yard was mostly slush, trampled rows of footprints, and bits of dirt. As I stepped over the garden path, I noticed small drops of reddish liquid darkening the trail. I leaned over to touch the crimson snow, my heartbeat roaring in my ears. The marks across the lawn were prints of bloody, naked feet.

I should have turned and run away. I felt like I had stepped into a horror movie, and I was the naive teenager about to stick her head into a slaughter room. But what was I supposed to do?

Jonah was in that house. He might be hurt and scared, and there I was, shivering outside, staring helplessly at clumps of bloody snow across his lawn. How could I forgive myself if I abandoned him now, when he needed me the most?

Gritting my teeth, I inhaled slowly and walked up to the door. It swung open at my touch. I peeked into the hall and shouted Jonah's name, hoping desperately that he would answer. The only sound I heard was my own echoing voice and the steady beat of music from upstairs. I climbed up to the second floor and paused in front of Jonah's room. There was no sign of him, no shouting, no swearing, no punching bag slam as I'd expected, just a rhythmic shriek blasting from his speakers.

I'm screaming louder, but you're walking away.

I'm screaming louder, but you're shutting me out.

I pushed Jonah's door open and peered inside. There was no one there. The room looked exactly as it had the day before. His iPod was propped up on his desk, and the walls were vibrating from the song that he'd set on repeat play.

I call your name.

Blood runs over my hands.

Please don't turn away.

You have to watch me go.

I stepped into the darkened corridor, and the music followed me, wailing and hammering in my ears. As I walked, my boot slid forward across the floor. I lifted my foot and stared at the reddish sludge beneath my heel. A trail of dark and sticky fluid was oozing from behind Jonah's studio door. I put my hand over my mouth and swallowed against a wave of nausea. *I can't go in there*, I thought, shutting my eyes. I was too scared to look inside. "Oh God," I prayed. "Please, please, let him be okay. Please don't let me be too late."

Shaking with fear, my eyes down, I crept along the hallway, calling out Jonah's name in a strangled whisper. Still no answer, only the screeching drone from his bedroom.

I'll make you watch, I'll make you watch, I'll make you watch—

I tapped on his studio door, took a deep breath, and pushed it open. The next moment, I was kneeling on the floor, my hands over my eyes, staring in disbelief at the scene in front of me. There was no one in the studio, but every painting in the room had been uncovered, the sheets tossed in piles across the room. The canvases were all stained in red, bleeding scarlet paint from top to bottom, dripping in streams across the hardwood. Not one painting had been spared. He'd overturned ten cans of dark-red house paint over his art and smeared the stuff across the pictures in destructive, bloody strokes.

Those were the tracks I'd seen on the lawn. He must have been covered in paint when he left that trail outside. But where was he now? Where could he have gone? He had destroyed years of hard work in a few wild moments. What else was he planning to destroy?

As I walked out of the house, I looked down at the muddied yard. Jonah had left footprints—clear, crimson marks across the snow. All I needed to do was follow the trail he'd made. And so I did. I tracked the prints like an amateur bloodhound, around and around in circles, up a nearby alley and then back onto my street, and finally straight ahead in the direction of my home.

When I finally understood the way he'd gone, I broke into a

run, picking up speed as I neared my house, panting for breath as I burst in through my door. There was no one in the living room. I called out for Kris and Katie, cried out their names over and over. The tracks of pinkish snow ended in a melting clump next to the kitchen table, and from there, small puddles of water extended in a trail up to my bedroom door.

I walked slowly to my room and listened. There was a noise coming from the room, the low sound of whispered muttering and the clunking jangle of a piano note, one key being pressed over and over again. I reached out to open the door when a hand rested on my shoulder. I screamed and wheeled around, then exhaled in relief when I saw Kris standing behind me.

"God, April, what's wrong with you?" she demanded, stepping forward. "I heard you calling so I came up. Katie and I were downstairs watching a movie. What's going on?" She paused and listened at my door. "Is someone in there?"

The muttering sound stopped just as she spoke; there was a padding of footsteps toward us. The doorknob turned, then stopped, and Jonah's voice called out to us. "Who's there? What do you want?"

I felt Kris's eyes on me. I could hear what she was thinking. *Who breaks into their girlfriend's room and then demands an explanation?*

"Jonah, it's me," I answered. "Can I come in, please?"

The door swung open, and he stepped into the light. Kris gasped behind me, and I drew back in shock. I expected him to be a mess, but I hadn't been prepared for this. He was dressed in a light T-shirt and shorts; his bare legs were tinged pink and blue with cold. His hair was windblown and crusted with ice, and streams of melting snow were dripping down his face and neck. From his shoulders to his hands, his skin was stained blood red, like a warrior who'd slaughtered an enemy and then dipped his arms into the corpse. Clenched between his dirty fingers was my mother's silver butter knife. He was looking at me with blazing, wild eyes, and as I stared at him, he reached out and grabbed my hand.

"Where is it?" he demanded in an urgent voice. "Where did you hide it?"

I had no idea what he was asking. I glanced past him into my room. Two keys from my keyboard lay in pieces on the floor. "Jonah, what happened to my piano?" I demanded in a shocked whisper. "What did you do?"

But he shook his head impatiently. "We don't have much time. They've bugged your keyboard. They've been inside my studio. When they find out that I've blocked them, they'll come here next. I need to know *now*—where is that painting that I gave you?"

I could see that he'd made some disorganized efforts to search my room. Some of my books had been knocked out of my book-case; the rug had been pushed aside. He'd opened up my closet and tossed around my shoes. That was the closest he'd gotten to it. I had faithfully hidden the portrait like he'd requested, and it was hanging covered up behind my clothes. But I wasn't going to tell him that.

"Jonah, I'm not giving you the painting so you can destroy it like you destroyed the others. And I'm not talking to you until you put that knife down."

He looked annoyed. "It's a *butter* knife, April! And you're missing the point. I didn't destroy the paintings! I *protected* them. They've been stealing them and trying to steal your music. Haven't you felt it? Haven't you felt them sucking away your talent? I've been feeling it for months now! Poisonous little bugs feeding on my brain! We have to block them now before they get here."

"Before *who* gets here?" I shouted. "No one is coming to get you—"

I would have tried to finish the useless argument, I would have tried to reason with him a while longer, but at that moment, we were interrupted by the sound of wailing sirens.

Jonah froze in place, and his mouth fell open in alarm. "I *told* you, April. I told you they were coming. Stand next to me, quick. We'll face them together."

Kris, who until then had remained paralyzed behind me, now began to back away from us. As the sirens came nearer, she flung open the front door and rushed out into the yard. "In here! We're in here," she called out, waving her arms wildly as an ambulance and a police car pulled up to the curb.

A moment later, a policeman was on the lawn. Mrs. Golden jumped out of the passenger side and ran toward us, calling Jonah's name.

With a rough gesture, Jonah grabbed my hand and staggered outside onto the lawn, pulling me after him. The officer froze in place when he saw us, and one hand went defensively to his holster. I realized that Jonah still held the knife firmly in front of him. *What would the cop think of this wild-eyed boy with red hands who was waving around a knife?* I wondered. What would he do if Jonah didn't surrender?

"Put down the weapon and place your hands over your head!"

the man commanded and slowly drew his gun out of its holster. "Let the girl go now."

Jonah wasn't going to do it. I could feel it in his clenched muscles and see it in his eyes. He was going to try to stand this policeman down. And if he advanced or threatened him, the cop would have to shoot. Jonah's mom was hovering behind the officer and calling desperately to her son, begging him to listen to her. But Jonah wasn't going to hear her. He wasn't hearing anyone now. There was only one way to end this.

Slowly, I stepped in front of Jonah and stood between him and the waiting officer. "Please, sir!" I called out. "My boyfriend's really sick. He doesn't know what he's doing. We have to get him to a hospital."

The officer wavered for a moment but didn't lower his gun. "He needs to put the weapon down," he ordered again.

"It's a *butter* knife!" I shouted. "He can't hurt anyone with it!"

The cop wasn't convinced. "Move aside, young lady!" he demanded. "Step away from him immediately."

Jonah leaned down and whispered in my ear. "What are you *doing*, April? I'm not going to the hospital with these people. I'm not going anywhere. This is my destiny, don't you understand? I'm a *messenger*. There's no way to fight this."

How do you save a person who refuses to be saved? I couldn't reason with Jonah; he was convinced that we were surrounded by enemies and spies. Nothing I could say would make him see that he was wrong. To him, everyone else was crazy; he was the only sane one in the world.

And then it came to me. The only way to get to Jonah was to

come into his world, to share his delusions with him, to embrace the fantasy. I would have to pretend that I believed only him and nobody else.

I turned around to him and gently put my hands over his cheeks. Slowly I drew his face to mine and brought my lips close to his ears. "Jonah, listen to me," I whispered to him. "You have to put the knife down and let the ambulance take you to the hospital. No, don't pull away, just listen to what I'm saying. If the cop arrests you, they'll take you to the station and throw you in a cell. I'll be all alone. And then they'll be able to get me too, because I won't have you to protect me." He was staring intently at me; I could see that he was hearing me. "Jonah," I pleaded, "if they take you to the hospital, then I can stay with you. We'll be together, and we can watch out for each other. I won't let them harm you, I promise. But if you try to fight, the cop will shoot you. Or he'll handcuff you and take you away. You have to tell them that you're sick and that you've made a big mistake. Please, Jonah. I'm begging you."

I'd expected him to argue or think it over for a minute. But instead, he smiled suddenly, as if a happy idea had just occurred to him, and stepped quickly away from me. With a careless gesture, he flung the knife aside, then suddenly, dramatically, clutched his hands over his head and dropped like lead to the ground.

The officer rushed over, his gun at his side; Jonah's mom threw herself onto her son and grasped his face between her hands. A medic climbed out of the waiting ambulance and ran across the lawn. I sank weakly down into the snow and watched them scramble over his limp body. Jonah didn't resist when the EMTs strapped him to the gurney and tied restraints onto his wrists. As they hoisted him into the ambulance, I called out to the EMT, "Can I ride with him to the hospital?"

The medic looked doubtfully at me. "Do you get sick at the sight of needles?" he asked.

I shook my head.

He shrugged and indicated a seat beside the gurney. "Ma'am, you'll drive behind us to the ER," he called out to Jonah's mom and shut the door behind us.

We rode to the university hospital without sirens or lights. The medic examined Jonah, muttered something about stable vitals, and then placed an IV in his arm. Jonah remained absolutely still throughout; he didn't even flinch when the needle went in. As they pulled him out into the lobby, Jonah opened his eyes briefly and winked at me. I leaned down to him.

"I think they bought it," he whispered and then shut his eyes again.

CHAPTER 23

THE EMERGENCY ROOM WAS BORING. THAT WAS A SURPRISE TO ME. FROM watching shows like *Grey's Anatomy* and *House*, I'd come to think of hospitals as places where exciting things happened. Patients would be screaming, needles and scalpels flying, everyone shrieking orders at each other, blood spurting in all directions, and doctors making love to nurses in the on-call rooms.

But it was nothing like on TV. We went through triage quickly and were assigned to a corner room. A nurse wandered in, checked Jonah's pulse, drew some blood, then wandered off again without a word. An hour and a half went by. Five more pulse checks. Jonah's mom and I sat silently and watched the door, waiting for someone to come in to talk to us. Jonah lay absolutely still; he hadn't moved since they'd brought him into the room. I tried to speak to him once, but he opened his eyes briefly and hissed, "Don't say anything in here. They're listening." Then he shut his eyes again.

Finally, after what seemed like hours, a tall young woman came in. She leaned over Jonah's bed for a moment and then flipped quickly through his chart. "I'm Dr. Wilde, the attending emergency physician," she said, addressing the clipboard in her hand. "I understand that Jonah has been having some behavioral trouble? Can you tell me what happened today?"

Behavioral trouble? Is that how she described this? Like calling out in class and throwing spitballs?

"Well, it's been going on for a while," Mrs. Golden told her in an apologetic voice. "I was worried about depression at first. Or drugs. But I'm not sure what's going on with him now."

Dr. Wilde was still looking at her chart. "I see his blood tests were normal. Drug and alcohol screen was negative." She appeared disappointed by the results. "So has he seen a doctor about this?"

"Yes, we took him to the pediatrician last week. Dr. Steiner said—" Mrs. Golden hesitated and glanced over at Jonah. "He said that he was worried about psychosis," she finished in a lower tone. "But I didn't believe him—"

"Hold on," the doctor interrupted. "*Hold on.* His pediatrician was worried that Jonah was hallucinating?"

"That's what he said."

"You're telling me that he suspected that his patient was psychotic and yet he didn't call anyone in?" the doctor demanded. "Social work? A psychiatrist?"

Mrs. Golden shook her head. "We didn't really give him a chance. I'm sorry, Doctor, I thought that we could deal with this at home. I never thought I'd end up calling the police on my own son."

Dr. Wilde had opened her mouth to answer when she was interrupted by a high-pitched yell and a clatter from the bed. Jonah had opened his eyes and was pulling furiously at the wrist restraints that bound him to the bed. "You called the police on me?" he shouted at his mother. "It was *you*?"

The doctor jumped back in surprise and began flipping through her chart again. "What is going *on* here?" she muttered angrily. "They told me that they restrained and sedated him!"

Jonah was thrashing about and screaming; his mom ran over to his side. "Jonah, I'm sorry! I didn't know what was going on! April's friend called and told me that somebody was robbing our home. I didn't call the cops on *you*. I thought you were in danger. Baby, listen to me—"

That was the end of Dr. Wilde's evaluation. I think she found out everything she wanted to know about Jonah during the time it took the nurse to draw up and inject the sedative into his IV.

Jonah stopped yelling at his mother and fixed his burning eyes on the doctor, who was standing quietly by the door. "I know what you're going to do to me!" he shrieked at her. "You're going to pump me full of pills. And then you're going to plant a probe inside of me and rape my brain with your machines and replace my thoughts. But I won't let you! I'm going to fight you! I know exactly who you are and who you work for! I have a surprise for you, Doc! Dr. Wilde, right? You said your name was Dr. Wilde? Are you really wild, Doctor? Are you a party girl? Do you like getting wasted at parties? Be careful about those frat boys. They have rape pills, Doctor. Frat boys are wild too, aren't they? They never call you the next day, right? That's what happens when you're wild, Doctor! What did you think would happen? You wait and wait and they never come. You know what that feels like, right? To wait and wait for your friend forever and he never comes. Because he's *abandoned* you! You know exactly what I'm saying, Dr. Wilde. I can smell the guilt coming from your face.

You were there with him, weren't you? You know what happened. You *watched* it happen, didn't you? *Didn't you?* Answer me!"

The doctor didn't say a word. She stood over Jonah with crossed arms as the nurse administered the antipsychotic. The fluid had barely left the syringe when Jonah sank weakly against his pillow and turned his face to me. "I told you this would happen," he whimpered. "I knew what they would do. But you promised me you wouldn't let them. April, you *promised* me—"

The medicine swallowed up the rest.

Twelve hours, thirty vital checks, two nurses, four medical students, and three doctors later, Mrs. Golden signed Jonah's admission papers, and he was transferred to the adolescent psychiatry unit at Shady Grove Hospital.

CHAPTER 24

AS DAWN NEARED, I MANAGED TO DOZE OFF FOR A FEW MINUTES, MY HEAD resting against the metal bar of Jonah's gurney. Mrs. Golden remained tearfully awake throughout the night. When the third and final doctor informed us that they'd found a bed for Jonah in their new facility, his mom nodded dully and put her head into her hands.

By the time the transport team finally arrived to take Jonah to the psych ward, my mother insisted on taking me home. Mom walked into the triage area just as he was being wheeled out. He was awake and calmer now but completely disoriented. He seemed to think that he was back in Boston, and he kept asking for a ride to the 7-Eleven. When he saw my mom, he appeared confused, and then his eyes widened in recognition. "Mrs. Wesley," he whispered to her urgently. "You need to take April out of here. I'm stabbing her with my mind."

Mom grabbed me firmly by the arm and pulled me away from him.

As we headed out, Mrs. Golden took my mother aside and begged her to watch Katie, promising to get her as soon as Jonah was settled. They hugged each other, and we left the hospital. On the way, we picked up Katie from the neighbors' and brought her back home with us.

It took a while to explain to Katie why she wouldn't be sleeping in her own bed that night. I finally managed to distract her with a pile of my old dolls and a pair of scissors. As she busily covered the carpet with plastic hair, I tiptoed out of the spare room into the hallway and closed the door. My mother was waiting for me with her arms crossed. There was no way I was going to avoid her now. I followed her into my room and sat down on the bed.

My room was still a mess from Jonah's meltdown, but I saw that my mom had tried to fix the damage to my keyboard. She noticed me looking at the piano and shook her head. "We might need to get a new one."

I nodded. "I know. I'll pay for it."

"Don't be ridiculous, April. It's not the money. I just don't understand why Jonah would do something like that."

I sighed and leaned back against my pillow. "He thought it was bugged, Mom. Didn't Dr. Steiner tell you about his meeting with Jonah?"

She shook her head. "He didn't tell me anything. Doctor-patient confidentiality, remember? I have no idea what's going on. Rachel didn't want to talk about it. And this is the first time you've been home in days."

"Fine," I said. "You want to know the details? I'll tell you. The doctors think that Jonah's psychotic. They wouldn't be more specific or tell us why he was sick. But I overheard one of the students say 'schizophrenia' twice. So maybe that's what it is."

She was suddenly stiff and at attention. "Are you sure that they were talking about him?"

"I don't know, but he was the only screaming patient in restraints in the emergency room."

"I'm sorry," she said and reached out to take my hand. "I knew something was wrong. But I never thought…"

I wished I hadn't been so honest with her. "He's *sick*, Mom. I get it. That's why he's in the hospital. So they'll give him some pills and he'll get better. You don't have to look at me like that. He isn't dead."

"I know, April, but…do you know what schizophrenia is? Have you looked it up?"

"No, I haven't. What does it matter? It won't change anything."

"But, baby, you need to be prepared. When I was growing up, I had a neighbor whose son was diagnosed with schizoaffective disorder. The boy spent the rest of his life in institutions. He never got better. It was just awful for his family. They never talked about it—they were so ashamed."

This was exactly the kind of information I didn't want—other people's horror stories. I knew what was coming next: the shoulder pat, the sympathetic look, and then "*don't worry, you'll get over him.*" I would *never* listen to that.

"What do you mean your neighbors 'were *so* ashamed'?" I demanded. "I'm not ashamed of Jonah. He's *sick*, Mom. He hasn't committed a crime. You haven't been around him these last few weeks. You have no idea what you're talking about. Whatever I've been going through, whatever his mother is going through, Jonah has been hurting a hundred times worse. Before he got really sick, he knew that we were worried about him. And it was *killing* him. He wanted to stop it, but he couldn't. He needed help. I'm actually *glad* that this happened, because at least now I know what's going on and I can help him…"

My mom was speechless for a minute. For that brief moment, I felt as if I'd won the argument.

But then she found her words—a whole lot of them. They came at me like bullets. "April, what are you trying to say? That you're planning to stick with this relationship? That you're going to visit your boyfriend—in a *mental* ward? Baby, you're fifteen years old! You should be concentrating on your schoolwork and spending time with friends, not playing nurse to a psychotic boyfriend…"

"Psychotic boyfriend?" I screamed, pulling away from her. "Mom, you *know* him. How can you talk about him like that? You want me to abandon him *now*, when he needs me the most? Would you be giving me the same advice if he'd been diagnosed with cancer? Would you tell me to wave good-bye and get on with my life? 'Aw, sucks to be you, buddy. Good luck with that.' Is that really who you want me to be?"

"Don't compare this with cancer. It's completely different."

"How? How is this different?"

"Because, April, with cancer, you either get better or you die. I'm sorry to be blunt, but that's the way it is. What Jonah has is *never* going to go away. And you'll be waiting for him in hospital lobbies for the rest of your life."

How could she talk like this? I thought bitterly. How could she crush my hope as if it was nothing to her? She could never know how much he meant to me, never understand that he'd become everything to me. If I lost him now, I'd be completely alone. I wanted Jonah to get better because I loved him, but I *needed* him to get better because I couldn't face my life without him. And he needed me too, more than ever. He'd been shattered once by the death of his best friend. After months of loneliness and pain, he'd finally given his heart to me, and I'd actually made him happy. How could I take that away from him now?

I *knew* that my mother was wrong. I was absolutely sure that he'd come back to me. It seemed impossible that the Jonah I loved, the boy who'd always been so gentle and kind, so vibrant and talented, could have disappeared. If my mom only knew him like I did, she would have understood that too.

"Please, Mom, I really need you to listen to me," I said in a calmer voice. "I need you to remember Jonah before all of this happened. He loved me—he really did—and I know that he still loves me. He would stand by *me* if I got sick. You know he would. I'm not doing this because I feel obligated. I *want* to be there for him. And if he stays sick forever…well, at least then I'll know I did everything I could."

She shook her head and sighed. "I think you're idealizing Jonah. You're only remembering the positive."

"What negative is there besides his illness, Mom?"

"I can't *say*, April! I didn't know him like you did. So I just have to take your word for it."

"No, you don't!" I exclaimed, an idea suddenly dawning on me. "You don't have to take my word for it." *Why hadn't I thought of this before?* "I want to show you something!" I pushed myself off the bed and stepped over to my closet.

Reaching behind my clothing, I lifted Jonah's portrait from its nail. My mother watched me silently as I took it out. Slowly,

I pulled back the covering and waited, holding my breath for her reaction.

She rose from the bed and stared openmouthed at the painting in front of her. "My God," she whispered. "I had no idea that he was this talented."

"No one knows, except maybe his teachers in Boston. He stopped showing people his work after he moved here. But he let me keep this one. Look at it, Mom. Look at how he drew me."

She was looking. I saw a flicker of indecision on her face; she squinted and stepped closer and then froze, her eyes widening. "Sweetheart, did he explain the background of the painting to you?"

I held it out and studied the canvas for a minute. "You mean the water? I'm standing on an island."

"No, you have to look closer. Look at the palm trees near the horizon. They're nearly covered in waves. You've climbed onto a hill in the middle of a flood."

"Okay, a flood then. I still don't understand what you're getting at."

"April, I think you've missed the real meaning of the painting. Did he explain why he drew you holding that little bird?"

"No, I just thought, you know, that the bird was an artistic touch. Like flowers or a bowl of fruit. I thought the sparrow was pretty."

She sighed and shook her head. Her eyes had glazed over with tears. *What was she seeing that I had missed?*

"It isn't a sparrow, baby. Look closer at the painting."

"Mom, just tell me already, please. I don't know that much about birds." Was she drawing this out on purpose? Did she have to be so mysterious?

"Do you know what Jonah's name means?" she asked. "Do you know its biblical background?"

I laughed. "You kept that stuff away from me, remember? Are you talking about the story of Jonah and the whale?"

"No, no, not that. I'm talking about the meaning of his name. Jonah is the anglicized version of the Hebrew word *Yonah*. And in Hebrew, Yonah means dove."

I stared blankly at her, then glanced again at the painting. How had I not noticed that before? I was holding a bird with broken wings, a little injured dove. I didn't know my Bible very well, but I remembered the story of Noah's ark and the flood that destroyed the world. And I remembered the part about the dove too. It was the symbol of hope at the end. But in Jonah's painting, the dove had been devastated by the storm. There was no hope in its shattered body.

"Oh, April, he *knew*," she murmured. "He realized what was happening to him. And this was how he tried to tell you."

I laid the canvas down and sank weakly onto my bed. This new insight was worse than anything that had happened until now. *What had that been like for him?* I thought miserably. I had pictured a clean break: a healthy mind and then confusion. But what if Jonah had seen this coming? Could it have started slowly? Could he have had moments of clarity when he knew that something was very wrong? It would have been like the minutes before a plane crash. You know exactly what's coming and yet you're powerless to stop it.

"Everything is different now, April. Things are changing for me," he'd told me more than a month ago. He'd *known*, even back when our lives seemed absolutely perfect. He'd tried to warn me. Why hadn't I heard him?

"I'm going to visit him tomorrow," I told my mom quietly. "And I'll stay with him as long as they'll let me. I don't have a choice."

It seemed so obvious to me, so perfectly simple. I couldn't believe that anyone would blame me for wanting to stand by the boy I loved when he needed me.

"April," she said in a steady voice. "I'm sorry. But I will not let you go."

I didn't say anything for a minute. At first, I couldn't find the words. She wasn't suggesting or advising. She was forbidding me from going. I didn't care how sweet and understanding my mother had been just a moment ago. It didn't count for anything if she was going to turn on me like this. And I wasn't going to just sit back and take it.

"You have no *right*!" I shouted at her. "You can't tell me that I'm not allowed to visit him."

She crossed her arms and glared at me. "I have every right. I'm your mother, and it's my job to protect you. And if you think that I'm going to sit by while you spend all your free time at a mental hospital..."

"It's my time and my choice where I spend it!"

"No, not really. You're my child. And besides, I'm not telling you that you can't visit Jonah. On the weekends maybe. Once in a while. But *that's it*. I'm not going to let you throw your life away—"

"I'm not throwing my life away," I spat back and then choked.

I was so mad it was hard to think straight; I'd been reasonable and patient, and she still didn't understand. "You're really one to talk!" I cried. "I'm following *your* example, okay? I'm choosing Jonah. Just like you chose my father, even though it broke your parents' heart!"

"I'm sorry for what I did every day," she responded in an even tone. "And your situation is completely different."

"That's right!" I retorted. "Because I'm not hurting you in any way."

"You're hurting yourself…"

"That's *my* business!"

"It's mine too."

I folded my arms. "Whatever. You're a real hypocrite, you know that?"

"Excuse me?"

I rolled my eyes. "You're all about independent thought, making your own decisions, forging your own life. That's why you left your family, wasn't it?"

"April, this *isn't* the same—"

"But the minute I decide to do something that you don't agree with, you react just like your parents."

It was a low blow. I knew it as soon as the words were out of my mouth. My mom looked like she was going to cry. I hesitated for a second and then slowly turned away from her. "I'm going to be on the bus to Shady Grove tomorrow after school," I said in a gentler tone. "I'm really sorry if it upsets you, Mom. But that's what I'm going to do."

CHAPTER 25

On a canvas painted red
This beautiful fire's fed
And I'll wait for you
Angels shuddering through a winter day
There are no more words to say
But I'll wait for you

STILL, I HAD TO GO TO SCHOOL. THAT WAS THE ONLY THING THAT SEEMED to stand between me and my real life. My mom hadn't exactly agreed with me by the end of our argument. But she hadn't threatened to tie me to my bedpost either, so for now, that was enough for me. Under no circumstances could I allow my grades to suffer though. She was very clear on that. There would be no more absences, no missed assignments, and no excuses. So the following morning, instead of jumping on the bus toward the hospital, I found myself trudging into history with my head down, trying to avoid the looks of my hovering classmates.

Unfortunately for me, Ms. Lowry chose that day to be late to class, and before I could escape, Cora took the opportunity to sail over to my chair. She planted herself in Jonah's empty seat and leaned toward me, a look of pity puckering up her face. I was praying that the news of Jonah's hospitalization hadn't reached the school yet, but that hope died as soon as Cora spoke.

"So Miles ran into Jonah a couple of days ago, did you know?" she began innocently, as if trading harmless gossip. "Apparently your boyfriend was wandering around the street barefoot and knee-deep in snow."

I could feel the blood rushing to my face. I knew what was coming, and there was nothing I could do to stop it. I focused on my clenched hands and tried to block her out, tried to think about something else, anything but the picture she was about to paint for the class.

"Miles tried to talk to him," she murmured sweetly. "But Jonah didn't seem to hear him. It's a good thing too, or who knows what could have happened? I told Miles that he should have run the other way. But of course he wanted to know what was going on. He wanted to understand why your boyfriend was wandering around a freezing street. And why he was all covered in paint. And *half naked.*"

She let her last words flutter in front of her. She wanted me to charge at her; she was waiting for me to rush to Jonah's defense so she could drive a sword through my heart. But I wouldn't give her the satisfaction.

"I just wanted to make sure Jonah was all right," she continued in a sympathetic singsong voice. "Miles saw the ambulance coming down your street. So of course we were all very worried."

That was all she knew, I reasoned. She couldn't possibly know what had happened in the ER or where they had admitted him. She could only be guessing from here on.

"So I called Kris, to see if she'd heard anything," she went on. "I wanted to bring Jonah a get-well card. Kris told me that they were admitting Jonah to Shady Grove."

There was an awful hush after she'd finished. But Cora was obviously not done yet; her pause had been just for effect. Everyone was staring at me now, but I couldn't think of anything to say. It hurt to swallow and breathe. *My life at school is over*, I thought bitterly. I'd be the girlfriend of "crazy boy" forever, long after they forgot him. As much as I'd hated being invisible before, it was infinitely better than being known for something like this.

"I don't think anyone was surprised really," Cora said with a smirk. "We all realized that he was nuts from the way that he'd been acting recently. But *I* knew something was weird even on that first day, when he decided to—when he chose to sit—well, *you know*." And she waved her hand in my direction. "But it's nice to know that it's official finally."

There was another uncomfortable silence. Where was the teacher when I needed her? Why did she have to choose that day of all days to be late to school?

I glanced around the room again. A few of my classmates— Miles, Robby, and his friends—were grinning at each other. But many of them were turning away from Cora and exchanging guilty looks and shifting uncomfortably in their seats.

And then, to everyone's surprise, Tessa spoke up. She had a shrill, nasal accent, but at that moment, no sound could have been sweeter than her voice. She started small, as if testing out her thoughts, but her words carried clear across the room. "You don't know what he's there for, Cora," she said. "Shady Grove has rehab clinics. And an eating disorder center. Maybe he drinks too much. Or has bulimia. My cousin had anorexia for a while, and she went to a place like that."

We all turned to stare at her, and I sent her a look of silent gratitude. She didn't have the face of a brave person; her cheeks were pale, and she was chewing nervously on a strand of hair. But she had defended an unpopular girl against the Princess of Fallstaff High. And for a moment, Cora didn't know how to handle it.

Cora cleared her throat a few times and tossed her hair over her shoulder. "People with bulimia don't wander around the street half-naked in the middle of winter," she said finally. "And they don't yell out strange things in class. Only crazy people do that."

But Tessa had broken the ice, and others were willing to jump in. "My uncle was admitted to that hospital," Michael called out. "He had PTSD and depression after he came back from Afghanistan. They kept him for a long time. If you want, April, I can tell you the name of his doctor. Maybe he can help."

I nodded gratefully. "Thank you, Michael."

"You know, when Jonah gets better, he'll have a great subject for Ms. Lowry's paper," Tessa remarked. She appeared more confident after Michael's comment, and she held her head a little higher. "It'll probably be the most interesting one."

As if on cue, Ms. Lowry sauntered into the room (a good fifteen minutes late) and dropped her purse onto her desk. "Who'll have a good subject for my paper?" she asked us cheerfully.

I groaned and sank deeper into my chair. I didn't want to hear Cora gloating over the details again. But she never got the chance to speak.

"Jonah was admitted to the hospital two days ago," Tessa called out before Cora could reply. "So we thought he would have a great story to tell us when he gets out. You know, for the assignment you gave us: How medicine changed our lives."

Ms. Lowry's smile faded, and she glanced at me briefly before turning back to Tessa. "That will be Jonah's choice, of course," she told her quietly. "If he feels comfortable sharing the experience."

Ms. Lowry's eyes skimmed over Cora's livid face and then followed her across the room as she slid back into her seat. "Maybe we should give April some space, Cora," she murmured. "But I'm sure she appreciates your concern." Her tone was just sarcastic enough to make her point.

When history was finally over, I gathered up my books and walked timidly toward Tessa's desk, hoping to thank her for her support. But before I could reach her, she slung her bag over her shoulder and was out the door. She clearly didn't want to stick around for either my appreciation or for Cora's wrath.

By the end of last period, the memory of Tessa's kindness was very pale. The whole day felt like a long obstacle course of nudges, smiles, and whispers behind sleeves. When the final bell sounded, I grabbed my schoolbag and fled the building, heading for the city bus that would take me to Jonah. On the way there, my phone rang twice, the first call from my mom and the second one from Kristin. I hit reject for both.

CHAPTER 26

SHADY GROVE LOOKED LIKE MOST HOSPITALS—MANICURED LAWNS, TALL brick walls, and gleaming, antiseptic hallways. There were small differences, but most of those were only noticeable on the locked wards. The first floor pretended to be a hotel lobby; there was a little fountain, a gift shop, and a meditation/prayer room. The main security guard was probably just there for show, because she barely looked at me as I passed her. But as I stepped off the elevator and walked over to the metal door of 11 West, I understood why Jonah had been so terrified of this place. The intercom bell's squeal and the clatter of the iron lock sliding into place made the entrance feel like a prison.

I announced my name into the call button and pulled at the heavy door when the buzzer sounded. A nurse waved me over to her station. As I crossed the room, a young boy ran over and intercepted me.

"I'm going home today," he told me as if he'd been waiting all day to let me know.

"That—that's great," I said and stepped back a little. He wasn't threatening at all; he looked no more than twelve years old. But there was a strange brightness in his brown eyes, and he'd brought his curly dark head so close to mine that I could literally feel the warmth of his excitement.

"That's enough, Shawn," the nurse called out. "I'm sure she's very happy to hear your news."

He nodded and moved away, but his entire body still vibrated with suppressed joy. "I'm going home in exactly twenty minutes," he declared.

"Okay, Shawn, we've been over this a hundred times," she told him crossly. "Your mother didn't give us an exact time. I've been calling to remind her that she has to come to sign you out. I'll let you know as soon as she phones, just like I promised."

Shawn didn't appear to hear her. He turned back to me and grinned. "Eighteen minutes now. My mom's coming to get me in eighteen minutes." His cheerfulness was contagious; his olive cheeks glowed, his teeth flashed, and his small hands twisted together.

"I'm really happy for you—" I began, but the boy slipped past me and began announcing his great news to another visitor.

The nurse was still watching Shawn as I approached her, but the irritation had faded from her face. She just looked sad now. "Shawn, if you can't sit still, I'll have to send you to your room."

He fell back and retreated to a corner, muttering happily. "Seventeen minutes. Seventeen minutes till she comes."

The nurse sighed and turned to me. "How can I help you?"

"I'm here to see a patient who was admitted yesterday," I said. "Jonah Golden?"

She nodded. "You must be April."

I stared at her. "Wait—how do you know my name?"

She smiled and pointed to a notebook on the table. "His mom listed you as an approved guest. It means I don't have to notify her if you visit or ask for her permission. You can go straight to the visitors' lounge. He's been waiting for you."

I thanked her and began to walk away, but someone touched me on the shoulder and said my name. I turned to look at the man behind me and then took a step back as I realized who he was.

I'd never seen him before in person, but I recognized him from Jonah's painting immediately. Dr. Golden looked just as I'd imagined him—and just as his son had drawn him. Tall, broad-shouldered, with dark brows, a square jaw, and smooth, sharp cheekbones, he reminded me of a model from an ad for expensive liquor. It was easy to see where Jonah got his striking looks; he was a gentler version of his dad. The elder man's hair was straight, combed back, and streaked with gray; the son's hung in thick, loose curls around his face. The father's lips were thin and drawn; his son's smile was fuller, soft, and dimpled.

I'd actually been afraid of meeting Dr. Golden. I'd imagined him as an awful ogre, a tyrant whose name we weren't allowed to mention. And yet, he didn't seem so terrible in person. His eyes were questioning, not critical, and he seemed genuinely nervous.

"My wife told me all about you," he said. (I noticed that he hadn't referred to Jonah's mother as his "ex.") "I've wanted to meet you for a while now."

"I'm April," I told him, holding out my hand awkwardly.

"Dr. Golden," he replied and gripped my fingers in a firm handshake. "I imagine you've heard a lot about me."

Was I supposed to say yes to that or no? The truth wasn't exactly complimentary.

He seemed to read my answer in my silence because he nodded sharply and released my hand. "I'll follow you in—"

"One minute, sir," the nurse called out to him. "You can't go in yet."

He wheeled around and glared at her. "What do you mean I can't go in? I'm his father. I just flew in from Boston to visit him. I have a right to see my son."

The nurse didn't flinch as he approached the desk. She seemed almost bored, as if she'd had this conversation ten times already before lunch and was gearing up for the afternoon routine. "I have instructions from Rachel Golden to call her when you arrive. She wants to be here when you visit him."

He grunted and crossed his arms. "Oh, she's still playing at that, is she?" He squinted at the nurse's name tag and pushed his lips into a rigid smile. "Listen, Becky, Jonah's mother and I are married, do you understand? Not divorced. We're just separated—*temporarily*. There's no custody battle here. I'm still Jonah's father. Legally I have every right to see him."

Nurse Becky was a battle-ax of a lady, almost as wide as she was tall, with her iron gray hair pulled back into a brittle, spiky braid. As she got up from her chair, Jonah's father took a step back. "Look, Mr. Golden," she growled at him. "Please understand that we're only concerned about Jonah's health. What your son needs now is stability and peace, not more conflict. If you have issues with his mother, then you should deal with those outside—*without* getting him involved. He's very sick right now, and we've only just begun his therapy."

"Don't talk to me about his *therapy*," he snapped. "I'm a physician. You don't have to dumb things down for me. I know all about the counseling crap that you do here. You'll get him to tell you some bull about how his parents didn't love him enough, and then six months later, you'll send him home with enough medicine to kill a horse."

She sank back into her chair. The bored expression had returned; her eyelids were heavy with it. She seemed immune to anger, as if she was used to swallowing obnoxious parents with her morning coffee. "You have a strange idea of what we do here, Doctor. But things have changed a little since you went to school. I'll ask you to respect our wishes and wait. Mrs. Golden will be here in a few minutes."

He sank irritably into a nearby chair. "Unbelievable," he muttered and crossed his arms. The nurse shrugged at me and gestured with her head in the direction of the hallway. I took her permission and slipped away. I felt guilty walking off like that and leaving Dr. Golden sulking in the waiting area. It seemed that I'd been given a pass that rightfully belonged to Jonah's father, who had, for better or worse, spent sixteen years raising his child. I didn't know what he'd done to deserve what had just happened, but it still felt wrong to me.

As I neared the visitors' lounge, all feelings of guilt faded, and I felt my stomach lurch. I had no idea what I would find when I went in; for all I knew, Jonah wouldn't even recognize me when he saw me. I didn't understand his illness, and I knew nothing about the medicines they'd given him. Could they change his personality? Would he still be the boy I loved?

But then I saw him, sitting huddled on a corner sofa, his head resting against the wall, and I realized that it didn't matter if he knew me or not. He looked so vulnerable; his knees were pulled up to his chest, and he'd wrapped his arms around them as if he was trying to disappear.

And then he glanced up at me and smiled—and all my worries vanished. It was Jonah's smile, the warm, happy one I loved, and it was all I needed. I ran to him and threw my arms around him, pulled his face to mine, and kissed him. *They've made a huge mistake*, I thought. Jonah didn't belong here. They'd be sending him home that afternoon for sure.

But then he put his hands on mine and pulled me away. His eyes narrowed in disapproval, and he bit his lip. "April," he whispered urgently. "Where's your hat?"

At first, I didn't understand what he was asking. What hat? He couldn't still be fixated on the tinfoil beret, could he? But as I watched him, I realized that he wasn't really looking at me. His eyes were focused a little to my right, and he seemed to be listening to something. He was shaking his head, not *at* me exactly, but at an invisible something that made his face darken and his muscles tense.

"Jonah, please," I begged him, placing my hands against his cheeks. "Tell me what you're hearing. I can't help you if you don't talk to me."

He seemed to hear me, but the frightened expression didn't change. He stared at me for a moment and then shook his head. "I don't know what you're talking about."

I sighed. "You're not being fair to me. You know I wouldn't lie to you."

He glared at his lap and plucked at the frayed edges of his sleeve. "Leave me alone," he said irritably. "I've answered enough

questions from doctors and nurses and medical students. I don't
need them from you too."

"What happened? What did the doctors do?" I asked.

"What I expected they would. They gave me pills. Three different ones. I wouldn't take them at first. I fought them for a long
time. They didn't realize how strong I was." There was a little
pride in his voice. "But there were a lot of them, so what else
could I do? I swallowed their poison in the end."

"Did it—did it help?" I regretted the question as soon it left
my mouth.

He frowned at me and clenched his fingers into fists. "Help
with *what*?" he demanded. "There's nothing wrong with me! Are
you siding with them now? I didn't think that you would do
that—that you'd believe their *lies*—"

"I don't believe them! I'm on your side. I'm just trying to
understand what's happening to you."

But he was no longer listening to me; he was staring at a point
outside the door. At first, I thought that he was hearing imaginary sounds again, but his expression was more focused than
before. He rose and began to back away, edging fearfully toward
the wall, his chest rising in fast, uneven breaths. And then I heard
the staccato rhythm of Dr. Golden's reedy voice and understood
Jonah's reaction. Mrs. Golden was pleading with her husband as
they approached. "Just listen to him, Aaron. That's all I'm asking.
Just listen."

Dr. Golden pushed his way into the room before his wife, but
she slipped by him and hurried over to her son. Jonah had flat-
tened himself against the wall and was glaring at his father. He

didn't seem to feel the hand that his mother laid softly on his shoulder or hear what she was whispering to him. "Give him a chance, Jonah. Please, baby, just let him talk."

I couldn't take my eyes off Dr. Golden's face. When he'd first come into the room, his expression was angry and severe, his face seemingly carved from granite. But then he saw his son, and the stone form melted in front of us.

I'd forgotten how much Jonah had changed over the last few weeks. Looking now at his father's pained expression, I saw my boyfriend again—but this time through a parent's eyes. I saw Jonah's pallor, the jutting ridges of his bones, the sunken deep blue eyes, the scabs and bruises on his knuckles. I remembered again what he'd looked like when I'd first met him, and I understood why Dr. Golden gasped and sank weakly down into a chair. "My God, Rachel," he murmured to his wife. "Why didn't you call me sooner?"

Jonah crossed his arms. He looked like a ghostly version of his father. The angry suspicion in his eyes was the same as the one I'd seen in Dr. Golden's just a few minutes ago. "What are you doing here?" he demanded.

Dr. Golden was making an obvious effort to stay calm. He swallowed several times and looked helplessly at the three of us before answering. "Did you expect I wouldn't come, Jonah?" he asked in a halting voice. "You've been admitted to a hospital, and you thought it wouldn't matter to me? If I'd known sooner what was going on—if someone had *told* me what was happening— I'd have been here a long time ago." Confidence was returning to his voice, and a shade of resentment too. "I tried calling—I tried everything I could think of—but you, both of you, seemed more interested in holding on to grudges than making things right again—"

"Aaron, please," Jonah's mother interrupted. "Now's not the time for this—"

"When's the right time?" he retorted. "How long will this go on? How many times do I have to apologize?"

"You *never* apologized—" Jonah said in a low voice.

But his father wasn't listening anymore. He rose from his chair and turned sharply to his wife. "You said he needed space, Rachel. You said we needed to give him some room. A new environment, a new school, a brief separation. And now I come down here to find that my son has wasted away to nothing and was admitted to a mental ward! They've refused to tell me his diagnosis, probably because they have no idea what they're talking about. And they wouldn't even let me see him right away. I have to wait for your *permission* as if I'm some sort of monster. As if I'm the one who caused this! That's what you all think now, don't you? That this is also my fault? *Is that what they're saying to you?*"

"No one blames you, Aaron," she assured him. "And you're jumping to conclusions. Listen, Jonah's doctor will be making rounds soon, and you can talk about his diagnosis then. We can discuss his treatment and come up with a plan. But for now, just sit down and talk normally to your son—like you used to do. You haven't seen each other for months. Please, Aaron. Both of you, just sit down for a minute."

Dr. Golden slowly sank onto the corner of the couch. Jonah glared at the chair in front of him suspiciously and began to edge toward it when a loud shriek from the hallway made him start. As the scream echoed through the ward, we rose together and rushed outside to look.

Just a few feet away, Shawn was wrestling with a young nurse; he was beating at her furiously and howling at the top of his lungs. Nurse Becky was trying to reason with him, but as she approached him, he swung at her with his palm, slapping her across the chin. She grunted irritably and wrapped her arms around him, tightening her grip slowly until he stopped struggling. Something about her seemed to calm him for a moment; he looked up at her with wide, bewildered eyes and whimpered miserably.

"You promised me," he wailed. "You promised I was going home today."

"I know, baby, I know," she said. "I'm really sorry. There's nothing we can do."

"Yes, there is!" he bawled, kicking at her. "Call her again! Go to my house and get her!"

The nurses exchanged frowns, and Nurse Becky shook her head. "We spoke to her already, Shawn," she said. "Your mom can't come to get you today."

It took a minute to sink in. Shawn swallowed a few times and gazed at the sympathetic faces of the staff. He was breathing hard, his chest rising in gasping hiccups.

"Let's go back to your room and rest, okay, baby?" Nurse Becky suggested pleasantly and loosened her hold on him.

But she'd let him go too soon. Shawn let out a furious shout and slipped out of her arms, then scrambled to his feet and darted down the hall in the direction of the exit. His flight didn't last long; he was intercepted by a large male nurse before he could get past the reception area. "We're going to the quiet room, Shawn," the man told him and hoisted him in the air, pinning the boy's arms behind him.

They disappeared around the corner, Shawn's screaming growing farther and farther away until it was cut off by the sound of a metal door.

Nurse Becky smiled sadly at the young nurse. "Having an interesting first day, Tina? Don't worry. You'll get to know Shawn very well. I doubt that he's going home anytime soon. Not if his mom keeps forgetting to pick him up."

Tina stared at her in disbelief. "His mother *forgot* to pick him up?"

Nurse Becky snorted and let out an angry little laugh. "Unbelievable, right? We all knew that this would happen though; it's not the first time. They need to stop telling Shawn his discharge date. It's just plain cruel."

The nurses disappeared down the hallway, and we drifted back into the room as the ward went quiet again. Jonah's mom seemed exhausted. She sat down beside her son and tried to put her arm around him, but he drew away from her and slid over to the wall.

Dr. Golden was shaking his head. "Our son doesn't belong here, Rachel," he muttered between his teeth. "This was a mistake. He's not like the children in this place."

She got up quickly and nodded brusquely toward the hallway. "You can't say that in front of Jonah," I heard her whisper as they left the room. "He needs to accept that he's sick—"

I settled down beside Jonah on the sofa and slipped my hand in his.

"I never thought I'd say this," he said after a minute of silence. "But my father's actually right about something. I don't belong here."

I didn't know how to answer him. Jonah *wasn't* like the patients in this place. He had a family who loved him. He'd been happy and well-liked and talented. How could he have ended up in a place like Shady Grove where mothers abandoned their children?

"Where were they taking Shawn?" I asked him. "What is the quiet room?"

I felt his hand tighten over mine, and his fingers gripped my knuckles. "It's like a padded empty cell. They use it to suck the energy from us."

"How—how do you mean?"

"It's one of the 'choices' they give you when they're having trouble controlling you. You can take a 'time-out' in the quiet room, or they can use other means to calm you down. Like pills or physical restraints. Most people choose the quiet room. They leave you in there until you have no strength left. And then they take you out and stick their pills down your throat anyway."

"How do you know? Is that what they did to you?"

He hesitated, turning his head away from me as he spoke. "When I first got here, I kept asking for you. I kept begging them to let me see you—but they wouldn't let me. And then I realized that they'd trapped me here, that they'd used you to get me into this place. They'd gotten what they wanted, which meant they didn't need you anymore. You were the only person I trusted, the only one who wouldn't betray me. They all knew that. After they took me away, I was sure they'd killed you. I had to punish them all. I needed to avenge your death."

If we'd been cast in an old medieval movie, and I was *Braveheart's* tragic bride, Jonah's speech would have been moving and romantic. But here, on the sterile plastic cushions of a hospital sofa, it was painful to hear him, and my last doubts about his illness faded away. Still, I couldn't argue with him, any more than I'd argued when he made me wear the tinfoil hat. I was the only one he trusted. I was the only one who would never betray him.

"What do you want me to do?" I asked him quietly.

His eyes flickered briefly, and then the light died out. "Just don't forget me," he said.

"Forget you? How could you ever think that I'd forget you? I'll be back again tomorrow, and every day for as long as you're in here!"

He shook his head. "No, I didn't mean that. I meant that I want you to remember me as I really am. Not what they tell you I am. And not what they'll turn me into. Remember *me*, the Jonah you knew before all this. Before they get to me. Otherwise, I might as well quit fighting and give up now."

"What are you worried they'll turn you into?"

He sank his voice to a low whisper and leaned close to me, his lips tickling my hair. "Their medicines are killing me," he told me. "I'll sit through their stupid counseling sessions if I have to. I'll go to their support groups and their *art* therapy if they make me. But those pills are bleeding me dry. They're getting what they want from me—for now. I'm not fighting them anymore—at least, not out loud. But I don't know how much longer I can hold on. I don't know how much longer I can breathe this bathroom sanitizer air."

"What do you want me to do?" I asked him again.

"Say nothing to anyone," he instructed. "We can't trust the people in here. Not even my parents. I'll do everything they tell me for now. I'll take their pills. I'll 'confess' to their psychiatrists. And in the meantime, I'm going to learn their weaknesses, so when the time is right, I can break out of here."

"But the door's locked, and they've got a guard…"

"People have busted out of maximum security prisons, April. This is nothing compared to that. Look, I'm not saying it's going to be easy. But as long as I know that you'll be waiting for me on the outside, I can work it out. Because that's where I'll need your help. On the outside."

"What do you mean?"

He drew closer to me. "Do you remember my navy spiral notebook?" he whispered. "You've seen me writing in it."

Of course I remembered. I'd been curious about his "independent project" since the day I'd first seen him scribbling away in math class. "Yes, I think so."

"Well, I want you to bring it to me. I'm going to need it."

I nodded quickly. "Of course, but can't your mother bring it?"

"No, they won't let her because of the sharp spiral binding. She won't break the rules, even for me. And anyway, I don't want her touching it. It's private. I'm trusting you with it. I need you to promise me that you'll bring it tomorrow. Please."

What was I supposed to say to him? *No way, Jonah. I'm leaving you here. You're on your own for this.* He put his arms around me and pulled me close, his rough cheek resting against my forehead, his lips brushing against my ear. It would have been a sweet and private moment, the first we'd had in weeks—except I couldn't shake the feeling that he believed somebody was watching us through it all. Even as he held me, I was conscious that we were not alone, that in his mind, we were surrounded by spies. His arms were only wrapped around me to protect me from the threat; his lips were close to mine not because he wanted to kiss me but because he didn't dare to speak above a whisper.

"I'll bring it with me when I come," I told him.

"And you have to promise not to open it. That's the most important part. You can't read it yet. It isn't ready. *You* aren't ready."

I wasn't ready. Ready for what? Did it even matter?

"I promise," I assured him.

He nodded and pulled away. "You can come at four. I'm supposed to meet with Dr. Hermann then. I'll tell her that I won't go to counseling without you."

"Jonah, I can't go to your sessions with you! There's no way they'll let me do that."

He shrugged and leaned back against the wall. "Then I won't talk to them. That'll piss them off. They're *obsessed* with talking here."

"But what do you want me to say to Dr. Hermann?"

"*Nothing.* That's the point, April. Don't you get it? Everyone is talking, talking, talking about me. Jonah's sick, Jonah's hallucinating, maybe we should raise his dosage, is there a special diet we should try, how long until the medicines start to work? *I want you to say nothing.* If she asks you questions about me, I want you to keep quiet. That way, I'll know that she hasn't gotten to you."

"Okay. I'll be back tomorrow after school then."

"Good. See you tomorrow."

I waited for a kiss or even some parting word or friendly gesture, something positive to take home with me. But he was no longer looking at me; he'd retreated back into his own chaotic world. I waved good-bye and left the room.

Jonah's parents were sitting next to one another in the reception area and arguing in low voices. As I passed them, Jonah's mom called out to me. "I'm so sorry for all of this," she said as I came up to them. "April, if you need to take a break, I completely understand. Jonah will understand too, I'm sure—"

"I'll be back tomorrow," I interrupted. "I'll see you then."

She gave me a doubtful look. "But his therapy could take weeks, or months even. It isn't fair to expect this of you. You have your own life. Jonah told me that you're hoping to audition for the art school. You should concentrate on that right now and not tie yourself to—" She sighed. "Listen, dear, Jonah's very sick…"

She paused as Dr. Golden rolled his eyes and muttered something about stupid psychiatrists. But I was no longer listening to them. A change in shadows down the hall caught my attention; Jonah had slipped out into the corridor and was eavesdropping on our conversation.

I turned back to his mom and shook my head. "I don't believe that. No one here is really listening to him; they just want to label him and stuff him full of pills. Yes, I *am* auditioning for the art school, because we're transferring *together* next year. I won't let him down. I'm not giving up on him."

And without waiting for an answer, I turned away and left the ward. I didn't really care to hear their response anyway. I hadn't actually been speaking to them.

When I got home, my mom met me at the door. She looked relieved to see me, as if she'd been worrying that my visit to Shady Grove might turn into a permanent stay, that Jonah's paranoia could somehow rub off on me until they were forced to commit me too.

"Kris called again today," she told me before I could escape to the safety of my room. "She seemed really upset."

"I'll bet she is," I replied darkly.

"Why are you ignoring her?" she demanded predictably.

"I'm not ignoring her," I replied. "I just don't have anything to say to her."

I had nothing to say to Kris because she was against me, like everybody else. She'd told Cora about Jonah being admitted to Shady Grove. But even worse than that betrayal was the knowledge that she'd seen Jonah at his worst and would never forget it. I would never be able to get that terrifying image out of her head, no matter what I said, and so she'd never understand how I felt about him. Even when he finally got better, I'd always feel that she was judging him.

"Everything is different now, don't you understand?" I told my mom. "Things have changed for me. I can't explain it. I'm sorry, I just can't."

"April, what are you talking about? You aren't making sense."

I didn't answer her. I'd just had the oddest feeling of déjà vu; my last words seemed strangely familiar, as if I'd unconsciously echoed someone.

CHAPTER 27

THE FOLLOWING AFTERNOON, I HEADED OVER TO THE GOLDEN HOUSE ON Jonah's errand. His parents were out, and Katie was home alone with a babysitter. Katie tackle-hugged me twice on my way up the stairs, and after I swore (twice) to read her half the princess stories on her shelf, I was released and allowed to enter Jonah's room. It took me less than a minute to find the notebook. For all its secret nature, Jonah hadn't bothered to hide it; it was at the bottom of his backpack.

As I held it, I couldn't help a little shudder of recognition; in some ways, this notebook represented all that was mysterious about Jonah when I'd first met him. Even then, there had been shades of his personality that I hadn't exactly understood—the sudden shifts in mood, the shroud of secrecy over his paintings, the random fear of dangers that no one else could see. I'd wondered what he'd been writing about during those first few months, what "project" he'd been working on so devotedly. And now it was actually in my hands. He'd instructed me not to read it, but as I stared at the tattered navy binding, my fingers unconsciously drifted to the edge, and I slowly lifted the cover. I had to see. What if the key to everything lay inside this journal, and I gave it up without a look?

But even as I turned the first page, I knew I couldn't go through with it. I couldn't break my promise to Jonah. He'd trusted me with this. I couldn't let him down.

I closed the book and slipped it into my bag. Maybe, deep down, I didn't really want to know after all. Maybe I was scared about what I would find inside.

I didn't touch the notebook again until I returned to Shady Grove and handed it to Jonah. I admit that it was kind of a disappointing moment for me. I'd been a little proud of myself and impressed by my own self-restraint. Most people would have read it. Maybe the first few pages, just to get an idea of what was inside. But I hadn't even peeked. I thought the accomplishment warranted a little gratitude, a hug or smile or something for the successful completion of a secret quest.

But he barely nodded as I drew it out. Without a word, he flipped back his blanket and tucked the notebook into his pillowcase, then glanced around the room as if he were expecting a SWAT team to suddenly materialize. When nothing happened, he swallowed nervously and muttered more to himself than to me, "It's time for our doctor's appointment."

Our doctor's appointment? Well, I suppose, in a way, it was my appointment too. I was now as much a part of this hospital as Jonah.

Dr. Hermann was a tall, pretty brunette with runway model legs. The legs confused me for a minute, as did the Chinese tattoo on her shoulder and the bangle bracelets. I think I would have dressed a little less like Angelina Jolie if my job was counseling disturbed young men. And I would probably have put away those legs, no matter how proud I was of them.

But Jonah didn't seem to notice the model/doctor who'd been assigned to cure him. He kept his eyes on me as she welcomed us into the therapy room.

"I'm glad to meet you," Dr. Hermann told me sweetly. "I don't normally agree to joint counseling for new patients. But I understand that Jonah is refusing to speak with me unless you're present, so for now, we don't have much of a choice."

I nodded and slipped into the chair that she pulled out for me. I was a little nervous; next to me, I could feel Jonah's tension radiating from him like an electric current.

"Maybe you can tell me a little about yourself, April," Dr. Hermann suggested. "Tell me how the two of you met."

It seemed a harmless question, but I remembered Jonah's instructions, and I shook my head. "I don't have anything to say," I told her quietly. Beside me, I felt Jonah's satisfied smile and heard his body relax into his chair.

Dr. Hermann frowned and glanced between the two of us. "You're not on the witness stand," she pressed me. "No one's judging you. You can say whatever you want."

But I *was* being judged, I wanted to tell her. Her patient was judging me. "I don't have anything to say," I repeated stubbornly.

She sighed and turned back to Jonah. "How were your first two days here, Jonah?"

He raised his eyebrows. "Oh, peachy, Doctor," he smiled. "Just what I needed."

"How are the medicines making you feel?"

He blinked at her. "Which medicine, Doctor? I'm getting three."

"Let's start with the Risperdal."

"Oh, the antipsychotic? Well, it's making me less psychotic. That's a good thing, right?"

She leaned back against her chair. "Jonah, you promised to cooperate if April joined us."

"I *am* cooperating. The medicines are fantastic. You're also fantastic, Doctor. This whole place is fan—"

"Okay, Jonah. I get that you don't trust me yet. But we'll get there. Why don't you tell me about the art therapy class? How do you feel about that? Your mom told me that painting is a hobby of yours."

I saw his eyes flame for a second, and then the anger died as quickly as it came. "You need some new stuff, Doc," he told her in a low voice.

"Sorry, what?"

"They gave me Magic Markers at first. Seriously. And the set of oils was dry and crusty. If I was a five-year-old finger-painter, it would have been a joke."

"The idea isn't to create great works of art, Jonah. The idea is to harness your creative side and use it in the healing process."

"Oh, I see," he replied in a dry tone. "Sorry. I thought the idea was to pass the time until you let me out of here. Fine then. I'll make you a nice picture of an elephant, okay? An elephant with emotional problems."

Dr. Hermann smiled and shook her head. "These meetings are part of the process. The sooner you cooperate, the sooner you'll be ready for outpatient therapy."

"What does that mean?"

"It means when we reach our inpatient goals, you'll be considered ready for discharge."

"And what are these goals exactly?"

"The first is to make sure that you're not in danger of harming yourself or anyone else. The second is to work through some of your fixed ideas—your belief that the government is shadowing you and planting thoughts into your brain, for example. That the doctors are trying to steal your creativity. And finally, we want to help you get rid of the voices that are bothering you."

Jonah's face froze, and his eyes flickered to the right; he seemed to be listening to something. "You *are* stealing my creativity, Doctor." His voice was quiet, deliberate, and emotionless. "I'm not the only one who says so. This isn't a delusion or a 'fixed idea' as you call it. Half of the patients here complain that they can't think when they're taking their meds. That's what they say in those group sessions that you make me go to. The medicine makes us dead inside. It turns us into zombies. Easy-to-manage zombies."

She seemed pleased that he'd confided in her. "It is a common complaint," she replied, smiling. "Each patient is different. We have to find the right balance of medicines to treat *you*. We increase or decrease the dosages to achieve the effect that we're looking for. The level we want is the one that lets you feel like your old self, but without the delusions and the voices that are hurting you."

Again the voices, the topic that put him on his guard each time it was mentioned. He glared at her, and his brows came down. "Is there anything else you'd like to know, Doctor?" he muttered. "Or are we done here?"

"I need to know what you're experiencing, Jonah," she insisted. "Are the voices quieter now than when you were first admitted?"

I could see him struggling, his mind screaming a silent protest. *I don't hear voices! Leave me alone.* But then he looked over at me, and he bowed his shoulders in defeat. *Don't make me admit it in front of April,* he seemed to beg her. *Don't make me say it in front of her.*

Why couldn't she hear him? It was obvious that he couldn't handle the shame of it, that he needed me to go before he confessed the truth. But I couldn't get up and leave him now. I had to sit and watch as the doctor leaned forward and pushed him again. "How are the voices today, Jonah?"

His answer came eventually in a shaky, embarrassed whisper. "There are no voices."

"Good," she said with a satisfied smile, as if he had just reported that an annoying rash had finally disappeared. "That's great to hear. It usually takes a long time to quiet the voices, so I'm glad that we're moving in the right direction. I hope that we can continue to work together over the next few weeks."

His eyes flashed. "Few *weeks*? I'm not staying here that long! You can't keep me more than twenty days without an admission hearing. They read me my rights when I got in here, so I know that you can't hold me against my will. Or make me take your pills either, if I don't want to. So I'll tell the judge I don't belong here. He'll see that and let me go."

She sighed and leaned forward over her desk. "Jonah," she said in a quiet voice. "We have several witnesses who will testify that you're a danger to yourself and possibly to others if you're discharged from the hospital too soon."

"Like who?"

"Well, there's the ER physician who first admitted you, the independent psychiatrist who examined you—"

"But they're all in on it!"

"Your parents."

He flinched and sank back into his chair. "Sorry. Time's up, Doctor. We're done here."

Dr. Hermann tried to coax him back into a conversation, but he closed his eyes and refused to answer her. Eventually, she gave up and reached out for his chart. "We'll meet again tomorrow then. Good progress today. Maybe next time we can do this without April?"

His eyes flew open. "No. With April—or not at all."

CHAPTER 28

"WITH APRIL—OR NOT AT ALL," WAS HOW WE ENDED EVERY SESSION OVER the next few weeks. They were all variations of that first one. Dr. Hermann made progress—or she seemed to think she did. Jonah began talking to her a little, mostly about stuff that didn't matter to him (or anyone), but she didn't appear to mind the pointless chatter. "It's all part of the process," she told me.

Once, when Jonah wasn't around, I took Dr. Hermann aside and asked her about his voices. "When this first started, Jonah seemed to be terrified of the voices and the things that they were saying to him," I told her. "He'd break into a sweat, put his hands over his ears, even yell back at them when he thought nobody was watching."

She nodded and gave me a knowing smile. "That's very common. The voices can be very hostile and angry sometimes. They're also very real to him, so real that he can find it hard to understand that no one else is hearing them."

"Yes, I realize that," I replied. "But shouldn't you talk to him about it? Find out what they're saying to him? I think the voices are what's bothering him the most, and what he's most embarrassed about."

"The voices are just another part of his illness," she said to me. "Our goal is not to understand them but to quiet them, maybe even to get rid of them. I think that we're doing pretty well too. He seems to be responding less to them now."

She was right about that, at least. Jonah did seem to be responding less to them, even though I couldn't help wondering if that was just an act. He'd stopped shouting at no one and covering his ears. But sometimes, when nobody was looking, I would still see his eyes flicker in response to something, even when the room was quiet. He was just hiding it better now. He understood that the voices were a brand of shame, that they stood between him and his freedom, and so he pretended not to hear them. It took all of his energy to pretend though—and it left him with very little strength to do anything else.

But he was gaining weight, and his face was filling out a little. I was encouraged by this at first, until one of the nurses told me not to get too excited—weight gain was a side effect of his antipsychotic.

Art therapy was also a big help—but not for the reasons that Dr. Hermann mentioned. Jonah produced a disturbed elephant as promised. Also a grieving hippo and a happy armadillo. His projects were funny to anyone who knew what he was really capable of creating. But the other patients loved it. There was a pale girl with purple scabs on her wrists who'd sit next to him when he worked and stare at him with an intensity that annoyed me. Her devotion didn't seem to bother him though; Jonah was used to being loved. He made her a rainbow butterfly as a reward for her support. For days afterward, I would see her walking around with it, cradling it in her arms as if she were holding a paper baby.

Shawn was Jonah's closest friend at Shady Grove. The kid had attached himself to Jonah a few days after his arrival, and he soon became his shadow. Shawn's outburst was considered a setback, and as Nurse Becky had predicted, his hospital stay had been extended because of it. It seemed wrong to me; I might also have had a breakdown if my mother had forgotten me in the hospital. But that logic didn't seem to apply on the psychiatric ward. Shawn had broken one of the goals of therapy when he assaulted the nurse, so they were no longer sure that he was ready for the outside world.

I never learned Shawn's actual diagnosis (that information was confidential), but from the bits of history that he revealed to Jonah, I understood that Shawn's "forgetful" mother had been just one of his many problems at home. There had been a steady stream of Mommy's boyfriends, and some of them were probably the reason that Shawn ended up in Shady Grove.

But the boy was a welcome distraction for both of us. I think those weeks of silence and fake therapy with Dr. Hermann would have driven me a little crazy if it hadn't been for Shawn. I was surprised to learn that he was nearly our age; he looked and acted like a sixth grader. Shawn was a little lightning bug, buzzing around, always talking a mile a minute, commenting on everything, excited by everyone around him. The few hours after his failed discharge were his dark time; I learned later that he spent most of the evening in the quiet room, throwing himself against the padded walls, swearing at the staff, and trying to tear the cushions apart. But there was no hint of that side of Shawn when he was around Jonah. He acted like my boyfriend's loyal disciple, and Jonah welcomed his enthusiastic follower. Shawn swallowed everything that Jonah said, never questioning anything, no matter how bizarre it sounded. "They're bringing in a new victim today," Jonah would tell him. "I can feel him speaking to me through his mind. He'll need us to help him."

Shawn would nod enthusiastically and then run off to hover near the entrance to the ward. And when they brought a new patient in a couple hours later, Shawn would gaze at Jonah as if he'd just witnessed a miracle of prophecy. Neither of them seemed to notice that the patient was female, not male as Jonah had predicted. Or that we'd all overheard the nurses talking about a new admission. For Shawn, Jonah's prediction had magically come true.

At first, I wondered if Jonah was using Shawn as a buffer between us, because he always seemed to be around whenever I was there. And I couldn't really talk to my boyfriend with Shawn in the room. I tried not to get frustrated. I was visiting Jonah to show my support, I told myself. It wasn't about me. But eventually my patience began to wear thin. *Nothing* was changing.

Each time my bus pulled up to the stop outside the hospital, I'd feel my heart begin to drum. "Maybe today will be the day," I'd think in spite of the previous evening's disappointment. Maybe today would be the day that Jonah would smile at me, would take me in his arms and kiss me. Maybe today we would finally get a few minutes alone. No doctors, nurses, parents, or Shawn. No voices. Just Jonah and April, like we used to be.

I'd walk into the ward, holding my breath. Praying.

And Shawn would be hovering by his side. Jonah's eyes would flicker over me. And then he'd smile, finally—at someone invisible at his side.

One day, as I was about to leave for home, Jonah asked me to wait. "Shawn, I think it's time to tell her," he declared.

"It isn't safe yet!" Shawn warned him. "It's too soon."

"We need help from the outside," Jonah said in a low voice. "We don't have a choice. They'll search my room the minute they discover that we're gone. Besides, April has been protected all this time. I've told her how to block them. She's on our side."

I suppressed a sigh and waited for him to continue. It was painful to admit it, but I *was* technically on their side. I still wore the ridiculous hat that Jonah had fashioned for me to keep out the mind-controlling radio waves. I'd even lined a few baseball caps with tinfoil and shown them to him to make sure that they were up to his safety standards. And I wore those too, after I tired of the beret. And no matter how many therapy sessions I attended with him, I still never said a word to his psychiatrist, just as he'd instructed me.

It pissed off Dr. Hermann in the beginning, but she eventually got used to Jonah's quiet girlfriend. "Psychiatrists have to be flexible," she told me. "We have to relinquish control in order to gain their trust. We have to listen to what they're saying."

And yet, we were weeks into Jonah's hospital stay—he'd passed all of Christmas break in Shady Grove's sterile hallways—and I didn't believe that *anyone* was actually listening to him. The medicines worked just enough to make him a passive mental patient, less likely to smack a nurse or scream at the hallucinations in his mind. But the doctors and the pills hadn't brought Jonah back to me.

It was a suspicious mental patient who was looking at me now, not the Jonah I knew and loved. He pulled the navy spiral notebook from beneath his pillow and turned it over and over in his hands. It was covered in strips of sticky gum that he'd stretched around the binding to seal it closed.

"It's all in here," he told me in a conspiratorial whisper. "And I need you to keep this safe until Shawn and I are ready to use it."

"What do you want me to do with it?"

"Take it quickly and hide it in your schoolbag." He glanced sharply over his shoulder as he spoke. "Now go home and rest. Tomorrow's going to be a big day for us."

CHAPTER 29

WHEN I GOT HOME, MY MOM MET ME AT THE DOOR. "KRIS IS HERE," SHE SAID in a hushed voice. "She's been waiting in your room all afternoon."

I'd been ignoring Kris's texts and calls for weeks. My phone had finally gone silent, so I hadn't expected her to just show up at my house. She was the last person I wanted to see.

I trudged into my bedroom without a word, slumped down on my bed, and leaned back against my pillow. Kris walked over and tried to put her arm around me, but I shrugged her hand off and glared at her.

"Why are you here?" I demanded. "Do you need more information about Jonah? Is Cora begging you for more gossip?"

She flinched and shrank away. "I know you're mad at me. But I swear I didn't mean to tell her anything. When Cora called, I'd just spoken to your mom and I didn't really understand what was going on. So I blurted out the part about Shady Grove. I'm really sorry. I regretted it the minute I said it."

"Oh, well. I'm glad you're sorry, Kris. Because that helps me a lot in school. I'll remember that you're sorry the next time Robby calls me Mrs. Crazy. Or Cora asks me what I did to drive my boyfriend insane."

"I *am* sorry," she insisted quietly. "That's what I came by to tell you. You've been shutting me out and not giving me a chance."

"Okay, let me guess. You want to join the April sympathy parade now? And drop little hints about how I should be 'getting on with my life.' Which is just code for 'dump that boyfriend already.' Thanks, but I already have my mom to tell me that."

"No, that's not what I think at all! Why can't you just listen? You've decided that the entire world is against the two of you, and so you're pushing everyone away. But I've been thinking about Jonah for weeks now. And I've wanted to tell you that I get it. I know that I was kind of suspicious in the beginning. I didn't realize what he meant to you before. I thought it was just a first crush, your first boyfriend. And frankly, he scared me a little, even at the beginning. No, don't roll your eyes. Just listen. There was something so intense about him, something that made me nervous for you. And then I saw him that day, all covered in red paint and holding a knife. Everyone was afraid of him; he looked completely out of it. And I thought—I was *right*. I saw it before anyone. I was actually a little *proud* of myself. I'm supposed to be the blind one, and you're the one with all the good advice. But this time—this time, you were the one in trouble."

Her eyes filled with tears, and she put her sleeve up to her cheek to catch them. "But then I saw the two of you out there on the lawn," she continued after a pause. "And I realized that even at the worst time, you two were closer than I'd ever been to anyone. You were able to go to him, to enter into his world. And he listened to you. He wouldn't pay attention to the policeman or even his own mother. But he heard *you*, April."

I'd never thought of it that way before. He *had* heard me, even as he blocked everyone else out. I was a little ashamed of myself, looking at Kristin's earnest expression. I really hadn't given her any credit. I'd just assumed that she would judge me. "Thank you, Kris."

"I've really missed you."

I reached out to hug her. "I'm sorry I shut you out."

"It's okay. I might have done the same thing if I was you."

"And you've been waiting for me here all afternoon?"

She shrugged. "A couple of hours. I didn't realize that you always go to Shady Grove after school or I would have called first. I have to be heading back now. But before I go, I want to ask you something. I've been waiting weeks to ask you."

"What is it?"

"I really want you to meet Danny."

I must have looked confused, because she answered my question before I spoke.

"He's the guy that I told you about a while back. We've been dating for a couple of months now, remember?"

I smiled. "Yeah, of course. The 'one.' How could I forget?"

She shrugged and shook her head. "Well, not yet. It hasn't happened yet. I've decided to wait a little longer, just to be sure. Anyway, I thought maybe I could bring him over. I've told him about you and Jonah."

"Awesome," I replied in a wry voice. "Maybe we could double-date."

"That's what he said! That would be so much fun."

"Kris, I was joking—"

"No, don't take it back! Jonah will get better soon, and then we'll hang out together."

"That sounds—fun," I admitted hesitantly.

"Also, I brought something for you. Danny and I have been doing some reading. He said that you should learn more about what Jonah has so you can help him. I brought you some articles about schizophrenia that we printed out from the Internet and this book we found in our library."

I glanced at the papers that she handed me. Each page was bordered by advertisements of pills with long names and showed women with patient, hopeful faces staring into the distance. There was a photo of a wise-looking bearded man standing beside a dirty alleyway with a caption that read, "This used to be my bedroom. I don't want to sleep here again. Zyprexa."

The ad made my stomach turn. I didn't want to think about Jonah turning into a smelly homeless man who shouted at nobody on a street corner. I shoved the stuff away and fell back against my pillow. "Thank you for this."

She nodded and stood up to go. "Whenever you need, just call, okay? And I'll try to come by as often I can."

"Okay."

After she left, I gathered up the papers and threw them underneath my bed. The book, a heavy paperback called *Living with Voices*, looked less threatening than the schizophrenia ads, but I didn't want to read stories about how some patients from Sweden got used to the voices in their heads. There was nothing in there that could help Jonah.

There was a knock on my door; I called out, and my mom entered, holding a letter in her hand.

"It came in the mail today," she said.

I took the sheet from her, glanced at it, then tossed it to the side. "The School for the Arts has accepted my application," I told her. "I'll be getting an audition date sometime in the next two weeks."

"Are you nervous about it?"

I shrugged. "I haven't had time to think about the art school. I don't really care that much about it anymore."

"But you practiced so hard!" she protested. "What happened?"

I didn't know what to say to her. Wasn't it obvious what had happened?

"You hoped Jonah would be home by now, right?" she suggested when I didn't speak. "You expected him to go with you to the audition, to hold your hand through it. But he's not there anymore, is he? He's not going to be there, and you're finally beginning to see that now."

"Please stop it, Mom!"

"Ignoring your own life isn't going to help Jonah."

"I'm *not* ignoring my own life. I practice whenever I can. You've heard me. I'm still planning to go to the audition. I just don't see the point anymore."

"*You're* the point, April. Jonah wanted you to do this for you, not for him. Think about how proud he'll be when you tell him you got in."

"*If* I get in, Mom. If."

But I wasn't thinking about the audition. I wasn't worried about whether I'd succeed or fail. I was wondering how I'd break the news to Jonah if I actually did get in. That dream had been the only thing pushing me to practice these last few months. The vision had once been such a happy scene, the letter in my hand, the two of us hugging, Jonah's triumphant smile.

But now, no matter how hard I tried, I could no longer picture it.

CHAPTER 30

"PLEASE, APRIL, I WANT TO COME WITH YOU."

It was not the first time I'd heard Kris say it. She'd been asking to visit Jonah every day for the last week. But I'd put her off with one excuse after another. I told her that he was too sedated, too confused, too everything. But she persisted anyway.

"I'm your friend. And I want to understand what you're going through. I want to see Jonah through your eyes."

So finally I said I'd call and ask. I didn't really want to. Kris didn't love Jonah like I did, so how could she ever see him through my eyes? Secretly I hoped that the nurse would say that he wasn't ready to see new visitors. But Becky answered brightly that because of Jonah's progress in groups, he'd earned a few extra privileges. An additional visitor was certainly acceptable.

When I told Kris, she acted like I'd just scored tickets to the hottest concert in town. "I'll be at your house as soon as I can! I just have to find a nice outfit and straighten my hair—"

"Kris."

"Yeah?"

"You don't have to put on a show. It's a hospital, remember?"

"*I know that.* But I don't want him to think that I didn't bother. That because he's in Shady Grove, I don't believe he's worth the effort."

Kris could be shockingly awesome sometimes. "You're right," I said. "Thank you."

I might have wished that she looked a little less perfect when she did finally arrive. That sheath of sleek hair and the miles of skinny jeans were a bit intimidating. But she'd inspired me to do the same while I waited for her. I dolled myself up for the first time in weeks. Makeup, hoop earrings, strappy heels—the works. I even put on panty hose. Jonah *was* worth the effort. I was embarrassed that someone else had to remind me.

I think we both overdid it a little though. Shawn's shocked face was the first warning sign that maybe I should have gone a little easier on the perfume.

"April!" he exclaimed when we entered the ward. "You smell so—different."

I didn't want to consider what he was implying about my earlier visits. "Thank you. Kris, this is Jonah's friend. Shawn, is Jonah in the visitors' lounge?"

He nodded solemnly. "I better announce you," he said and scurried off down the hall.

"What a cute kid," Kris remarked. "What's he in here for?"

"He's…I don't know, actually. Depression, I think. Something to do with his family. He's been in here forever."

"Depression?" She wrinkled her brows and sniffed. "He seems just fine to me."

"Yeah, well, Dr. Hermann decides who comes and goes."

"Have you talked to her?"

I shook my head. "About Shawn? Not really. It's not exactly my business."

"I meant about Jonah. Have you spoken to Dr. Hermann about Jonah?"

I motioned her to be quiet. We'd approached the visitors' lounge as we were talking, and I hadn't had time to explain Jonah's rules. *I never speak to Dr. Hermann*, I should have said. I don't betray my boyfriend.

Jonah was standing in the far corner when we entered.

"You were supposed to come alone today," Shawn whispered. Jonah nodded curtly, his gleaming eyes focusing briefly on Kris and then shifting back to me. "Why did you bring her to see us?" Shawn demanded.

Before I could answer, Kris barreled forward and extended an eager hand to him. "I wanted to visit you, Jonah," she declared cheerily, flashing an overbright smile. "April tells me that you'll be getting out of here soon."

Jonah's face went white, and he quivered at her. "How do you *know* that?" he asked under his breath.

I felt my skin grow cold. I saw now what was coming, what Jonah was suspecting. Kris had said something completely sweet and innocent. But that's not how Jonah heard it. He turned to me, his eyes narrowing. *Don't say what you're thinking*, I begged him silently. *Please, not now, not in front of Kris. I won't be able to handle it.*

"Jonah, she was talking about your therapy," I explained. "I told her you were progressing in therapy. That's what she meant. That's all."

Now give me a nod, I prayed. *Just give me a little smile or something and then sit down, like a normal person. Don't hover there like you're waiting for us to attack you. And for God's sake, call off your tiny guard.*

But nothing came, no smile, no nod, not even a flicker of acknowledgment from his cold eyes.

"It's okay, Shawn," I murmured after it was obvious that Jonah wasn't going to answer me. "Kris is just a friend."

"I am," Kris echoed beside me. Her cheery expression fell, and she began backing away. "I didn't mean to upset you. You're looking—really good, Jonah."

Her pause had been louder than the compliment.

I couldn't leave things like this. I needed to show Kris *something* redeeming. *He's still in there*, I wanted to cry. You just can't see it now.

"Jonah," I said in a calm voice. "I was hoping you could sit down and talk to us. I have a lot to tell you about school. I'm sure you have things to tell me?" I was approaching him slowly as I spoke, advancing in small steps as if he were a sleeping tiger. He frowned as I drew near him and began to inch away from me, backing up against the wall behind him. "Jonah, please sit," I begged. "Don't walk away."

He was glaring at me silently, his eyes still narrowed with suspicion. He didn't say a word, but I could hear what he was thinking.

Don't trust April. She's lying to you.

He'd never looked at me that way before. I'd done nothing at all, and suddenly, for no apparent reason, he was terrified of me. It was bad enough that he had turned on me, but why did it have to happen today in front of Kris? She was the only person who believed in us, the only one who actually supported my love for Jonah.

"Let's go," I said to her. "I don't think he's up for visitors today."

"I'm right behind you," she replied, but her eyes were still fixed on Jonah's face.

"I'll see you tomorrow," I told him curtly and then turned and walked out of the ward without looking back.

I was halfway down the stairs when I realized that Kris wasn't behind me. I glanced around nervously and called her name, but my voice echoed through the stairwell. Had she really fallen behind? Had I walked so fast I'd lost her?

I doubled back and hurried toward the ward, speeding up as I reached the corridor to 11 West.

It took a few minutes until Becky buzzed me back in.

"Forget someone?" she asked with a smile.

"I didn't realize she was still here—"

I bounded toward the visitors' lounge and then stopped; my breath caught as Kristin stepped out into the hallway. She paused for a second, glanced fearfully over her shoulder, and then reached out to take my hand. "It's okay. We can go now."

"What happened?" I demanded, pulling back my hand. "What were you doing in there?"

"I just had to say something to him," she said. "I'm done now." And she strode off down the hall before I could reply.

I was standing near the open doorway of the lounge, and as she walked away, I peeked into the room. Shawn had already gone, but Jonah was still inside, in the corner where he'd been standing. He'd sunk down onto the floor, and his head was down, his shoulders trembling. I could hear him crying.

YOUR VOICE IS ALL I HEAR

I wanted to run to him and hold him close to me, whisper comforting words to him and lay his head against my chest. I wanted to pull a kiss from his lips, to stop his tears. But I couldn't do it. I knew that he was hurting, and yet my instinct told me to turn around and leave.

So I walked away from him.

Kris was waiting for me outside the ward door. She looked a little scared; there was a sheen of sweat over her brow. "Before you say anything, I want you to know that I didn't do anything wrong," she said.

"What did you say to him?"

"I told him that you love him. And that he isn't being fair to you. I said that you'd suffered enough."

"You did *what*?" I shouted. "God, Kris, I trusted you! And you waited until my back was turned and then what? You laid a guilt trip on him?"

"It wasn't a guilt trip. I *know* it isn't his fault. I know he's sick—"

"Exactly!"

"But that doesn't mean that he's completely gone. That doesn't mean that he can't hear me."

"Of course he can still hear you! I don't understand what you're saying."

"Well, that's been your point all along, hasn't it? That Jonah's still there? That's why you keep on loving him. Because underneath the illness, he's still Jonah."

I leaned back against the door and put my face into my hands. "Of course he is. I *know* that."

She walked over to me and cautiously wrapped her arm around my shoulder. "April, I realize I'm not a psychiatrist or anything.

But I couldn't help thinking maybe it's time everyone stopped speaking to Jonah like he's a mental patient. Stop trying to protect him from the truth. And start talking to him like he's a person."

I laughed bitterly. "That's a very pretty thought. But mental patient Jonah hates me now. And I don't know what the real Jonah thinks about anything anymore."

CHAPTER 31

THERE WAS ONLY ONE WAY TO FIND OUT WHAT JONAH WAS REALLY THINK-ing. I had an obvious clue that I was ignoring.

His secret notebook.

It had been sitting in my room untouched, wrapped in nasty wads of chewing gum and hidden beneath a stack of books. He hadn't told me that I could read it. I was only supposed to guard it. But I'd been faithful and true to Jonah. I'd obeyed his every instruction to the letter—and he'd still turned on me. I couldn't see any reason not to open his journal now.

After Kristin left, I settled down on my bed and took it off my desk. The bits of gum had hardened into grime-coated strips that cracked and fell apart as I pulled back the wrinkled cover. I hesitated for a moment, took a couple of deep breaths, and turned the first page.

The American Revolution, I read. *During the last half of the eighteenth century, thirteen colonies in North America...*

What the hell was this?

I was holding his notes from history class! *That* was his big secret? I couldn't believe it. My heart was actually drumming in my ears, my hands were cold and clammy, and all he'd given me was some closely written chapter summaries of our history textbook. I flipped forward impatiently, skimming the pages with growing irritation. Had he been bluffing? Or did he really believe that there was something magical in here?

I was a third of the way through already, and there was nothing here—nothing at all.

And then I saw them.

Lists.

Dozens of lists.

Somewhere in the middle of the history lesson, the writing broke off completely and became something else. A complete record of everyone in our class. Their phone numbers, addresses, random facts I'd never known, all scribbled down in jagged columns. Some of the names were circled with black marker, some were underlined or highlighted, and some were crossed out with vicious pen strokes. Then came a record of teachers, the principal, and secretarial staff, even Steve, the janitor.

Ms. Lowry (I read): Metoprolol 25 mg take twice daily. Verapamil…

What did this mean? Had Jonah found out our teacher's medications?

A blank page followed the final list. And then a giant X. Ten pages of Xs and nothing else.

And then a transition, as his life at Shady Grove began. He'd drawn complex maps of the hospital grounds and marked them up with swirling lines and arrows. He'd recorded every nurse's name along with explanations for how each had been turned by the U.S. government. He'd put together a summary of cafeteria food with the word "contaminated" next to some of the entries. He'd made a list of Shawn's mother's boyfriends and then scratched them all out.

And then more Xs.

I remembered what Ms. Lowry had said about one of Jonah's class assignments. *I'm worried because Jonah stopped making sense.*

I kept flipping the pages. Where was I in all of this?

Finally there was a chart with my name in it, but otherwise you could never guess that the author of this journal even had a girlfriend.

Spy	Ally
Dr. Aaron Golden	April
Mrs. Rachel Golden	Shawn
Dr. Hermann	Katie (but they never let me see her)
Carla, the security guard	
All the nurses (especially Nurse Becky) except maybe Nurse Tina	Nurse Tina (probably will be a spy by next week— will watch for signs)
All medical students except Tracie	Tracie (same as Tina— more likely to go spy because in medical profession longer)

Five more sheets of Xs then.

And on the last page of his notebook, written over and over, in cramped and spastic strokes were the words:

April Wesley will not betray you.
April Wesley will not betray you.

April Wesley will not betray you.
April Wesley will not betray you.
April Wesley will not betray you.
April Wesley will not betray you.
April Wesley will not betray you.
April Wesley will not betray you.

CHAPTER 32

I WAS SICK OF THE BUS ROUTE TO SHADY GROVE. I KNEW EVERY LANDMARK by now, the gas station with the missing *S* in its sign, the roadside coffee shop, the strip mall beneath the bridge, where teenagers with sane boyfriends gathered in the afternoons to laugh and flirt with one another. I would see them as the bus slowed down before the stoplight, and sometimes I would watch them and wonder about their lives. I'd begun to recognize a couple of the girls; they met their dates here every day at three, just as my bus passed by them. The pretty one, a rosy-cheeked redhead, would do the same thing each time her boyfriend came into view. She'd jump up and wave, then run to him and throw her arms around his neck. He'd smile and kiss her, and they'd go into the café together.

It was those two strangers at the café—not the doctors or Jonah's parents or Kris or even my own mother—that finally got to me. Despite the teasing at school, the loneliness, and Jonah's awful silences, I'd still believed myself to be the luckiest girl in the world. It was all temporary; he was just sick for a little while. He'd come back to me, and then we'd be happy again.

I had my memories and my imagination, and they kept me warm while I waited for him to get better. Every night, I'd pretend that he was lying beside me, his flushed cheek next to mine, his curls tangled in my hair. He'd tease me, whisper "stalker girl!" in my ear, tickle me when I pushed him away. And then, when I couldn't bear it anymore, he'd finally kiss me, and I'd attack my pillow in a frenzy of frustrated love. My phantom Jonah was sweeter and sexier and better than anyone else. And if I was patient enough, one day he'd become real.

But as those two cheery teenagers faded from my view, I finally saw what I'd been refusing to see. Jonah wasn't getting better, and I was going to spend the rest of my life on the number 18 bus, watching other people live their lives. And I was so angry at everyone. I was furious with Jonah's parents, unhappy Shawn, the burly psychiatric nurses, Kris and her *Dr. Phil* advice, optimistic Dr. Hermann, and especially with the redheaded girl and her loving, healthy boyfriend.

But worst of all, I was angry with Jonah. For the first time since he had gotten sick, I was angry because he had betrayed me, he had left me, and he was never coming back.

I was raging mad as the bus pulled up to Shady Grove, my eyes stinging with hot tears, my throat tight and dry. As I pushed the buzzer and the lock to 11 West clicked open, Shawn ran up to greet me. "April," he whispered eagerly. "Jonah's been waiting for you! He has instructions for you."

"*Instructions?*"

His eyes flashed. "Don't worry. Jonah knows that you're on our side. He wants you to come right now. It's happening today. Just as he predicted."

I glanced at Nurse Becky, who was signaling to us to move back from the door. Shawn was bouncing on his feet in front of me and grabbing my arm. I shook him off and turned my back to him. I couldn't stand to look at him anymore. I wasn't going anywhere with him ever again. I wasn't going to wear their crazy tinfoil hats. I wasn't going to pretend to be a mute every time Dr. Hermann asked me a question. I wasn't going to take any more of Jonah's ridiculous orders. I'd finally had enough.

Shawn said my name but I ignored him. "Is Dr. Hermann in?" I asked the nurse. She nodded, and I headed down the hall, moving faster as I approached her office.

Dr. Hermann looked surprised when I entered and motioned for me to close the door. Jonah's parents were sitting with her, and their faces mirrored the doctor's surprise. It was the first time we had all been in the same room without Jonah and the first time that I'd sought out the psychiatrist on my own.

"Jonah is due for his session in a couple of minutes," Dr. Hermann said. "Did you want to talk to me before he comes? Is something wrong?"

"Yes, there's something wrong," I told her, my voice tightening. "There's been something wrong ever since he got here."

The Goldens exchanged concerned looks. Dr. Hermann leaned back against her chair and folded her arms. "I can see that you're frustrated. But Jonah *is* making progress."

"Oh, really?" I shot back. "Well, did you know that he's been trying to convince Shawn to escape from here? Did you know that while he's been scribbling away in your art therapy class, he's actually been plotting to break out of Shady Grove?"

Dr. Hermann laughed and motioned me to a chair. "Oh, April," she said. "Do you think he's the first paranoid schizophrenic to try to run away? I'm sorry to hear that he's gotten Shawn involved in his plans, but honestly, I'm not surprised. It's pretty typical actually. They'll plot and plot, and in the end, they'll just do something silly like try to break through the main door. Jonah's too disorganized to come up with a realistic plan."

It was true, I realized. Nowhere in the notebook had he sketched out anything that looked like a real escape route or even a coherent diagram.

"Well, he's still hearing voices. He's still paranoid."

"I know," she answered evenly. "But I believe that I'm slowly gaining his trust and getting him to talk about what's bothering him. That's what's important."

I laughed bitterly and reached into my schoolbag. "You think so? Then maybe you should look at this!" I threw Jonah's notebook down in front of her.

With a rough gesture, I flipped it open and pointed to the "Spy/Ally" chart. "Does this look like you've gained his trust?" I asked her bitterly.

She scanned the sheet and glanced up at me, her face hardening. Jonah's mom leaned forward to look at her son's writing. Her eyes widened as she read her own name in the "Spy" column.

Dr. Golden was the only one who seemed pleased by my revelation. His lips curled up, and he shook his head at the psychiatrist. *Nice try*, his smile seemed to say. *You have no idea what you're doing.*

Dr. Hermann seemed to be considering her response. But before she had a chance to speak, there was a knock at the door, and Jonah walked into the room.

I'm not sure if Dr. Hermann wanted Jonah to see the notebook on her desk. I think that if she'd thought quickly enough, she could have covered it with something. But she didn't flinch, even as his eyes scanned the room and stopped, alarmed, at the sight of his journal open before us. None of us moved or breathed as we waited for the storm to hit.

It's all over between us, I thought as I watched Jonah's face. He'd never forgive me for this. In a moment, he'd turn to me and demand to know why I'd betrayed him.

And yet, he wasn't looking at me. His lips were moving silently, his hands trembling. His eyes were fixed on the open notebook.

Finally, with deliberate coolness, as if she'd been preparing for this moment, Dr. Hermann motioned for him to sit down. "Jonah, would you like to join us?"

He didn't answer her. Instead he wheeled around suddenly and glared at his father.

"How did you do it?" Jonah hissed at him. "How did you steal my notebook from April?"

His father started to defend himself, but Dr. Hermann raised her hand to quiet him. "One minute!" she said. "Jonah, what makes you think that your father stole your notebook?"

"Don't you see?" he shot back. "It's so obvious now! He's been trying to keep me quiet, to protect himself! As long as I was locked up, he knew that no one would listen to me. Who would pay attention to a mental patient, right, Dad? Who would believe a crazy person?"

"Oh, Jonah, for God's sake—" But Dr. Golden never had a chance to finish.

"You think that your little plan worked, don't you?" Jonah cried out. "You think that you'll get away with it?"

Dr. Hermann rose quickly and pointed to a button on her desk. "Jonah, if you don't calm down, I will call the nurse in. This is your last warning. *Sit down.*"

He hesitated for a moment and then slowly sank into a chair, his eyes still fixed on his father's bewildered face.

"That's good," the doctor breathed, relieved. "Now maybe you should explain to us why you're so angry with your father. Or would you prefer April left the room before you speak?"

"No. I want April to stay. She needs to know why they've locked me up in here."

"Okay," Dr. Hermann replied indulgently. "Then why don't you tell us why you believe you've been hospitalized?"

"There's no point," he muttered darkly. "He's already filled you with his lies."

"Why don't you tell us your side of things? Your father has already told me his side."

"He has no *side*," Jonah retorted. "This isn't an argument, don't you understand? He did what he did, and now he's trying to cover it up by locking me away. And he's convinced my mother to go along with him."

Jonah's mom was weeping quietly. "Please, Jonah—" she began.

But Dr. Hermann motioned her to keep silent. "Go on, Jonah. Tell us what your father did. Tell us why you're angry at him."

"You already know, Doctor," Jonah spat back. "You were watching all along, weren't you? You know exactly what happened."

"You know that isn't true. I only met you two months ago. But this isn't about me at all. So why don't you tell us what happened last year before you moved to Baltimore?"

"You already know."

"But I want to hear it from you. I want to hear what happened to your friend. Tell us what happened to him."

"You know what happened—"

"I *don't* know. What was it? What happened to Ricky?"

"*Don't you say his name, don't say it...*"

"Tell me, Jonah. Tell me about your friend."

"You want to hear about Ricky, Dr. Hermann?" Jonah shrieked, leaping from his chair and fixing his eyes on his father's face. "All right then. You asked for it!" Jonah took a long deliberate breath and pointed an accusing finger at Dr. Golden. "My father *murdered* Ricky. My father let my friend bleed to death, and he did *nothing*! Are you happy now, Doctor? Is that what you wanted to hear? *My father did it! My father killed my best friend!*"

They were all shouting now, Dr. Hermann demanding that Jonah take his seat, Mrs. Golden wailing her son's name, and Dr. Golden protesting that he wouldn't stand for this insanity a moment longer. I sat silently and listened to them scream, but my eyes didn't leave Jonah's face. He stood apart from all of them, his face flushed with triumph and his lips curled in a strange smile. Common sense told me that his father hadn't actually killed anyone; if Dr. Golden had been guilty of murder, he wouldn't be walking the streets a free man. But the longer they shouted at one another, the more I realized that I was the only one who *didn't* take Jonah's accusation seriously. Mrs. Golden was weeping into her hands and calling her son's name. Dr. Hermann appeared to be debating whether to buzz security. Dr. Golden had risen to his feet and was thrusting his finger in Jonah's face.

"I've had enough, you hear me?" he yelled at him. "This is not fair to me or to your mother. I've already apologized! What else do you want me to do, Jonah? What else do you *want* from me?"

"Tell April what you did!" his son shrieked back at him. "Tell everyone what you did! Tell them that I'm innocent and make them let me go! I don't belong here. I didn't do anything. I'm only here because of you!"

"You're here because you speak to voices in your head!" Dr. Golden retorted.

Jonah paled and took a step back from him; his hands were shaking at his sides. "That's not true. I don't hear—"

"This has *nothing* to do with me, and you know it," his father added in an acid voice. "This *never* had anything to do with me."

"Dr. Golden, sit down, please," the psychiatrist ordered suddenly. She had finally found her voice. "I'll stop this session now if the two of you don't quiet down and speak calmly to one another."

"I have nothing more to say to him," Dr. Golden responded, taking his seat. "This therapy of yours has been a disaster. And just to clear the record, in case you're wondering, I never killed anyone. I've spent the last fifteen years of my career saving lives, Doctor, which is a lot more than you can say. As for Ricky, I am really, really sorry about what happened to him. Jonah knows that. He also knows that I had nothing, *nothing* to do with his friend's death."

"If it weren't for you—" Jonah began.

"If it weren't for me, you might also be dead!" Dr. Golden cut in. He sighed and turned back to the psychiatrist. "I prevented Jonah from going to meet his friend that night, Dr. Hermann. *That* is my crime. I felt that those two boys spent too much time together. How was Jonah going to find a girlfriend if he spent every single day with—" He hesitated as Jonah's face contorted. "Anyway, we'd fought about it before. But now my son blames me for Ricky's death, as if I could have predicted what would happen."

"I told you he was waiting for me," Jonah protested. "He was still waiting for me when those guys showed up."

"Ricky was being bullied," Dr. Golden explained. "His parents reported it to the police, and a couple of the kids involved got into trouble. We thought that it was over. But that night, those boys ran into Ricky outside the theater. At first, they just laughed and teased him. One of the kids swore that they never meant to touch him."

"And you believe that?" Jonah demanded, his voice rising again.

"You were at the trial with me, Jonah. You saw the evidence. Ricky tried to fight them. He was all of ninety pounds, and he tried to beat up five guys who were twice his size."

"So what? How can you blame him?"

"I don't blame him! I blame the bully who knocked him down. Just one blow, to the temple—that was all it took. He never meant to kill Ricky. Don't you remember how he went to pieces on the witness stand? Jonah, I understand that you hate that kid because he killed your friend. So blame him all you want! But you can't blame your mother or Dr. Hermann or me even. And you definitely can't blame yourself."

"But I could have saved him if I'd gotten there in time. I promised I'd protect him."

Dr. Golden sighed and ran a hand over his face. "I'm sorry. I really am. I don't know what else to say."

Jonah nodded slowly without looking up, his shoulders drooped lower, and he brushed a finger beneath his eye.

The tension in the room melted; Dr. Hermann sat back in her chair, and Mrs. Golden dabbed at her smeared makeup with a tissue. I moved my chair closer to Jonah. I hoped that he would turn to me now that this was over. I pictured us hugging, Jonah's troubles melting away in my arms. I imagined Dr. Golden and his wife embracing tearfully as Dr. Hermann beamed at her recovering patient from behind her shiny desk. But I forgot that I wasn't living in a Hallmark movie and that endings like that rarely happen on 11 West.

"Let's go, April. We're leaving," Jonah said and held his hand out.

I took it gratefully. His grasp was warm and strong, and I had the sudden urge to throw my arms around him and hold him close. *You're coming back to me*, I wanted to cry. *You're finally coming back to me.* Because in that moment, for just a second, he was almost with me again. His clear, blue eyes were seeing only me, and he smiled that sweet, perfect smile. I saw it; I'm sure I felt him there—even if no else did.

So I can't forgive Dr. Hermann for her next words, even if she never understood what they did to Jonah or how far she set him back.

She folded her arms across her chest and nodded pleasantly at her patient. "That's fine, Jonah. I think we've done very well today. You can go back to your room now, and we'll pick up again tomorrow."

And just like that, the moment vanished. Jonah was gone. And now, for the first time, I could actually *see* the voices in his head. I could see him drowning beneath them. His fingers tightened over mine, and through their pressure, I could feel them hurting him. I could feel them screaming their fury. He closed his eyes and inhaled slowly. He seemed to be listening to the storm roaring in his ears.

"Pick up again tomorrow?" he echoed, turning toward the doctor. "What are you talking about? I'm going home now."

Dr. Hermann looked confused. Her cherry lips twitched, and she uncrossed her shiny legs. "We aren't finished. There's still a long way to go before you're ready for discharge."

"But—but what else do you *want* from me?" he pleaded, his voice breaking. "I gave you what you wanted!"

She sighed and rose quickly from her chair. "It doesn't work that way. I think you know that."

"*I don't know that!*" he screamed at her. With a sudden gesture, he let my hand go and started toward the doctor. "You lied to me! I gave you what you wanted! I gave you everything! What else do you want?"

Dr. Hermann backed away, one hand extended in front of her, the other pressed firmly to a button at the corner of her desk. "Jonah, sit down, or I will ask the nurses to restrain you."

His parents started toward him; they were pleading with him in one voice to listen to the doctor. I called his name and reached out to him, but he threw me off and grasped at his hair, like a person in agony.

"You got to me!" he screamed at the frightened psychiatrist. "How did you do it? How did you get into me? How did you get inside of me?"

"Jonah!" We were all shouting in unison now, but he was no longer hearing us.

"Did you put yourself in the medicines?" he demanded, circling the desk to draw closer to the cowering doctor. "Is that how you did it? Did you inject yourself into my pills? Oh my God, you're in my brain! *Your voice is cutting into my brain!*"

He would have lunged at her, but just then, the office door flew open, and two male nurses barreled into the room. With a quick movement, one of them grabbed Jonah in a bear hold and squeezed, and the other drew a syringe out of his pocket and jabbed the needle deep into Jonah's thigh. They were talking to him calmly as they wrestled with him, the nurse who held him whispering gently in his ear, as if trying to calm a fussy infant. Jonah fought harder and longer than he had in the emergency room, but he was no match for the nurse. The man never flinched, even as Jonah shrieked and struggled, kicked and bit at the air around him. He remained still and never relaxed his hold. Finally, after what seemed like hours, Jonah weakened; he breathed deeply and moaned, then slumped forward in the nurse's arms like a rag doll.

He looked so sad to me, even in his drugged sleep. I reached out to touch him, but the nurse pushed me back and shook his head. I couldn't understand why he did that; I wanted to shout *but he's not a danger to anyone right now*! And yet somehow I didn't have the energy to argue. Nothing I had done had helped Jonah, and I was worn out from trying.

I could feel Dr. Hermann behind me, exuding disappointment. I could hear Jonah's mom crying softly and Dr. Golden patting her on the shoulder. But I couldn't look at them; I was disgusted with all of them and sick of their tired faces. I wanted to get home, to be far away from them, from the sterile tile walls and disinfectant smell, the plastic mirrors, and the bolted windows. I needed fresh air, the sound of traffic and people, my little piano, my pillow, my mother, even my school.

Without a backward glance, without saying good-bye, I pushed past the nurses and ran out of the office.

CHAPTER 33

FOR THE NEXT FEW DAYS, I WAS A GIRL WITHOUT A BOYFRIEND. ALTHOUGH I never planned to cut Jonah and his family out of my life, I felt that we could all use a little break from one another. I didn't have anything to say to them, and I doubted they wanted to talk to me. I'd sensed that Mrs. Golden was becoming increasingly embarrassed by her son's illness and that every time I showed up on 11 West, she blamed herself for the hours that I spent with him.

So I took her unspoken advice and stayed away for a little while. I went to school as usual, hung out with Kris, played with Katie, and banged away at my keyboard.

My classmates at Fallstaff finally stopped making fun of Jonah. It was a relief to me at first, until I realized that the only reason they'd stopped talking about him was that they'd forgotten he existed. That hurt worse than the teasing, and if it hadn't been too crazy, I might even have wished them to start up again, if only to remind me of him. The empty chair in front of me was quickly becoming the only sign that Jonah had once walked the halls of Fallstaff High.

One morning after history, Ms. Lowry asked me to stay after class. After everyone filed out, she waved me into a seat beside her desk and then settled at the corner of her table.

With characteristic bluntness, she came right to the point. "April, I wanted to ask you how Jonah is doing," she said. "I tried calling his home to speak to his parents, but no one answered."

I shrugged and looked away. "He's pretty much the same. The doctor keeps talking about progress, but I don't see any. I don't really understand what's going on—"

"You don't know anything about schizophrenia?"

Her question took me by surprise. We'd never spoken about his diagnosis before, and I was shocked that she'd bring it up so confidently, as if it were a well-known fact. Until then, when anyone had asked me, I'd insisted that Jonah had been hospitalized for severe depression.

"My uncle had schizophrenia," she explained after an awkward silence. "So when Jonah started having those symptoms—that unusual outburst in class, the homework assignment—I recognized the signs. That's why I was worried about him."

It was strangely comforting to hear that. She wasn't pitying me or judging Jonah. That was the reaction I'd gotten from everyone—my classmates, my mom, and even Jonah's parents. Ms. Lowry seemed to really care about what I was feeling and how I was reacting to my boyfriend's pain. She actually wanted to hear how I was doing.

"I don't understand anything that's going on," I told her. "I can see that Jonah is hearing voices, of course; everyone can see that. It's so strange for me, knowing that they could be talking to him about me and I can't hear what they're saying! And yet everyone seems to be brushing it off and telling him to ignore them! Like the voices are an itch that he just has to remember not to scratch."

She nodded thoughtfully. "That sounds familiar. The medicines don't always control the voices."

"The medicines aren't doing anything for him!" I exclaimed. "They dull him down a little, make him less edgy, but he isn't himself. And the anger, the outbursts, they happen anyway. The last time I saw him, he needed to be drugged; he was almost violent. That isn't progress, no matter what his doctor says. I'm scared she'll raise his doses again and he'll turn into a drugged-up zombie. But I can't say anything to Dr. Hermann. It's not like I can understand this stuff."

"Why do you think you can't understand it?"

I stared at her for a moment and then looked away, embarrassed. The question had never occurred to me before. "I haven't gone to medical school," I answered lamely. "There are so many medicines. I can't even pronounce some of their names."

"Don't you think you ought to try though?" she suggested. "Pick out a book about mental illness and do some reading. You don't have to get a degree in psychiatry or anything. Just educate yourself, so when Jonah reacts to a medication, you'll be able to ask intelligent questions. You may even be able to help him. April, you're a smart girl. You don't have to be powerless."

I didn't know what to say. I realized that she was right, but for some reason, I didn't want to follow her advice. Maybe I was afraid that reading about Jonah's illness would make me more depressed and frightened about the future; I wasn't sure what I would find in the large red textbooks that I'd seen in Dr. Hermann's office, but since they were linked to the mental ward, I didn't want to touch them.

"Dr. Hermann won't listen to me anyway," I protested weakly. "I'm only in high school."

"So what?" Ms. Lowry replied. "You can still read, can't you? Look words up in the dictionary? Give it a try. Why do you think I gave your class that assignment in the beginning of the year? It's because I learned from my own experience in the hospital that nothing is more terrifying than ignorance."

I'd actually forgotten all about her "medical history" assignment. I'd been barely keeping up with my daily homework; long-term projects had been completely neglected. But as I listened to her, an idea started to form slowly in my mind. And from it, a strange hope began to grow.

"I guess it can't hurt," I told her cautiously. "I'll think about it."

I could see that she was dissatisfied with my answer, but at that moment, it didn't matter to me. My plan was only half formed, and I wasn't ready to share it with anyone. But I was sick of Jonah's helplessness, and worse, I was sick of my own. And since Jonah wasn't able to speak for himself, I would have to find a way to do it for him.

CHAPTER 34

When roaring silence covers everything you touch
Splits the very air your lungs inhale
Your shadow girl will try her best to walk ahead
While her breadcrumbs leave behind a crooked trail

I STARTED WITH SIMPLE INTERNET SEARCHES AND PILES OF LIBRARY BOOKS. I spent hours poring over case reports and journal reviews, listening to interviews on YouTube, memorizing medicines and side effects. After only a few days, I realized that Ms. Lowry was right—it wasn't as difficult as I thought it would be. I began to recognize patterns in people's stories. The same phrases kept popping up over and over: "flat affect, tardive dyskinesia, flight of ideas." The words meant nothing to me at first, but after a while, I began to match these phrases with signs that I had personally seen, either in Jonah or other residents of 11 West. It was strangely empowering. I felt as if I were making little diagnoses in the privacy of my bedroom. And my discoveries made me curious to learn more.

Some of my reading depressed me, as I'd expected it would. There were a lot of dismal prognoses discussed, awful things that I would have to look forward to. Drug addiction, alcohol, homelessness, suicide attempts—the authors of the psych books didn't sugarcoat the outcomes of untreated schizophrenia. But every so often, there were glimpses of hope, cases of success and remission of symptoms. I clung to those nameless patients like a security blanket and reread their stories over and over.

In addition to all my extracurricular reading, I was also practicing piano harder than ever. A few days after my conversation with Ms. Lowry, I got my audition confirmation from the Baltimore School for the Arts. It was nothing special, just a simple note with a time and place written in bold. I brought the letter to Shady Grove the following day and handed it proudly to Jonah.

He looked at it blankly at first, as if he was having trouble understanding why I was showing it to him. "What do you want me to do with this?"

There was no spite or sarcasm in his voice; he just seemed confused by the paper in front of him. Everything baffled him lately; simple statements took him ages to process.

"I'm going ahead with it. I'm auditioning for the art school."

He nodded slowly and handed the letter back to me. His blue eyes were vacant, like windows into an empty room. "That's good, April."

Normally I might have been happy with that pale bit of encouragement. But today, I needed a little more. This was his idea, after all. I was doing it for him, and I couldn't let go of the dream that somehow we would make the move together, just like we'd once planned.

"So I was thinking that you should start working on your portfolio," I suggested. "I'll help you with the application and written statement, but you'll need to have a few paintings to show them."

"My portfolio? What for?"

"I called the visual arts department at the school, and they told me that the deadline is next month. So I was thinking, since most of your paintings are…covered up now, maybe you should start working on new ones. I'm sure the staff here would be happy to get you some supplies—"

The old Jonah would have laughed at my last statement; he would have made some sarcastic remark about happy hippo drawings and finger paint. I'd actually been hoping for that reaction, some hint that his sense of humor wasn't completely gone. But medicated Jonah didn't take the bait. He shook his head slowly and shrugged. "My hand hurts," he told me finally. "I don't think I can hold a paintbrush."

And that was the end of the conversation.

But Jonah was doing very well, Dr. Hermann assured us. He was participating in group therapy, cooperating in private sessions, keeping up with his schoolwork, and earning more and more privileges every day. He was no longer under constant supervision; he was even allowed to take short walks around the hospital grounds alone. He was quiet and respectful, and the paranoid delusions seemed to have faded away—or at least he no longer acted on them. Everyone was feeling the difference, the doctor told us, even Shawn. Dr. Hermann wasn't free to share his medical information with us, but she did mention that the boy was improving also, now that his friend had stopped filling his head with conspiracy theories and escape plans. Even Jonah's parents appeared satisfied with his progress. Mrs. Golden's eyes were no longer watery and swollen, and Dr. Golden looked a little less pissed off at the world. By the middle of March (Jonah's twelfth week in the hospital), everyone seemed optimistic that he would be out before Passover, as long as there were no more setbacks.

Things were going so well that Dr. Golden felt comfortable returning to his practice in Boston. There had been talk about relocating to Baltimore, but in the end, it was decided that he would work in Boston and fly down on the weekends to be with his family.

By the end of March, there was no longer any doubt that Jonah had met his goals and was ready for discharge. His parents were so pleased that they finally allowed Katie to visit him in the hospital. They hadn't seen each other since that December morning when she'd shown up shivering and terrified on my doorstep. Katie had been begging to see Jonah forever, but her parents kept postponing or canceling the visit. Better to keep her away, they said, than risk Jonah flying into a rage and terrifying his little sister.

But no one was scared of him anymore, and five days before Jonah's discharge, they finally brought Katie to see him.

As we walked up the paved path to the hospital, she clung to my hand and pulled anxiously at my sleeve. "Will Jonah have tubes in him?" she whispered to me.

I shook my head. "What kind of tubes?"

"Like needles. A girl in my class went to the hospital once, and I visited her there. She had needles and tubes all over her arms."

I smiled at her and squeezed her hand. "No, he doesn't have tubes or needles. He'll be just like you remember him, Katie."

I regretted the sentence as soon as I said it. While it was true that Jonah had regained some of the weight he'd lost, he'd still changed a lot since Katie had last seen him. He was much paler, the shadows beneath his eyes were darker, and his hair had grown into a thick tangle of long, black curls. He looked a bit like a former rock star just out of rehab.

But Katie didn't seem to notice any of that when she saw him. She ran to him, threw her arms around his neck, and squeezed him hard. The Goldens settled down next to her on the bed, and I pulled up a chair opposite them.

"I've missed you," Katie said. "I wanted to come but they wouldn't let me."

"I know," Jonah told her. "I was sick before."

"So? I can't catch it, can I? But Mommy kept saying it wasn't safe."

"No, they were right," he said after a pause. "It wasn't safe."

"Are you better now?"

His eyes flickered and shifted to the right; he stared off into space for a few seconds, then refocused on his sister.

"I think I am," he replied. "My doctor says I'm better."

"So you're coming home?"

"Yes, I think so. Soon."

Katie fell silent for a minute. Then she glanced around, cocked her head to the side, and turned back to her brother. "What are you listening to, Jonah?" she asked him. There was no fear or suspicion in her voice; it was just an honest question. But her simple frankness terrified me. She was the only innocent person in that room; the rest of us were pretending that we weren't seeing it. Jonah was still listening to sounds that no one else could hear. He hadn't fooled Katie for a minute.

"I'm listening to you, baby girl," he said. "Who did you think I was listening to?"

She shrugged. "Your imaginary friend? I have one too, for when I'm lonely."

He smiled and shook his head. "He's not my friend, Katie. He isn't very friendly to me."

I saw the Goldens exchange surprised looks. We all realized the same thing—Jonah had, for the first time, admitted that he was hearing voices. Any time the topic had come up before, Jonah had immediately denied the symptoms, sometimes aggressively. But just now, he'd actually acknowledged it, and he'd even described the illusion as unfriendly.

But Katie wasn't satisfied. "Tell him to be quiet then. He keeps interrupting when I'm talking to you."

The smile faded from Jonah's face. He looked confused and a little frightened. "You—you can hear him, Katie?"

"No. But you can. And it's annoying."

Jonah's mom sprang up from the bed and gently pulled her daughter up. "It's time to go now. Your brother has his session with Dr. Hermann soon."

Katie began to argue, but then her eyes met Jonah's, and she flinched beneath his quiet stare. Her lip quivered, she swallowed hard, and after a moment's hesitation, she allowed herself to be led out into the hall.

I followed Katie and the Goldens out and closed the door behind me. Katie looked like she was fighting back tears, and her parents appeared completely lost. I don't know what they had hoped for from that visit, but they definitely had not expected their eight-year-old to rip apart their faith that Jonah was getting better.

Dr. Hermann chose that moment to appear. She waved at Jonah's parents, and they smiled, but before she had a chance to speak, Katie stormed over to the doctor and let loose. "What did you do to Jonah?" she demanded. "What did you do to my brother?"

The doctor didn't seem upset by Katie's question. She reached out her long, manicured fingers and patted her hair. "He seems different to you?"

"He isn't *different*," Katie spluttered furiously. "He's missing. *What did you do?*"

Dr. Hermann smiled indulgently at Jonah's parents. "You have a very perceptive little girl."

"Where is he?" Katie persisted. "You made a mistake! You have to bring him back!"

"Where do you think he is?" Dr. Hermann asked her patiently.

"I don't *know*," Katie replied. "I just know he isn't Jonah anymore."

The doctor gave her an understanding look, the same look that I'd grown to hate over the last few months. It said *thank you for sharing your opinion. While it is very interesting to me, I hope you realize that I know better.*

"What do you mean, Katie?" Dr. Hermann asked.

"He didn't tease me once. Or smile when I came in, or get angry when Mommy pulled me away. I brought my book with me so he could read to me. But then I didn't want to ask him."

"That's a shame," the doctor said. "Why didn't you want him to read to you?"

"Because he wouldn't have been able to do the voices," she replied sadly. "He always does the voices when he reads to me. But you took the voices away."

"Katie—"

"I liked him better before," she declared before the doctor could finish. "And I don't want to come here anymore."

CHAPTER 35

You're beautiful, he says
Why can't you see it?
I stare into his eyes, but nobody looks back
My reflection is fading
Sheets cover the mirrors, the glass is now black

JONAH WAS DISCHARGED FROM THE HOSPITAL LATER THAT WEEK. WE'D ALL waited so long for that day, and yet, when it finally came, no one felt happy or festive. My mom and I had talked about hosting a welcome back party, Kris brought up the double date idea again, and his parents planned a neighborhood barbecue. But in the end, we let the plans fall through. Maybe none of us truly believed that Jonah was really coming home for good.

The only emotional thing that happened on his discharge date was a hysterical display from Shawn, who clung to Jonah until the security guard had to pry him off. I felt sorry for the boy. Besides the hospital staff, Jonah had been the only reliable presence in his life. No one had visited Shawn in the months that he'd been in the ward, and I overheard one of the nurses grumbling that he would be on 11 West forever, because every time they tried to discharge him, Shawn's mother would "forget" to pick him up.

Jonah promised to write and visit, but Shawn knew what we were all thinking: nobody discharged from 11 West ever willingly came back.

I stayed with Jonah for a couple of hours in his room that afternoon, curled up next to him on his bed, his laptop balanced between us. We tried to watch a movie, and I tried to ignore the fact that he was barely reacting to anything that happened on the screen. He only laughed once, toward the end, when nothing funny had actually happened. When Kris called to ask if she could stop by my house, I welcomed the suggestion and was embarrassed by the feeling of relief that washed over me as I left the Goldens'.

Kris was waiting for me on the porch when I got home. It was good to see her again. I knew I hadn't made enough time for her over the last few weeks, but it wasn't until I saw the person standing next to her that I realized just how absent I had been. "April, I want you to meet Danny," Kris said as he stepped forward.

I tried not to stare as I greeted him. I knew that Kris had wanted to introduce me to her boyfriend ever since they'd met, but between Shady Grove and piano practice, I'd somehow never found the time. I didn't even know what Danny looked like. I'd avoided Facebook since Jonah's hospitalization, because the ever-changing relationship statuses of my classmates had started getting on my nerves, so I'd missed all of the photos Kris had posted of them.

So this sweetly smiling, freckled, round-faced boy came as a bit of a shock. He didn't fit Kris's type at all. Danny wasn't tall and blond, he wasn't intensely aware of his hotness, and he looked like he'd be more comfortable scoring guitar chords than a winning touchdown. While not exactly unattractive, Danny wasn't going to be on a magazine cover anytime soon.

I had to be missing something, I decided as the two of them settled on the sofa opposite me, and Danny gingerly curled his arm around my best friend's waist. He was shy and a little awkward; he didn't take control of the conversation or crack hilarious jokes or come up with interesting stories to tell.

It was a few minutes later, when Kris was returning from the kitchen with a drink, that I finally saw what I'd been looking for. Danny turned toward her as she came forward, and when he glanced up at her, their eyes met. Kris looked as she always looked: royally, confidently beautiful, with the glow of a girl who knows that everyone is staring at her. But it was Danny's eyes that made me catch my breath, the flame in them as she approached him, the sweet adoration of a boy who could hardly believe his luck.

It was that look that made me understand why Kristin was so blissfully happy. And it was that look that finally broke me and made me cry.

Kris hurried over and wrapped her arms around me, and I fell against her shoulder and sobbed. I should have been embarrassed to be weeping like a baby in front of a complete stranger, but at that moment, I just didn't care. Kris had told Danny about Jonah, and if her boyfriend was as gentle and thoughtful as he seemed, he'd understand.

And he did. He got it right away. He didn't say a word, and while Kris held me, he rushed around the house trying to be helpful, coming back with piles of tissues, a hot drink, and finally (out of desperation) a bag of Cheetos from his backpack.

When I quieted down, he sat next to us and smiled nervously. "Was Jonah discharged from the hospital today?" he asked.

I nodded and tried to speak, but nothing came.

"Maybe we should have come another time then?"

I shook my head and wiped my wet cheeks with the back of my sleeve.

"Jonah hasn't gotten any better?"

I shook my head again. "Not really."

"Are you worried he'll go back to the hospital again?"

"No, that isn't it," I replied. "I mean, of course, I know Jonah might have to go back. But that isn't why I'm crying. I just realized all of a sudden how much I miss him."

Kris squeezed my arm and smoothed my hair back. "We could walk you back to Jonah's house now if you want."

"No, I was just at his house. You don't understand, Kris. He isn't there. I've been by Jonah's side for months now, and I'm *always* missing him. I miss that—that *look*." I pointed my finger at Danny. "I haven't seen that look in months. I'd give anything for that."

"What do you mean?" he asked, but his blush told me that he knew what I was talking about.

"The way you looked at Kris just now," I continued miserably. "Jonah used to look at me like that all the time. Even when I wasn't doing anything special. I'd catch him staring at me, like I was the only person in the world. And now he barely realizes I'm there. I think he wants to. I really do. But he just can't. He can't see anyone anymore."

"He knows you're there," Kris reassured me. "He has to. And when he comes back, he'll remember what you did for him, how you stood by him."

"But I need him now! Did you know that my art school audition is tomorrow? And he was supposed to come with me, to support me. I kept telling myself that if only he could get out of the hospital in time, maybe there was still a chance. But now—"

"So I'll come with you!" Kris suggested. "I'll be with you the whole time, okay?"

"I'll be happy to help too," Danny put in.

"Thank you," I told them. "I think I might actually take you up on that."

"I'll switch my guitar lesson to Wednesday," Danny said to Kris, "so I can come with you guys."

"It's okay, Danny." I smiled. "You don't have to. My mom and Kris should be enough support."

"Well, let me know if there's anything I can do. I really do want to help."

"Actually," I said hesitantly, "there's something I've been working on for a while. A history project for school."

"Did you need help with the research?"

"No," I said. "I've already done that. What I need is someone who can record soundtracks."

Danny's face lit up. "I can record anything you need! Instrumental, vocal, drums… We'll have to do it at my house, but I can't do guitar and bass. I can ask some friends—"

I shook my head. "No, no instruments, Danny. I just need your voice. Both of yours."

They stared at me for a minute, and Kris giggled. "April, you know I can't sing."

"You won't need to sing!" I assured her. "I'm going to ask you to scream. And I want Danny to record it."

"You want us to…scream—what?"

"Don't worry," I replied. "I'll tell you exactly what to say."

CHAPTER 36

FIVE MINUTES AFTER WE ENTERED THE ART SCHOOL, I WAS SURE I WAS going to make a fool of myself, that the judges would stare at me patiently and then roll their eyes the minute I left the room. I couldn't go through with it. Until then, I'd only performed for friends and family, people who were obligated to be supportive and kind. But the audience behind the painted brown door was different. They knew what real talent sounded like. I could hear strains of music echoing through the building as I paced the hall in front of the audition room. The walls vibrated with sound, the trill of a flute floating over us, the rising notes of a singer practicing her scales. The students in this school were true artists. The nervous little violinist next to me who was plucking her strings and sweating was probably a prodigy, a future star. And I was nothing.

"What's the point?" I whispered to my mom as a beaming clarinetist brushed past us. "They only accept a handful of incoming juniors. Why am I even bothering?"

"Because you owe it to yourself," my mom said. "You've been practicing so hard. And you'll never succeed if you don't try."

"Oh, Mom, that's such a cliché. Who cares if I don't succeed? If I leave now, I've only wasted my own time. At least I won't embarrass myself."

Kris folded her arms. "I'm missing a class trip for this. So if you don't go through with it, you've wasted *my* time. Stop whining and get in there. They've just called for the next applicant."

Sometimes the best advice is a kick in the ass. It was exactly what I needed.

As I introduced myself to the three smiling music instructors, my voice sounded small and scared. My knees felt weak as I slid onto the stool, and my palms had gone slippery with sweat. *How could I play like this?* I couldn't even control the trembling in my hands.

The silence closed in around me as the judges waited for me to start. But all I could do was wipe my hands over and over on my corduroy skirt. "Anytime now," someone said good-humoredly, and I laughed nervously and nodded. Had I disqualified myself before I even began? Were they thinking who cares if she has talent if she freezes on stage?

This isn't how this was supposed to happen, I thought. Jonah should have been here with me. He was the one who believed in me, who encouraged me. I'd wanted to become the confident girl he'd painted, the one he saw when he looked at me. Today I'd hoped to make him proud. Jonah was the real artist, not me. This was his school, his world. And he'd wanted to bring me with him.

I remembered his vacant eyes, the baffled expression, the Jonah who shut down when I spoke about painting. And then I finally understood: he wasn't coming with me after all. And I wasn't going to make Jonah proud, no matter how I played. Even if I burst into his room waving my acceptance letter, he wouldn't be happy for me, because he couldn't feel anything anymore. Who was I doing this for? My mom and Kris would love me no matter what school I attended.

The only person I could disappoint was me, and I was used to disappointing myself.

So what was I scared of? I had nothing to lose. I could be the confident girl in Jonah's painting, if only for a few minutes. Over the last few months, I'd been through hell, and I'd survived. I could survive this too. I would show those judges that a five-minute audition was nothing compared to watching the boy I loved disappear in front of me. The students who were waiting in the hall didn't matter to me. These teachers didn't matter. Even this school didn't matter.

Jonah was the only one who'd mattered, and he was gone.

So I was the only one left.

And I would show them that.

My hands raised themselves as if by magic, and I sounded the first chord. My fingers traveled along the keyboard, and the first few bars rang as clear and perfect as a recording. I wasn't thinking or planning; the music just came. Before I knew it, I'd played through half the page and still hadn't slipped or missed a note. I heard the melody that I'd rehearsed five hundred times, and yet it seemed to have nothing to do with me at all. The song had somehow learned to play itself.

I didn't hear the teacher call out to me at first; I was too absorbed with the piano in front of me. When I heard my name shouted again, I pulled my hands back and clasped them in front of me.

"Thank you," one of the judges said, smiling. "That will be enough."

I sat rooted to my piano bench. Why had that been enough? I hadn't gotten to the hardest section yet. I could do even better if they'd let me!

Or had I been fooling myself? Had it sounded so awful that they couldn't wait to get me out of the room?

But the judges didn't look irritated or critical. The male judge was scribbling something in his notebook while the two female judges nodded approvingly. "We *believe* you!" one of them said, and the other one laughed pleasantly.

What does that mean? I wanted to ask. *Are you telling me I was good?*

The male judge murmured, "You'll be hearing from us soon, April," and before I knew what I was doing, I had stumbled into the hallway and my mother was hugging me.

"That was *amazing*, April," she gushed. "We were all in shock out here!"

"You did it, you did it!" Kris squealed and threw herself at me. "Those judges are probably peeing themselves!"

"I can't go in there after *that*," wailed the sweaty little violinist. "Oh God, they just called my name."

The tension and fear were gone, and I was suddenly filled with love and generosity. "You'll be great," I assured my fellow applicant, whose pit stains had spread nearly to her waist. "Just pretend that none of this matters."

CHAPTER 37

IT DID MATTER THOUGH. I REALIZED JUST HOW MUCH IT MATTERED DURING the next few weeks as I waited for that letter to come. I went to school, I visited Jonah in the afternoons, and I got together with Danny and Kris and worked on my history assignment. But everything was colored by that day; I now thought of events as "before the audition" or "after the audition." I couldn't practice the piano anymore. I was afraid to touch the keys; my performance at the art school was still tinged with magic, and I didn't want to ruin it.

So instead of music, I decided to focus my energy on doing something for my mother. She'd been really supportive before my audition, and I wanted to show her that I appreciated it. So I started a thank-you note to her. I wrote a few poetic lines—and then I quickly tore it up. She didn't need poetry. I wanted to give her something useful, something that might actually make a difference in her life. I just didn't know what that could be.

One evening, I was chatting with her about my history project when I noticed that her attention had drifted. She was gazing over my shoulder at the neighbors' house again. "Mom, why do you keep looking at that home?" I asked her. "What's so special about the Greenwalds?"

She shook her head and shrugged. "It's—nothing."

I turned around and followed her gaze. Mrs. Greenwald was at her dining room window; her children were gathered around her in a circle. She lit one candle, passed the match onto the second, then placed her hands over her face in silent prayer.

"What is she doing?" I asked. "Are those Sabbath candles?"

My mother nodded. "It's Friday night."

I finally understood why Mom had looked so sad when I'd asked her about the Greenwalds. She'd been watching her neighbor light the Sabbath candles every Friday night for weeks.

"Mom, do you want to do the candle thing with me?" I asked her quietly.

She slid off her chair. With a quick motion, she reached out and drew the curtains, shutting out the light.

"Why? What would be the point?" she said.

"I don't know. Because it meant something to you once? It was so important to your family that they pushed you away. But you don't have to accept that. They're not the gatekeepers of your religion. It's *yours*. And I've been thinking about your traditions, ever since you told me about Jonah's Hebrew name. I realized you never told me mine."

She gave me a strange look. "I didn't give you a Hebrew name. I never thought you'd care."

"Oh." I felt disappointed, as if there was a part of me that she'd lost, and now it was gone forever.

"But you can give yourself one, if you want," she suggested, smiling. "If it would make you happy."

"I can?"

"Sure, why not? Choose a name that's meaningful to you."

"Would that make *you* happy?"

She seemed to consider for a moment before replying. "Yeah. It would, actually."

And that was how I got the idea for the letter. It started from a name, my Hebrew name, and ended with a letter, written late at night, after a long search in the attic for an address on a fifteen-year-old envelope.

The letter began:

Dear Bubbe and Zayde,

I hope it's okay if I call you by the Yiddish words for Grandma and Grandpa. My name is April—but if you would rather call me by my Hebrew name, I've just chosen Shira, because it means song...

It wasn't a long note. I wasn't sure it would get to them and even less sure they'd reply. But I understood how my mother felt now; she missed her family just like I missed Jonah. I was sure I'd never give up on the boy I loved, and I didn't want to see her give up either.

And I hated that the neighbors' candles made her sad on Friday nights. So a few days later, I stopped by a Judaica store on the way home from school and bought two candlesticks. I set them on the windowsill, lit the wicks, and waved my hands around in circles.

"April, what on earth are you doing?" Mom was standing behind me and staring at the dancing flames.

"I'm lighting Sabbath candles. I found an instructional video on YouTube." I began to mumble the blessing—or what I could remember of it.

"But it's Wednesday."

"So what? I'm practicing."

She laughed. "I appreciate what you're doing, sweetheart. But for me, those candles are about family. And I lost mine a long time ago."

"Okay. But you didn't lose everyone."

By Friday night, I'd learned the blessing by heart. I didn't know what the words meant, but the expression on my mom's face was all that mattered to me. She didn't say the blessing with me and didn't wave her hands over the fire. But she watched the flames until they flickered out. When the candles finally died, her eyes filled up with tears. I'd wanted to make her happier. But I'd only made her miss her family more.

So I hoped for two things every time I heard the creak and clatter of the mail slot: the acceptance letter of the art school and the acceptance of my grandparents.

I told Jonah about my secret letter when I went to visit him the next day. He seemed very interested in my story, and he smiled when I told him my new name. "I like Shira," he said. "But do I have to call you that now?"

I grinned and shook my head. "Only if I get accepted to the art school."

He laughed. "A new life and a new name?"

"Sure, why not?"

It felt so good to laugh with Jonah again. I'd been noticing a change in him since my audition day. He was a little less withdrawn; his eyes had regained some of their brightness. He smiled when he saw me and looked sad when I got up to leave. He wasn't back to his old self—not even close—but it was pleasant to be with him. His mom didn't have to remind him to shower and change, he began to do little chores around the house, and he even started reading to Katie. She still complained that his skill at doing all the voices wasn't up to par, but around him, she never let on that anything was lacking.

One afternoon, a couple of days before Passover, I stopped by to ask Jonah's mom if I could help her prepare for the holiday.

"Thanks for your offer," she said. "But I'm almost finished in the kitchen. Why don't you help Jonah instead? I told him he had to clean his room before tomorrow, and I don't think he's even half done yet."

Jonah wasn't in his bedroom when I knocked. But the art studio door, which had remained closed since his hospitalization, was wide open now, and the light from the window spilled out over the hardwood.

I approached the room slowly. My last memory of the studio was not a pleasant one. But as I peeked inside, I saw that the room had been cleaned up. Fresh canvases were set up next to a desk covered in brushes and tubes of oil color. The floor still bore faint traces of red paint, but the walls had been scrubbed clean and the room smelled of fresh varnish and turpentine.

Jonah was sitting with his back to me in front of an easel, a palette of colors in his lap. As I came in, he turned around with a smile and beckoned me over.

"I haven't gotten it right yet, but it's a start. What do you think?"

He turned the canvas toward me, and I stepped forward to get a better look. The painting was the beginning of a self-portrait. I recognized his features right away, his long black curls, his blue-gray eyes. He'd gotten the resemblance right. And yet, I couldn't help feel that something was missing. He'd drawn himself sitting alone in the middle of a sterile white room with padded walls, the quiet room on 11 West.

The scene was supposed to be stark and sad; it should have sent a chill through me, especially considering what I'd watched him go through. But I didn't feel anything. The portrait left me cold. The Jonah in the painting was as sterile as his padded cell.

"It isn't done yet," he said apologetically. "There's a lot of shading work left—"

"It's very good. It looks exactly like you."

That wasn't what he'd wanted to hear. He pushed the easel away and tossed his palette and brush onto the desk. "I just can't get it right," he muttered, rubbing his hand over his face. "I can't see things the way I used to."

"You've only just started painting again. It'll come back." I reached out and touched his face, running my finger over a smear of paint across his cheek.

He caught my hand in his and turned it over, then with a sudden movement, he bent down and pressed his lips to my wrist. The unexpected warmth against my skin sent a shiver through me; it had been so long since he'd kissed me that even this light touch made me go weak.

"I never said thank you for what you did for me, April," he said, his head still bowed over my hand. "I don't think anyone else would have stood by me for so long and waited for me the way you did."

"I was waiting for this," I said. "I was waiting for you to feel better—"

I trailed off, uncertain how to finish.

He looked up at me as I spoke, a vague smile in his eyes. "You're right. I'm finally feeling better. Not a hundred percent yet—but I'm actually *feeling* again."

"Dr. Hermann said it would take time until you got used to the medications…"

"Dr. Hermann has *nothing* to do with this!" he retorted, dropping my hand. "Dr. Hermann doesn't understand anything. The medicines made me dead inside. They're the reason I can't paint anymore! April, I thought you understood that."

His anger didn't upset me; I was actually glad to see him flare up. It had been so long since he'd gotten passionate about anything that I welcomed his outburst now, even though he'd directed it at me. "Never mind," I said calmly. "You're coming back to me. That's all that matters."

"Exactly! I beat her at her own game. Can't you see that?" he continued, rising from his chair in his excitement. "While I was under her influence, I couldn't care about anything. She had complete control. I couldn't feel anything, not hate, not happiness, not even love. April, *I couldn't love anyone*. I couldn't feel anything for you. I wanted to, so badly, but I couldn't."

Something was wrong; something he'd said seemed off to me. His hatred for his psychiatrist wasn't surprising. And the medicines *had* dulled him and made him miserable, but still…

But I didn't have time to analyze what Jonah meant, because as he spoke, he stepped over to me and pulled me close to him. Before I could say a word, he bent his head down and kissed me, not softly as I'd expected, but with a bruising force that made me gasp. Again and again, he kissed me, running his fingers through my hair and down my back, pressing me so close to him that I could feel the pounding of his heart against my chest. I couldn't catch my breath; I backed away and tried to speak, but with a rough gesture, he pushed me up against the wall, placed his hands over my cheeks, and forced my mouth open with his tongue.

I want this, I told myself. *This is what I've wanted since we first met; this is what I dreamed about every night while he was in the hospital.* I was trying so hard to want it. I wrapped my arms around his neck and tried to kiss him back, but he was moving too fast for me. His lips left mine and traveled to my collar; I felt him pulling at me, tearing at the buttons on my blouse, tugging at the cloth until it dropped around my hips. He was everywhere at once, his fingers skimming my legs, my belly, my chest, so sudden and urgent that I didn't know if I was excited or terrified. He never paused, not for a second, not even when I caught his wrists as he grasped my bra straps and began to slide them off my shoulders. "Someone could come in," I whispered. "Jonah, stop."

He walked over to the door and turned the lock, then caught me by the waist and pulled me down onto the floor. "I want you, April," he breathed. "I couldn't before; they wouldn't let me. But I want to show you how much I love you."

I love you too, I wanted to tell him; *I'm so happy that you're finally coming back to me.* But the words just wouldn't come.

The pressure of his body on mine was cutting off my circulation; the cold, hard floor beneath my naked back was hurting me. This was nothing like the moments we'd shared before. He'd touched me gently then, like he couldn't believe I was actually in his arms. That was the Jonah I'd been longing for. The one who waited for me to kiss him back. But this Jonah wasn't waiting for me; I could barely catch my breath. I wanted to shut my mind off and make him happy. I wanted to love him and just let go.

But I was scared. I couldn't shake the feeling that something was very wrong. Something he'd just said…

"Jonah, I want to stop," I gasped. "I'm not ready for this."

He pulled back, and I slipped out from under him. Jonah was breathing heavily, and his eyes were shining. But he wasn't really looking at me; for a moment, I wasn't sure if he'd heard what I had said. As I buttoned up my shirt, he sighed and rubbed his hands over his forehead. "I don't understand. I thought that you'd be happy, that you want to be with me—"

"I do! I've missed you so much! But you've changed so quickly. I was wondering what happened—"

"Oh, come on," he replied, grinning. "Isn't it obvious what's different?"

My mind was beginning to clear, and with a sinking feeling, I realized what he was trying to tell me.

"Jonah," I whispered, "Are you still taking your medicine?"

He laughed and folded his arms. "If I was, do you think that I could have kissed you like that?"

CHAPTER 38

I DON'T REMEMBER HOW I GOT OUT OF THERE OR WHAT EXCUSES I MADE. I believe I mumbled something about school, deadlines, and piano lessons. Jonah didn't seem to mind; I think he was so happy that he'd taken some control over his life that my rapid exit didn't upset him too much. But I was in total shock. I didn't trust myself to speak calmly, so I grabbed my schoolbag and fled the house.

On the way home, I heard my phone buzz twice inside my bag, but I ignored it. I needed to think. Alone, without distractions.

What was I supposed to do? I knew I was obligated to tell Dr. Hermann what Jonah had just admitted to me, but what would happen if I did that? If his psychiatrist suddenly called his parents and demanded that they monitor his meds, he'd know I sold him out. He wouldn't be able to blame his father for it this time.

But what choice did I have? I'd learned enough about his medication to understand that sudden withdrawals were dangerous. I wasn't sure how abruptly he'd stopped taking the pills, but still—

How long would it be until he suffered a relapse? Would his symptoms be worse this time? And what had just happened in his studio? Was our romantic moment part of his illness too? Could I trust anything Jonah did now? Or would I be examining every kiss and smile and touch from now on?

I needed advice, but I had no idea whom to ask. I couldn't talk to my mom; she was just waiting for a relapse so she could tell me that she'd had enough, that my relationship with Jonah was over. I couldn't trust that she wouldn't freak out on me and make things worse.

I was thinking about calling Kris when I rounded the corner of my street. My mom was waiting for me on the porch; her arm shot up into the air as I came into view. She was waving a white envelope over her head, and when I saw it, my heart dropped into my stomach.

I broke into a run, shouting at her as I raced across the road. "Did you open it? What does it say?"

"I didn't open it! I've been calling your cell all day! I just called Jonah's house, and he said that you were coming home—"

"Oh God, just *open it*!" I screamed, and as she ripped apart the envelope, I bounded up the stairs and snatched the letter from her hands.

We are pleased to inform you of your acceptance to the Baltimore School for the Arts...

"I got in!" I shrieked and threw my arms around her. The next few moments were a wonderful blur of hugs and bouncing and happy tears.

It was an almost perfect moment—almost like my dream come true—until I felt my mom stiffen and step away. I turned to follow her gaze and saw Jonah coming up the street.

As he approached, his face brightened into a sincere smile. I waved the letter in the air and began to shout the news, but the words were hardly out of my mouth before he bounded up the steps and caught me in a warm embrace. I felt a tickle at my neck as his lips brushed away my hair. Then he let me go and beamed at my mom, who was bashfully pretending to study the ivy on the porch railing.

"How are you, Mrs. Wesley?" he inquired politely.

She didn't seem to know what to say. "I'm—I'm excited for April," she replied after an uncomfortable pause.

"Why don't we all go inside?" I suggested. "We can talk about this in the living room."

"I can't, I have to go to work," my mom said. "I was waiting for you to come home, so I'm already late." She gave me a doubtful look and glanced over her shoulder at the house. "I suppose you two will be okay until I get home—"

"We'll be fine. We'll order a pizza or something to celebrate."

She shifted uneasily and cleared her throat. "April, maybe you could invite Kris over while I'm gone," she suggested quietly. "I'm sure she'll be glad to hear the news."

"I would, but Kris went to visit her grandmother this week. I'll call her later and let her know. Jonah and I will hang out here until you get back from work."

"Okay, I'll phone Rachel then. She can come over until I get home—"

"Jonah's mom is cleaning the house for Passover," I said irritably. "I really don't want to bother her."

"Okay, but it's just—I thought—April, I'm not sure—"

"You can go to work, Mom. We'll be fine."

Jonah had moved away from me and was standing with his head bowed and his hands clasped behind his back. "It's all right,

Mrs. Wesley," he told her softly. "I completely understand. I'll go home now so you don't have to be scared about anything."

"*No*, Jonah, stop it!" I cried out, my voice breaking in anger. "Mom, we're fine. Jonah's *fine*! You have nothing to worry about!"

She looked ready to protest again, but a glance at Jonah's mortified face seemed to silence her. She followed us into the house and shuffled around the kitchen for a few minutes, pretending to have lost her keys and purse, and then finally, after I glared furiously at her, she hurried out the door, leaving it open—just in case I needed to escape quickly, I suppose.

I felt awful for Jonah. He looked so unhappy sitting hunched over on the sofa next to me. I reached out and pulled him close to me and leaned my head against his shoulder. "I'm so sorry—"

"Don't worry about it," he said. "I'll just have to get used to that. People being afraid of me and not trusting me. Even my own mother—she won't leave Katie alone with me. I don't know what she's afraid I'll do, but we have a babysitter now, even when I'm home."

"It'll get better," I insisted. "Everyone will see that you're okay and they'll forget—"

"They'll never forget! No one forgets stuff like this. My parents definitely won't. My mother watches over me like I'm a toddler. She doesn't want me going out alone; I had to sneak out to see you just now. And when I go back to school, I don't even want to think about what people will say."

"So you can finish this semester at home and then transfer next year." I smiled hopefully. "Talk to the admissions committee at the art school. Maybe they'll make an exception and accept your application late."

He laughed shortly. "You're still holding on to that, April? You still think we'll transfer together? God, and they call *me* delusional!"

"I don't want to go without you. We were supposed to do this together."

He said nothing for a moment; his head was bowed near mine, his black curls brushing my cheek. "We were supposed to do a lot of things," he said sadly. "*I* was supposed to do a lot of things. But there isn't anything left. My art is gone. No, don't say anything. I'm telling you—I don't have it anymore. The hospital took everything from me. My parents look at me differently now, like I'm a stranger to them. They used to be so proud of me—even my father, in his own way. He used to say that I'd gotten my 'talented hands' from him." He sighed and shook his head. "I'm sorry, April. I shouldn't be dumping this on you right now. You were so happy a second ago, and as usual, I've ruined it."

"You haven't—"

"You're crying," he said and brushed a finger over my wet cheek. "How many times have you cried this year because of me? Have you lost count? That's too bad. I think somebody should be keeping track."

I gave him a playful shove. "I wouldn't worry about my crying. I do that a lot anyway. I tear up during TV shows, remember? Stop blaming yourself."

"Who else am I supposed to blame? And I can't help asking myself—if you're crying more than you're laughing when we're together, why are you still with me?"

"Jonah—"

"No, *I mean it*. Haven't you wondered, even once over the last few months, if maybe you'd be better off without me?"

"Did you want me to abandon you?" I demanded. "Would you have abandoned me if I had, if I had a—"

I stopped, confused. Was I allowed to say the word? Or were we still pretending that he was the victim of a horrible government conspiracy?

"So that's what it was then?" he asked me quietly. "You felt obligated to stay with me?"

"No! I didn't—that wasn't it…"

"And I let you, of course. Because I love you. And because— because I'm just that selfish."

"Jonah—"

"No, I see it now. You won't leave me, will you? Not if you feel that I still need you."

"I need you too…"

"*No, you don't*. Why can't you see that? You'd be much better off if—"

"Don't say it! I won't, I *won't* break up with you. I won't leave you. I'm sick of people telling me I should! If you want to leave me, go! But I'm not leaving you."

He sighed and closed his eyes again. "I love you, April. You know that, right?"

I took a deep breath and leaned against his shoulder. "I know. We'll get through this together, okay? And you can stop worrying—I'll stick by you, always, no matter what."

He nodded but didn't open his eyes to look at me. "No matter what."

CHAPTER 39

I HAVE A DATE TONIGHT.

I have a date tonight.

I have a date tonight.

I repeated the words to myself as I watched the clock tick closer to the final minute of last period. Jonah had called me that morning and asked me to meet him at the mall. *The mall.* Not a doctor's office or a hospital. Just the mall. As if that was normal. As if we'd been hanging out there each day like everybody else, trying on clothes, buying ice cream, making out in the back row of the movie theater.

I couldn't wait.

We were going to be a normal couple again.

I was so lost in my daydream that I didn't notice the strange looks that Miles kept shooting me or the pucker of Cora's red lips. It wasn't until the school bell rang that I finally paid attention to my classmates' whispering and understood that they'd been talking about me the entire afternoon.

As soon as the English teacher left the room, a circle of students formed around my desk, and Cora swept up to me like an army general leading an attack.

"I'm not staying in this class if he comes back," she declared shrilly. "I'm going to complain to the school board."

"Me too," Miles chimed in. "I sit right next to him."

I didn't understand what they were talking about; Jonah hadn't mentioned anything to me about starting school again.

"Jonah isn't dangerous," I told them, trying to keep my voice steady and failing. "You have no idea what you're talking about."

"He's *crazy!*" Cora shot back. "My mom heard from Kris's mom that he's actually insane. The doctors kept him locked away as long as they could, and now his parents are pushing the school to let him back in."

I yanked my schoolbag off the floor. "Shut *up*, Cora. Jonah's never hurt anyone."

"*Who cares?* You don't know that he won't snap all of a sudden. Go apeshit and start screaming and stabbing people. How many personalities does he have anyway? Is one of them a rapist? Because I don't want to meet that one behind the gym one day."

"He doesn't have other personalities!" I shouted. "You don't understand anything about schizophrenia!"

I realized what I'd said too late; the word was already out, and I couldn't take it back. I knew that they'd all guessed Jonah's diagnosis. And I'd wanted to stand up for him and defend him against their prejudice. But I'd been planning to do it in my own way.

Cora flipped her hair over her shoulder and gave Miles a triumphant look. "I told you so, didn't I?" she crowed. "Depression, my ass."

The other students began to whisper and nudge each other. But I didn't stay to listen to the rest. I wasn't going to waste another second on them.

I arrived at the mall a little earlier than I'd meant to; as the bus pulled up, I saw Jonah stepping out of the corner hardware store, clutching a small, black plastic bag in his hands. I called to him, and he looked up with a guilty start and quickly shoved the bag into his backpack.

"April! You startled me. I was expecting you in half an hour."

I shrugged. "I was excited. And the kids in school were obnoxious. So I left early."

"Oh." He smiled wryly as he led me to a corner café table. "They heard the news?"

"Yeah, they heard. Before me even. You never told me you were coming back to school."

"I'm not. But my parents seem to think I am."

"Do you have a choice? You have to go back eventually."

He shrugged. "I always have a choice." He looked away from me as he said it.

"Well, Cora will be relieved to hear that. She wasn't very nice this afternoon."

"I told you, didn't I? There's no going back for me."

"Jonah, that isn't—"

"No, please don't argue with me. Not today. It's our first date in a long time, right? So let's forget about these last few months and just be us again, like we used to be. No doctors, no stupid therapy appointments, no medicines. Just Jonah and April. This one time. Please."

I nodded and took a sip of Coke. "Okay. Just us."

And it *was* just us that night; it felt almost like old times. We didn't leave the mall until closing hour. I didn't want the evening to end. Maybe I sensed that the calm was too good to last.

But that evening, he actually seemed okay to me. So when he invited me to his room, I told him yes, even though I was still unsure of what I really wanted—or how far I wanted to go with him that night.

His family was asleep, so we tiptoed upstairs. I was excited and nervous; there was an air of mystery and romance in the dark stillness of the house. Was he going to grab me when we got to his room? Pull me onto his bed and kiss me? Our last kiss had frightened me, but tonight I was sure he would be different.

But when we entered his bedroom, he didn't try to touch me; he didn't even bother to shut the door behind us. His expression was tense, his eyes focusing on some faraway point, his lips drawn in a grim, determined line. *I have to be patient*, I told myself. I needed to pretend that everything was fine.

"We could watch a show if you want," I suggested in a light voice. "I have a midnight curfew, but we have a little time until I have to leave—"

"Can you help me?" he asked abruptly. "There's something I need to do."

I followed his gaze; he was staring at the punching bag hook in the ceiling. "What do you need?"

There was a nervous thrill in his voice. "I want to take my heavy bag down," he told me. "Can you hold it steady while I unhook it?"

I should have asked him why he needed to remove it now, in the middle of the night. But Jonah had made so many bizarre requests over the last few months that this one didn't stand out as anything unusual. "You want to stop training?" I asked as I took my place beside the bag.

He flexed his calloused fists and climbed up on a chair. "I'm not going to need it anymore. Dr. Hermann said that I should find some other way to channel my anger."

His comment surprised me a little. It was true; his doctor had said that he should try some other exercise. Anyone would have suggested the same after examining Jonah's bleeding knuckles. But he'd never taken any of Dr. Hermann's suggestions seriously before; he tried never to refer to her at all if he could help it. Was this a positive sign? Was he finally coming to terms with his illness?

I heard him grunt as he detached the bag's chain from the swivel hook, and together we grasped the smooth vinyl and let it slide slowly to the ground.

"Thank you for your help," he said, leaning over and kissing me lightly on the cheek. "Good night, April."

And then he turned his back to me.

I couldn't believe it. Our first date in months, and he'd dismissed me with a brotherly little peck! How could he have treated me so casually? Didn't he realize how long I'd waited for tonight? Didn't he understand how much his coldness hurt?

I left his room without saying good-bye. He didn't deserve a kind word after that cold farewell. With a rough motion, I pushed the front door open and stepped out into the street. I took a deep breath and felt my muscles relax. *I need to calm down*, I told myself as I headed home. I wasn't being fair; he hadn't meant to treat me badly. Maybe he was just taking things slow. He'd asked me to try and leave the past behind us for just one night, so we could start again and rediscover each other, like a couple on a first date.

Just Jonah and April, he'd begged me. This one time.

This one time.

This one time.

It was that little phrase, chiming over and over in my head, that made me freeze then, that made me stop suddenly as the shock of understanding hit me. Then all at once, each sign, each word, each hint, came rushing back, overwhelming me.

There's no going back for me, April. There isn't anything left.

You'd be much better off…

Why hadn't I heard what he was saying?

And today—it had been in front of my eyes all day.

The black plastic bag from the hardware store.

The guilty look when I'd interrupted him.

Can you help me, April? There's something I need to do.

The vacant punching bag hook in the ceiling…

I screamed, there in the empty moonlit street, alone. I shrieked his name. Then I was running, my heels pounding against the pavement, gasping as the night air burned my throat. I kicked off my shoes and flew down the road, hardly feeling the stones as they tore at my bare feet.

The Goldens' front door was still unlocked, and I threw it open and dashed up the stairs and down the hall to his bedroom. The knob turned easily, but the door wouldn't budge; I threw my weight against it and felt it push me back. There was something jamming it shut.

All doubts had vanished. I screamed Jonah's name and beat frantically at the door, hurling myself against it, begging him to open it and let me in. No answer came; there was a faint scraping sound and then total silence. I clawed at the wood frame and tried to wedge my fingers through the opening, then shouted for help again and again, my voice echoing through the still house.

Then Dr. Golden was in the hallway, blinking and rubbing his eyes.

"What's going on?"

"I can't get in!" I gasped, drumming my hands against the door. "Jonah's blocked the entrance!"

There was no need for further questions; my frantic eyes, my bare feet, the eerie silence from Jonah's room, told his father everything he needed to know. He was beside me in a second, and together we hurled ourselves at the door until it moved, scraping forward inch by inch. The gap was finally big enough to squeeze through. Dr. Golden went in first, and I followed after. I heard him shout; the room was dark, but through the shadows, I could see Jonah's quiet form hanging limply beneath the ceiling hook, a rope twisted around his neck, his head bowed before us.

Dr. Golden sprang forward, grabbed Jonah by the hips, and lifted him. The taut rope went slack, and Jonah's head lolled forward, an awful flaccid drop, like a rag doll's. Behind me, I heard a high-pitched shriek, and the room flooded with light. Mrs. Golden was beside me, her hands over her face, screaming wordlessly at her husband. He was shouting back at us, ordering me to call an ambulance, begging her to find a knife to cut the rope. But she was frozen, paralyzed with shock, her mouth open in a final silent cry, her eyes fixed on the mottled, dusky face of her son.

I couldn't panic; there wasn't time. I pulled my cell out of my pocket and dialed, then thrust the phone into her hand and squeezed her fingers. "Tell them your address. I'll help get Jonah down."

She nodded dumbly, her eyes still vacant, and lifted the phone up to her ear. I dashed over to Jonah's desk and yanked open the drawer, grabbed a pair of scissors, and ran over to Dr. Golden. There was a chair near Jonah's feet, and I climbed on to it, squinting my eyes against the glare of the ceiling light. Carefully, I reached above his head, grasped the rope, and cut, sliding my fingers between the twine loop and his neck. I could see the red mark that the noose had left on Jonah's skin, a raw and angry wheal at the corner of his jaw. The sight made my stomach lurch; I felt hot acid burning my throat as the room began to swim around me. Below me, I heard Dr. Golden grunting beneath Jonah's weight; he was begging me to hurry, because his arms were getting weaker. I shook my head to clear my sight and gripped tighter at the scissors. *Stay calm*, I told myself. *Don't pass out now.*

Then suddenly the rope went slack, and Jonah began to slip downward; I grasped him beneath the shoulders, and together his father and I eased him to the ground.

"Is he breathing?" I asked. "Please tell me that he's breathing!"

Dr. Golden dropped to the floor and put his ear against his child's purple lips. "Just tell me that he's breathing!" He nodded quickly, and as he did, I saw it too, the slow rise of Jonah's chest.

"He's unconscious, but his pulse is good, and his breathing's regular. He couldn't have been up there longer than a minute," he reassured me. "You got here just in time, April."

That's all I wanted to hear. He kept talking, but I wasn't listening. His hands were on Jonah's chest and neck, and he kept babbling about airways and cervical columns, arteries and blood flow.

I dropped down to the floor and closed my eyes.

I didn't open them again until three red-faced paramedics barreled through the door to take Jonah away.

CHAPTER 40

I HADN'T APPRECIATED HOW GOOD JONAH'S FIRST HOSPITALIZATION HAD been until he was readmitted to 11 West. It was one thing to be a psych patient on a locked ward; it was quite another to be a psych patient on suicide watch. During his first stay, Jonah had not been judged high risk, so he'd been allowed small freedoms. Toward the end, they'd even allowed him to walk around campus unescorted. Now, a nurse accompanied him everywhere, even to the bathroom.

They searched our bags when we came to visit. We weren't allowed to bring in anything that he could use to harm himself. It didn't matter that he promised the nurse that he wouldn't try to hurt himself again. Nobody believed him. Nurse Becky held on to my spiral school notebooks and pocket mirror while I sat with Jonah, just in case. She even took my house key from me.

Physically, Jonah recovered quickly. The doctors assured him that he was very lucky; most attempted hangings ended in brain damage or worse. This information wasn't much of a comfort to Jonah. He hadn't wanted to be lucky.

I'd been dreading the therapy meetings with Dr. Hermann; I cringed at the thought of her condescending sympathy. But Jonah received an unexpected blessing during his second hospitalization. Dr. Hermann had just gone on vacation, so a covering physician took over his care.

I was introduced to Dr. Mina Vardi a week into Jonah's hospital stay. He'd already had several sessions with her and, amazingly, hadn't hated her guts. At Jonah's request, the doctor agreed to have me sit in on a session.

So with my mother's reluctant permission, I returned to 11 West to meet yet another psychiatrist. Since Jonah's readmission, I'd only been to see him once. My mom had forbidden daily visits this time around. Finals were coming up, I still had Ms. Lowry's medical history project to finish, and my mom wouldn't let me fail the tenth grade because my boyfriend had tried to hang himself. She'd actually said those words to me before ordering me to my room.

When I'd visited Jonah the first time, he was still groggy from his pain medications, so we really hadn't talked much. Now as I stepped into the psychiatrist's office, I realized that I didn't know what to expect. Would Jonah be hostile? Would he refuse to let me speak to his psychiatrist again? Would he be sorry for what he'd done? Or would he just be sorry that he hadn't succeeded?

He looked okay, all things considering. He was sitting in his usual chair, and as I entered, he smiled at me and nodded toward the seat beside him. The marks of his recent injury had begun to heal—his skin had regained its normal color, the little red freckles under his eyes had disappeared (Dr. Golden explained that was from the rope's pressure), and even the stripe beneath his chin had faded.

"You're looking good, Jonah," I told him.

The truth was that it upset me to see how healthy he looked.

Maybe it was selfish of me, but it didn't seem fair that I'd spent the last week fighting off nightmares, trying to block out the vision of his purple face, while he was resting comfortably, his memory of the whole thing wiped away by his blackout.

The doctor behind the desk nodded pleasantly and reached out to shake my hand. Dr. Vardi was a soft, round doughnut of a woman, white-haired and olive-skinned, with two sharp little black eyes sparkling over plump cheeks. "It's good to meet you, April." I noticed a light Middle Eastern accent when she spoke; the *r* in my name sounded exotic when she said it. "I've heard a great deal about you."

"I haven't heard anything about *you*." My voice was sharp and hostile, and I didn't return her smile. *I've already been here*, I wanted to tell her. *I've already spent hours in this office. And after months sitting in this chair, you guys failed him anyway. And I ended up having to cut my boyfriend down from the ceiling.*

"I can tell that you didn't want to come here today." There was no criticism in her tone.

I glanced at Jonah and saw that he was watching her calmly; he didn't seem upset by her remark.

"I realize that you're disappointed and frustrated, April," Dr. Vardi continued. "It's only natural to feel that way after what you've gone through—"

"What I've gone through? We aren't here because of what *I've* gone through! We're here to talk about Jonah. But we're not going to do that, are we? You're just going to throw a basketful of medicines at him and then send him home again."

I couldn't believe that I'd spoken to her that way. It wasn't like me to yell at a complete stranger, especially one who looked like the Pillsbury Doughboy's grandma. But she didn't seem offended. She nodded again, as if she was actually pleased and wanted to hear me yell some more.

"You're right. I did recommend a medicine to Jonah," she said. "One medication, at a fraction of the dose that he was originally taking. He's been on it for a few days. Why don't you ask him how he feels?"

I looked over at him again and saw that he was watching me. But he didn't seem unhappy or suspicious as he'd been in front of Dr. Hermann. He was gazing at me frankly, and his eyes were clear, untroubled. "The medicine makes me calmer," he said. "Less confused. It actually helps."

I didn't know what to say. What had Dr. Vardi done to him? Who was this person in front of me? "What do you mean, it helps?" I demanded. "Helps you with what?"

"With most things," he replied. "My mood. My thoughts are more organized now. It doesn't take everything away. But—"

"What doesn't it take away?"

I was sorry I'd asked the question right after I said it. Jonah's cheeks flushed, and he glanced helplessly at Dr. Vardi. She nodded encouragingly. "Go ahead, Jonah," she urged him. "It's what we wanted to discuss today."

He cleared his throat and threw me an uneasy glance. "The medicine doesn't—it doesn't help me with—" He stopped abruptly.

"Go on, Jonah. We've talked about this already. It's okay."

"I'm sorry, Doctor. You don't understand. *They won't let me tell you.*"

She didn't seem disturbed. "They don't want me to find out about them?"

He shook his head and swallowed. "They're telling me—they say that you are—"

"What do they say about me?"

Jonah exhaled slowly and shook his head again. There was a light sheen of sweat over his forehead, and he was breathing hard, like a boxer after a tough fight. I couldn't take my eyes off him. I couldn't believe what I was hearing. Jonah was actually telling Dr. Vardi about his hallucinations. He'd just admitted to them in front of both of us.

"They're saying that I shouldn't trust you," he finished in a miserable voice. "They're saying that you're evil."

She smiled pleasantly again. "Then why don't you tell them how you feel about me, Jonah? Why don't you explain to them what I told you before?"

He stared at her blankly. "What do you mean *explain* to them? You want me to talk to them?"

She nodded briskly. "Yes. Haven't you ever spoken to them before?"

"Sure I have, all the time," he responded bitterly. "It doesn't help. It only makes them louder and angrier."

"What have you said to them in the past?"

"What do you think? I've told them to shut up and leave me alone. What else would I tell them?"

"Why don't you try a different way then?" she suggested. "How about talking to them just like you're talking to me? Address them as your friends."

He stared at her. "Are you serious? You want me to *talk to the voices in my head*? Jeez, and they call *me* the crazy one!"

"Jonah, what did I tell you during our last session?"

"About what?"

"About voice hearers. I want you to tell your voices what I said to you yesterday."

"Right now?"

"Right now."

"Out loud?" He glanced apprehensively at me again.

"Yes. If April doesn't mind."

"No, I don't mind," I told him. "But if I'm making you uncomfortable, I can leave the room."

He shook his head. "No, I'd rather you stayed."

"Whenever you're ready then," the doctor said. "Feel free to answer them. Disagree with them if you want. Be respectful, but speak your mind. The next time they say something, tell them how you feel."

"The next time they say something? They're saying something all the time! They're talking through you right now."

"Good. Then go ahead."

He sighed and gave her a doubtful look, then turned his head away so I couldn't see his face. I felt him listening—I saw the muscles in his shoulders tense—and then he spoke, hesitantly at first and then with growing confidence and strength.

"I don't like it when you call her names," he began. "I don't think they're true." A brief pause and then a head shake. "If she's trying to hurt me, then why do I actually feel better? That doesn't make sense."

I glanced over at Dr. Vardi and saw that she was looking calmly at her desk. Once in a while, she'd glance up at Jonah and nod thoughtfully, as if she were listening to a discussion between two colleagues. It was all so strange to me, like eavesdropping on a telephone conversation where we could only hear one party. And it was scary too; I felt like I was finally meeting my boyfriend's invisible evil twin.

Dr. Vardi waited until Jonah stopped speaking. "Well, what happened when you talked to them?" she inquired. "How did they react?"

He gave her a cautious smile. His face was pale and drawn, but his eyes were shining. "They got a little…quieter. I don't get it. Why did that happen?"

She grinned at him and leaned back in her chair. "You've stopped fighting them, Jonah. That's the first step, to acknowledge their existence. The next step is to learn to reason with them, to find a place for them in your life. That's the only way that they'll make room for you. Think of them like annoying relatives; they'll never really go away, but you can learn to deal with them so that they don't disrupt your life."

"You don't *understand*, Doctor," he retorted. "They *hate* me. How can I reason with that?"

"The same way you just did. If you tell me what they say to you, I can help you with a response."

He drew back from her and shook his head. "No, I can't do that. I can't tell you what they say." There was a thin note of rising panic in his voice. "I'm not allowed."

"Ask them for permission then."

"*What?*"

"Explain yourself to them. They might actually understand."

He rolled his eyes. "You've *got* to be kidding me."

"Why not? The first time worked, didn't it? So why don't you give it a shot? Come on, Jonah. Indulge me."

He sighed again and rubbed his knuckles over his eyes. There was a moment of silence, then his figure tensed again, and his hands shifted to cover his ears. "God, shut *up!*" he shouted suddenly. Dr. Vardi cleared her throat, and he looked up at her with a shamefaced expression, like an older brother who'd just yelled at his little sibling. "I'm sorry." I wasn't sure who he was apologizing to, the doctor or his voices. "I didn't mean to yell," he continued wearily. "But I'm going to tell the doctor what you're saying if you keep talking to me like that."

"Don't threaten, Jonah," chided the psychiatrist. "Just explain yourself. Patiently."

A mischievous smile flickered over his face. "You're right, guys. She's completely nuts." He grinned. "But you know, I kinda like her." There was a brief pause. "Well, I do. And I'm going to tell her about you. Because I don't think you can actually do anything about it. No matter what you say."

I could almost hear them now; the same way you can imagine what the person on the other end of the telephone is saying, I could guess now what they were shouting at Jonah. I watched his expression, and I listened with him. I could actually taste their venom as they slowly tightened themselves around him.

We'll kill you if you tell her about us. We won't let you out of here alive.

"How will you do it?" he challenged them, his voice breaking. "Tell me what you'll do."

It won't be just you. We'll get your sister too. And your parents.

"How?" he demanded. "Why won't you tell me how?"

"Softly, Jonah," Dr. Vardi urged. "Stay calm, please."

We'll kill April just like we killed Ricky. But we'll save her for last. We'll make her suffer. And we'll make you watch.

"I don't think you can," Jonah replied, his expression struggling to stay composed. "You're all just talk. You've threatened me before. And nothing ever happened."

Everyone knows why you're here. You're here because you're worthless. We put you here.

"No, I'm here because of what I tried to do. You didn't put me here."

We told you the truth about yourself.

"You told me that I didn't deserve to live. You told me that I had no choice. And I believed you."

We told you the truth about April.

"You were *never* right about April and you know that!" He turned to face me for the first time now, and his clear eyes filled with tears. "Not once were you right about her."

She hates you. She's going to leave you.

"She won't. She'll never leave me. She's been here through everything, even through this—"

He broke off. He was shaking now, his pale cheeks streaked with tears.

"Jonah, I'm not going anywhere," I said. "I told you I'd never leave you—" But I couldn't finish the thought. It was so confusing; I didn't know to whom I was speaking. I was looking at Jonah, I was trying to talk to him, but he was still addressing *them*.

And then he spoke to me, his eyes focused on me, just me, and his words were only mine. "That's why I decided to leave you, April," he told me softly. "To save you from this. I tried to leave, I really did. But you wouldn't let me go."

Dr. Vardi rose quickly from her chair and walked over to him; she laid a gentle hand on Jonah's shoulder. "You had other choices," she said. "I hope you'll learn to see that."

He nodded, his eyes still fixed on me. "I know. I see that now. I just felt so guilty. And it seemed the only way out."

"But now you understand what your actions did to the ones you loved."

He nodded dully. "I knew that it would hurt them for a little while. But in the long run, I was sure it was for the best—"

"You thought it would be for the best?" I exclaimed. I could feel Dr. Vardi's eyes on me. She raised a calming hand and shook her head. But I couldn't help myself. I had to tell him how I felt—and how much he'd hurt me. "Do you remember how awful you felt after Ricky died? Do you remember how you blamed yourself, even though it wasn't your fault? Jonah, if you had died, I would never have forgiven myself. You had me *help* you! You made me part of it!"

"I know. I'm sorry." He hung his head. "I don't know what else to say."

"Okay, April," Dr. Vardi interjected. "Your anger is natural, of course. I understand that you felt betrayed by Jonah—"

"I *didn't* feel betrayed," I interrupted. "I just wanted him to talk to me a little, to make me understand what he was experiencing. I wanted to help him! But in the end, I only helped him try to kill himself."

She was right though. I *was* resentful and angry. I did feel betrayed. I didn't know if I could get past it.

"You understand now why he couldn't confide in you, don't you?" she asked me. "Not only was he afraid of what you'd think of him, he was afraid of what would happen to him if he went against the voices' instructions. So he couldn't bring anyone in. Not even you."

I nodded slowly. "I get that."

She turned back to Jonah. "Do you want to talk about it a little more? Or would you rather take a break?"

He glanced at me. "No, I'm okay to talk. They're quieter now for some reason. I can concentrate."

She walked over to her chair. "Let's start from the beginning then. Do you remember the first time you noticed the voices?"

He raised his eyebrows at her. "Of course I remember. It's not something you forget."

"Tell me about it then."

"It was about a year ago, at Ricky's funeral. I was watching them lower his casket into the ground. And then I heard his voice. I swear it came straight from the pit. It sounded just like him! It was so real, I actually started toward it. My father held me back. He thought it was just grief, I guess. Later, that's what I thought too, that my mind was playing tricks on me. There was no other explanation. Ricky *couldn't* have called to me. None of the other mourners had reacted at all. But it had been so loud, so clear. I couldn't believe that no one else had heard him."

"What did Ricky's voice say to you?"

He hung his head again and closed his eyes. "He said, 'Jonah, please don't abandon me.'"

"But you realized then that it wasn't really him speaking."

"I—I didn't know what to think."

"And Ricky's voice kept coming back to you? You heard it again?"

"No. That was the only time. After that, the voice changed."

"How did it change?"

He hesitated, and his eyes flew open suddenly; I saw his muscles tense again. But then he glanced at Dr. Vardi. His figure relaxed, and he took a deep breath.

"I can't talk to you right now," he said, addressing something invisible at his side. "I talked to you earlier."

Dr. Vardi nodded approvingly; she clasped her hands together and smiled broadly. "That's it, Jonah. That's perfect. Address them like a friend. Ask them to come back later, because you're busy now."

"*Ask them to come back later?* You're not serious? I don't *want* them to come back, ever. I want them to leave me alone."

"Remember what I told you before? You're in control. But remember, you have to make reasonable requests of them. They won't go away completely, because they're a part of you. So compromise a little. Go ahead and make an appointment with them for later in the day. Just try it now, for me. Try it and see what happens."

Jonah was shaking his head at her, his expression alternating between mockery and disbelief. "You're completely nuts, Doc, but whatever." He looked away from her. "The shrink wants to know if you guys can come back later." He laughed shortly and then stopped; his mouth fell open in surprise. "I…I don't know. What time is best for you?" A quick nod, and he smiled suddenly, his face glowing with amusement. "After dinner is better. Okay then. Yeah, we'll talk about it then, no problem."

"They've left you alone for a little while?" Dr. Vardi remarked as Jonah looked up at her in awe.

He smiled timidly and looked around the room as if he were seeing the place for the first time. "I don't understand how you did that. They're always so loud in here. Whenever I'm stressed or scared, they rise up and choke me. It's horrible. I can't think; I get swallowed in them. I have to believe them, everything they say. I have to listen or they get louder and louder. And some of the things they tell me—"

"Can you speak about it now? Do you feel safe?"

He nodded shortly. "It's just a dull roar now. Like in a restaurant. They've—retreated a bit. I don't mind this at all, really. It's the best it's been for a long time."

"How many are there? Voices, I mean."

"It shifts, depending on the day, what's going on. There's one main voice. It's low and sharp, a man's. I call him the boss. Because he's in charge of all the others."

"What's he like, Jonah?"

He sighed and looked embarrassed. "He's an asshole. He hates me. He's always screaming at me. He tells me…"

"Yes?"

"He tells me that I deserve to die. Because of what I've done."

"What does he say you've done? Why does he hate you so much?"

"I don't know. He keeps changing his mind. Sometimes it's

about Ricky. That I failed him. He tells me I'm a murderer, that I'm evil. And then he'll shift all of a sudden and start trying to protect me. That's what he says he's doing anyway. He tells me to get rid of all my electronics, that the government is spying on me through my cell phone. He warns me about my food, tells me that it's poisoned. That they've planted bugs in my chili that will worm their way into my brain and drain my thoughts."

"Does he ever tell you to do things? Give you instructions?"

"Sometimes. Yes." He glanced at me and cleared his throat. "Not—not anything harmful to other people," he assured me, as if anticipating the question in my mind. "Mainly it's about myself. *Don't leave your room today, Jonah. It isn't safe.* That kind of thing."

"Does he ever tell you that other people are evil?"

"He doesn't trust anyone. Even the people that I love."

"So how do you deal with that?"

"I try to ignore him. If I play my music really loud, sometimes I can block him out. It's really hard though. When I ignore him, other voices join in, like his little fan club in my head."

It was all coming together as I listened to him; all the signs and clues that I'd seen over the last few months were beginning to make sense. The absentmindedness, the paranoia, the loss of appetite—it was all part of this illness, all part of the slow torture that his own mind had created for him.

There was just one detail though, one memory that I had to understand. I needed to ask him about it, even if it hurt to hear the answer.

"I was wondering," I began hesitantly, my eyes focusing on a corner of Dr. Vardi's desk. "That afternoon near Quarry Lake—"

"Yes," he said, finishing my thought. "I heard the voice. After the first time we kissed."

I forced myself to look at him. His shoulders were bowed, his hands clasped together like a prisoner's, begging for forgiveness.

"But you told me that you'd heard Katie scream."

"I lied," he admitted. "I hadn't heard Katie. But I was sure that something bad had happened to her."

"Why? What made you think that?"

He winced and looked away. "The voice told me so. I know I shouldn't have believed him. I'm so sorry, April. You hadn't done anything wrong. I don't know what made him say those things about you."

"What did the voice say about April?" Dr. Vardi asked.

"He said—it said..." He swallowed, choked; he seemed to be strangling on the words.

"Take your time, Jonah."

I wished she would stop pushing him. He looked so miserable, so guilty. *Don't make him tell me*, I begged her silently. What was the point of dragging the memory of our first kiss through the dirt?

Jonah covered his face with his hands. "The voice said, *Katie's dying—that bitch April is killing her.*"

I couldn't believe it. The voice didn't make any sense, and yet he'd listened to it anyway. He'd run to save his little sister—from me. The voice, to him, had been as real as I was.

"You're disappointed, April," Dr. Vardi remarked.

That was an understatement. I was actually fighting the urge to scream. It didn't matter to me that she was helping Jonah, that he was thinking clearly for the first time in months. I hated her because, little by little, her healing conversation with her patient had torn me apart.

"Was *nothing* between us real?" I asked him bitterly.

I didn't stay to listen to Jonah's answer. I couldn't bear to hear the truth.

I left them there, Jonah reaching over to me, trying to catch me as I ran, Dr. Vardi calling my name, and the door slamming between us and swallowing them both.

I needed quiet, to think, to be alone, to fill my lungs with air. All of a sudden, I couldn't breathe. Their voices had drowned me out.

CHAPTER 41

When the chorus stops screaming
And the prophets go hoarse
When the preacher falls silent and the church bells don't ring
They'll gather in circles
To hear the mockingbird sing

BY THE END OF HISTORY, MY ENTIRE CLASS WAS GOING TO BE HEARING voices. That was my medical history project. At the beginning of the period, Ms. Lowry instructed everyone to hand over their iPhones and a cable. I collected them and set them on my desk next to my laptop.

The principal would be getting a few complaints by the end of the day, I was sure of that. But I didn't care. I had Ms. Lowry's full support. She believed that the best lessons were the ones that sent a few students home whimpering.

The subject that day was the civil rights movement. Ms. Lowry began her lecture by scrawling the topic on the board and jotting down the relevant dates. Then she turned around to face us and instructed each student to put in their earbuds and select the track that I'd just downloaded onto their phones.

"During the duration of our lesson, I will ask you not to turn your player off or remove your earbuds," she said. "Right now, all of you should be hearing relaxing music; it shouldn't bother you too much. But even if it does," she continued with a smile, "I don't want you to react to it. I want you to pretend that you are hearing nothing. I want you to pay attention to my lesson; at the end of the hour, we will have a quiz on the civil rights movement. Those of you who followed my instructions will get ten points added to your quiz grade. April will be standing by the door and recording your reactions. Okay then, before we begin, does anyone have any questions?"

Michael raised his hand. "I don't get it. Why are we doing this? This music is getting on my nerves. I won't be able to concentrate on the quiz."

She laughed. "I promise you'll understand before the end of class, Michael."

From where I stood, I could see everyone's faces—expectant, confused, a couple of students already nodding off to the Enya track that I'd recorded. *Not much longer*, I thought. Another couple of minutes before the first reaction.

It came sooner than I expected. Ms. Lowry had barely read out the first sentence in her syllabus when Cora suddenly sat bolt upright in her chair.

"What the hell?" Her exclamation came at the same time as two other girls'. One started out of her seat and stared helplessly at the teacher; her hands flew to her ears.

"What the hell is this?" They were shouting in unison now, their faces red and white with fear. "Whose voice is this? Why is he saying this stuff?"

"Girls, sit down," Ms. Lowry said in a calm tone. "This is part of April's project. Your job this morning is to try to pay attention to what I'm saying, no matter what you hear on the recording. Ignore it as best you can. And remember, no one else is hearing what you're hearing. So you can't react, no matter how much you may want to."

But Cora wasn't going to cooperate. "I don't have to do this," she declared. "I know what she's trying to do." She rose from her chair and pointed a manicured nail at me. "She's trying to make us all crazy like her boyfriend."

"No one is forcing you, Cora," I replied. "You can take the earbuds out anytime you want. This is only a challenge—try to listen to Ms. Lowry while that voice is yelling in your ears. If you don't want to participate, that's fine, but at the end of the lesson, everyone will be discussing what it felt like, and I think you'll want to know what your friends are talking about."

There was an uncomfortable silence. Cora slumped back in her chair and hunched over her notebook. Her fingers went to her ears. She plucked nervously at her hair and then slowly lowered her hands again. It was hypnotic, the voice that Danny had recorded with me. Not one person removed their earbuds. As Ms. Lowry began her lecture again, I scanned their faces and noted their reactions.

Many of them couldn't help themselves. They bit their lips and flinched; their breathing was fast and panicked. The voice was shouting warnings and threats; it would be impossible to ignore it and concentrate on Ms. Lowry's quiet teaching. Some of the boys were trying very hard though. They sat stony-faced and solid in their seats, eyes fixed straight ahead, stoic through the storm raging in their ears.

And though I couldn't hear what they were hearing, I remembered what we'd recorded, and by their expressions, the blanched cheeks, the staring eyes, I could guess what they were going through.

Get out now, the voice ordered them. *Go home before they get here. They're coming for you!*

I saw Miles shake his head; his jaw tensed, and the fingers around his pen turned pale. He was scrawling furiously in his notebook, trying to grab on to Ms. Lowry's words while his mind battled with the voices that surrounded him. Tessa had given up completely; she sat entranced and openmouthed, like a mute and terrified prophetess receiving divine instructions. Even Cora was struggling. She kept shooting furious looks at me, but her earbuds stayed firmly in place. Taking them out would have been admitting defeat, and she wouldn't be the first one to cave.

She's in on it. That bitch Lowry is trying to make you insane. Don't listen to her. Listen to me.

I felt sorry for them as I watched them squirm. I'd listened to the recording at home, and it disturbed me more than I'd expected. It only took a little imagination to picture what it must be like for someone who lived with this every day, every hour, whose every thought was colored by the chaos in his ears. I'd gotten used to the idea of hearing voices months ago, and yet the experience still gave me a sleepless night. But this was a completely new experience for my classmates, and none of them had been prepared for how horrible it would be.

Not one of them lasted until the end of Ms. Lowry's lecture.

Cora was the first one to yank the cord out of her ears; Miles followed shortly afterward, and then, one by one, everyone else. Ms. Lowry surveyed the class grimly, then nodded at me and motioned for me to take her place before the blackboard.

It was the moment I'd been dreading. I wanted so much to do this for Jonah, to get through to my classmates and make them understand. But speaking in front of my peers terrified me, and at that moment, I was just as afraid of their attention as I'd once been of their indifference.

A few of the girls were crying quietly; Tessa was shivering in her chair and staring at me with large, bewildered eyes. "Is it like this all the time, April?" she asked me. "How does he fall asleep?"

"It's very hard," I told her. "He can block it out sometimes with music, but usually it's impossible to control. At first, he tried to ignore them and pretended that nothing was wrong. But after months of that…"

"*Months?*" she interrupted. "He was going through this for months before he told someone?"

I nodded. "That's pretty common. Many people with schizophrenia find ways to cope and to disguise their symptoms in the beginning. But after a while, it becomes too much. They begin to withdraw from people. Some of them become paranoid, and they lose touch with reality and believe things they would never have believed before they became sick."

"Is it because of the voices in their head?" she asked me. "They have to do whatever they say?"

I shook my head. "Not really, no. I thought that at first too, and it really scared me. Who can predict what a person with schizophrenia will do, if he's completely under the control of voices that no one else can hear? But it doesn't really work that way. They don't blindly follow everything the voices tell them. But they often find it difficult to relate to other people and even to take care of themselves every day."

"It would make me want to kill myself," Miles said. "I couldn't take that noise all the time, yelling at me like that."

I felt my stomach lurch. *He doesn't know*, I told myself. None of them knew what Jonah had tried to do.

"More than fifty percent of people suffering from schizophrenia will attempt suicide at least once in their lives," I told them. "About ten percent will succeed. Many believe it's their only way out."

"Were you ever scared that he would hurt you?" The question had come from Cora. There was no malice in her voice now. "Did you ever feel like he was completely gone?"

"I was never worried for myself," I assured her. "But sometimes it did feel like I no longer knew my boyfriend. Sometimes it was hard to see that he still cared about me."

They were all listening to me, their expressions sober and thoughtful. I couldn't believe how absorbed they were. I'd never experienced anything like this before; not only were they interested in Jonah's illness, they also wanted to know what I'd experienced, how I had felt when I was with him. I actually mattered to them.

I went on for a little longer, giving a few more facts I thought would interest them. There was a ripple of shock when I explained that symptoms of schizophrenia usually begin in high school or college and that it affected nearly two million people in the United States.

"There are so many who suffer from this," I concluded, "but each one feels like they're completely alone. It's not like other illnesses. A person who's sick with cancer has the support of the community. Everyone bands together and tries to help. Friends organize runs for a cure and put together bake sales and blood drives. Next-door neighbors bring tuna casseroles to the patient's family.

"There are no casseroles for schizophrenia," I said. "People are afraid, so they keep away. The families are embarrassed, so they hide. They pretend their son or daughter has gone abroad or is busy at school—anything to avoid telling the truth."

There were a few minutes of silence after I finished speaking. Ms. Lowry asked if anyone had questions, but no one spoke; no one even moved.

When the bell rang, everyone gathered up their books and filed out without a word. As I headed for the door, Ms. Lowry called me back and told me she was proud of me.

"Thank you for helping Jonah," I said.

"You're welcome. But it wasn't only for Jonah."

She was right, I guess. Getting through to my class was an exciting first for me. It was hard to believe they'd actually cared. I was worried that they'd forget what I'd told them before the final school bell rang. But those few minutes they'd listened were enough for now.

Before math, I slipped into the bathroom to wash my face.

The cool stream felt good against my cheeks; I cupped my hands and let the water spill over my wrists, then bathed my forehead and neck. I was smoothing my damp hair back when I heard the door open and the sound of heels on tile. I rubbed my eyes and turned around, then shrank back against the sink and gripped the porcelain edge.

Cora was staring quietly at me. She didn't say a word at first; she craned her neck around the bathroom, then stepped over to the stalls and checked that they were empty.

I didn't know what she was planning, but the fact that she didn't want witnesses wasn't very reassuring. At five foot four and a hundred pounds, she was hardly a threat, but I couldn't help eyeing the exit as she approached.

"I want to talk to you," she began. "I've been thinking about what you said."

"O—okay." I squirmed uncomfortably; I could feel small rivulets of water snaking down my neck.

She leaned over and plucked a paper towel out of the dispenser and handed it to me; I took it gratefully and rubbed it over my wet face.

"I wanted to tell you that I'm sorry," she said simply.

I didn't believe what I was hearing. Could this be some kind of twisted joke? Were her friends hiding somewhere, waiting to mock me if I fell for it? No, that couldn't be it; I'd just seen her check the stalls to make sure that they were clear.

Could she actually be serious?

"You're—you're sorry?"

She nodded, her large eyes wrinkling at the corners. "I've been awful to you these last few months. And I know you're leaving Fallstaff next year. So I just wanted to tell you that I'm sorry while I had the chance."

I nodded again and searched for something to say. "Thanks, Cora," I replied after a pause. "It's—it's fine."

I wasn't really sure that I'd forgiven her. Still, it seemed the only decent thing to say.

She swallowed nervously and edged slowly over to the door. "Could you do something for me?" Her eyes flickered doubtfully over my face. "Just one small thing."

"Yeah, sure, I guess." *Okay, here it is*, I thought irritably. She hadn't been sincere, just as I'd suspected. She'd only apologized because she wanted something from me.

"Could you tell him what I said?" she whispered. "Can you tell him that I'm sorry?"

"Are you—are you talking about Jonah?"

She nodded. "Yeah. He still remembers things, right? The stuff that happened before he got sick?"

"Of course he does. His memory is fine." He wasn't senile or demented, I wanted to tell her. He doesn't have amnesia, like some character in a soap opera.

"I don't want him to hate me," she said. "Those three days he pretended to go out with me—" She took a deep breath and pulled open the door. "I know it wasn't real, but fake happy sometimes feels like the real thing. Anyway, just tell him that I'm sorry, okay?"

I shook my head. "Cora, I'm sure he doesn't hate you—"

But she wasn't listening. "Just tell him for me, okay? Maybe those things I said—maybe it made him worse. Even if it doesn't help now, I want him to know I'm sorry."

I would have tried to reassure her if she'd stayed. I would have told her that Jonah hadn't gotten sick because of her and that he probably would've forgiven her on the spot if he was there. But she was through the door and down the hall before I could stop her. And when I saw her in class later that day, she wouldn't look in my direction.

When I got home from school, my mom was sitting in the dining room waiting for me. Every muscle in her body was tense with waiting, and her face was whiter than I'd ever seen it. I was scared for a moment. I thought, *Oh God, something's happened to Jonah*. And then I saw the envelope on the table in front of her.

"It's my father's handwriting," she said, her voice quavering. "But it's addressed to somebody named Shira."

I picked it up and turned it over. "Why didn't you open it?"

"It's not for me," she said. Her voice was sharp with pain. "He didn't write it for me. *Who is Shira?*"

I handed it back to her and slipped my arm around her shoulder. "Shira is the Hebrew name I chose," I explained. "I wrote to your parents a few weeks ago. I thought that maybe I could get through to them."

She stared at me silently, her eyes wide with hope and disbelief.

"I know your family hurt you, Mom," I continued. "But you love them anyway. So this letter is really yours. You can decide what you want to do with it."

She was shaking when she took it from me, and her fingers

trembled so hard that she had trouble opening the envelope. In the end, I had to do it for her. Then I sat down next to her and watched her read it, her face crumpling, tears running down her cheeks, her eyes devouring the words that her father had written to me.

Sometimes, Shira, when you're angry, you make mistakes you can never take back...

"Do you want me to call him?" I asked when she'd finished the letter. "He wrote his number at the end."

She didn't answer my question. Her eyes had wandered to the windowsill, and she was staring at the melted wax splattered on the ledge.

"I need to go to the store," she told me.

"Okay." I hesitated, confused by the sudden change in topic. "I can go for you if you want. What do you need?"

"I need candles," she replied, smiling. "We're going to need a lot more candles."

CHAPTER 42

JONAH WAS GETTING OUT OF THE HOSPITAL. I COULDN'T BELIEVE IT WHEN his mom told me. I'd stopped by his house the day after my presentation to drop off a couple of Katie's toys, and his mother met me at the door. She smiled when she saw me and blurted out the news before I had a chance to say hello.

"When—when did they say he can come home?"

"Tomorrow morning. Dr. Vardi believes he's met all of his discharge goals."

"But—but it's only been two weeks. Do you really think he's ready?" I glanced over her shoulder toward the staircase. The last time I'd climbed those stairs, I'd taken them two at a time because Jonah was getting ready to die. How could they be sure he wouldn't try something like that again?

"I hope so," she said. "He's doing so much better than he was before. I'm not scared to have him home now. Dr. Vardi has this new approach; she calls it cognitive therapy. He's learning how to communicate with us again! He's even had a session with his father—and they really talked. I was in shock. Anyway, Dr. Vardi believes that Jonah will progress faster at home, with daily outpatient appointments."

"But what about school? Will he go back?"

"He's been working with a tutor so that he doesn't fall behind. I think we'll finish up the year at home and then reevaluate in the fall. I've been in contact with the administration at Fallstaff High, and they've been very supportive."

"At Fallstaff?" I couldn't hide the disappointment in my voice. "But what about the art school? What about what *he* wants for the future? He hates Fallstaff High!"

She sighed and stepped back into the foyer. "I'm sorry, April, I know you two had big plans, but you have to understand that Jonah simply isn't ready—"

She hesitated for a moment and glanced over her shoulder. Her husband had just come into the living room, and she gave him a shrug that I didn't really understand. It was like she was waiting for him to speak, to help her out. She'd never been shy in front of me before. And why did she look so guilty all of a sudden? Why did Dr. Golden shoot her a warning look, as if urging her to be quiet?

"Rachel, I thought Jonah was going to speak to April," he told her. "He said he wanted to explain things to her himself."

"I know, I know! But we were only talking about school, Aaron. That's all. That's what you heard when you came in."

He looked uncertain for a moment, and then his brow went smooth. "Oh. I see. Never mind then."

It was my turn to be confused. "What do you mean?" I demanded. "What was Jonah going to speak to me about?"

"He'll be home tomorrow," Dr. Golden replied after an awkward pause. "You can talk things over then."

It was obvious that they were hiding something from me. "What's going *on*?" I pleaded. "Is something wrong?"

I would have pushed them for an answer. I'd planted myself firmly on their floral carpet and was getting ready to beg again when a little patter of footsteps behind me made me pause. Then Katie's thin arms were around my waist, and she pulled me into the living room. "I told you April was coming back to read to me," she declared. "I *told you.*"

I don't remember any details of the storybook that she handed to me; I can't even remember the title. There were ogres in it and magical trees, I think. My brief conversation with the Goldens had killed my concentration for the remainder of the day. I spent the rest of the afternoon battling my doubts and trying to reason with my fears. After I left their house, I circled the block and argued with myself, struggling to make sense of what I'd heard.

Jonah was going to have a talk with me; there was something he needed to break to me gently. Under different circumstances, I'd have assumed what every insecure girlfriend believes: he wanted to break up with me. But that was totally impossible. He still loved me; I knew he did. And he was getting better now! No, he wasn't going to break up with me. That didn't make sense.

Could it be that they were moving back to Boston? Was that the reason for all the secrecy? But Dr. Golden recently mentioned that he was applying for a medical license in Maryland, and he'd just spoken to the surgical department at Johns Hopkins. Why would he bother to do that if they planned to return to Boston?

But then why had both his parents looked so guilty?

What if Jonah was sick, truly sick, some awful side effect of the medications maybe, and the doctors had just told the family that there was nothing they could do to save him? What if *that* was the reason they were discharging him so soon, to let him spend his last days at home with his loved ones? Is that why Jonah's mom hadn't even given the art school a moment's consideration when I'd brought it up? Because she knew—she *knew* that it wouldn't matter in the end?

A few flips through old Internet searches brought up everything I needed to support my worries. The antipsychotic clozapine, I learned, could cause complete bone marrow failure in some, and several patients had died as a result of taking the medication. I didn't even know if Jonah was taking that particular pill, and I didn't consider the fact that he would have been hospitalized in the medical ward if something like that was going on with him. I *knew* that he was dying, I was sure that everyone had lied to me, and I was certain that when he came to see me the next day, I would be saying good-bye to him forever.

I was at my bedroom window when Jonah walked up to my house the following afternoon. I'd been at that bedroom window for nearly two hours, pacing back and forth and checking my phone every few seconds. I'd pretended to head off to school as my mom got ready for work, but I'd doubled back after I knew she'd gone and shut myself in my room for the remainder of the day. I couldn't have concentrated on class work anyway, so there was really no point in going.

Still, school might have distracted me a little. By the time Jonah came around, I was close to tears, having spent the entire night preparing for the worst of news. But he looked so good that morning; when I opened the door, he smiled at me. His sweet blue eyes wrinkled at the corners, and his lips curled into the little grin I loved. His hair was freshly cut, and his clothes looked pressed and new. As he leaned down to kiss my cheek, I caught the familiar scent of aftershave and mint chocolate. He didn't *look* like someone who was dying.

But then he smiled again, a sorry, heavy smile; his eyes filled up, and something inside me broke. I was afraid to speak because any moment he would tell me why he was crying in front of me, and I just couldn't bear to hear it. I didn't want to know; I wanted to hold on to that last moment of ignorance, because it was the only thing I had left. Those final seconds were all that stood between me and Jonah's tears, and in that space, I could believe that he was crying because he'd missed me and was simply happy to see me again.

"April, I'm sorry—"

"I already know," I blurted out. I was afraid to let him say it.

He stepped back and cleared his throat; I could see the confusion in his eyes. "What do you mean? What do you know?"

"I spoke to your parents yesterday…"

"My *parents*?"

"Yes."

He led me into the living room and sat down heavily on the sofa. "What did they *say*?" There was a hint of annoyance in his voice, but nothing else. Something seemed wrong to me; his irritated frown didn't fit with the dark picture I'd painted.

"They didn't really say anything," I said. "They just seemed upset."

"Well, that's because I'm upset. And they know how much I care about you."

I was completely lost. "What's going on? Are you—are you guys moving away?" There was no need to tell him what I'd been suspecting, I decided quickly. It seemed pretty stupid to me now, and I knew he'd tease me and call me the "crazy" one in the relationship if I told him what I'd been worried about.

But he didn't look like he wanted to tease me. His eyes were sad and guilty, just as his parents' had been when they'd spoken to me. He kept fiddling with his shirt sleeve, picking at a loose thread with nervous energy until it snapped against his fingers. "No, we're not moving anywhere," he said after a pause. "I think it would be easier if we were."

"*What* would be easier?"

He hesitated briefly. "It would be easier if we were moving away, because then you'd understand what I have to tell you now."

"Oh, Jonah, *nothing* could be harder than what we've already gone through!"

Why did he drop his face before me, his shoulders bowed, his eyes all red and crumpled as if he was ashamed to look at me?

"I'll understand, whatever it is, and I'll be there for you no matter what," I added weakly.

He nodded briefly and smiled to himself, as if I'd just spoken his thoughts out loud. "No matter what?" he echoed. "You've said that to me before, do you remember? That's kind of been your motto, hasn't it, throughout our whole relationship?"

"What do you mean?"

"I mean that you've stood by me, even when you should have left, even though no one would have blamed you for leaving me. You've waited and waited for me, and for months, I've rewarded you with nothing. I've felt you waiting. Even when I was completely out of it, I knew that you were hurting for me, and I still couldn't bring myself to do the right thing. And now I see that whatever happens, no matter how awful I make you feel, you'll never go. *No matter what.* Not as long as you believe that I still need you."

"Okay then, what do you *want?* Do you *want* me to leave you?"

He shook his head. "No, I don't. Because honestly, I don't think you can. And even if you did, I don't believe that you'd ever forgive yourself. You'd feel as if you'd wronged me somehow, that you were abandoning me while I was sick. So I realize now that it's time for me to do what I should have done months ago, when I first suspected that there was something wrong with me. No, don't interrupt me, April. Just listen to me, please. I should have set you free back then, back when I still could, when my mind was clear. But I was going under so fast, I thought that you were the only solid thing I could hold on to. So that's what I did. I held on to you through everything. Even during the worst of times, I thought that if I still had you, then I wasn't really lost. And so I wouldn't let you go."

"But I didn't want you to!"

"I know you didn't, and that's how I justified my weakness. Every time you visited me in the hospital, I told myself that you wanted to be there with me, that we were in this together, that it was the two of us against the world. But no matter how hard I tried, I couldn't stop feeling guilty for what I was doing to you, and as the weeks turned into months, I could hardly look you in the eyes anymore, I was so ashamed."

"You had nothing to be ashamed about! It wasn't your fault that you got sick."

"No, but it was my fault when I slowly began to use my girlfriend—when I turned her into my nurse. It was my fault when I painted that portrait of you, holding that bird—do you remember?"

I nodded silently.

"I *knew* what I was doing then. I suspected what was coming soon, and I didn't have the strength to tell you; I was too afraid. So I let you shelter me, just as I knew you would. But I couldn't get rid of that guilty weight. It killed me to see your patience; it made me hate myself even more. And then the voices started in on me. They're part of me, Dr. Vardi says, and so they know exactly where I'm the most vulnerable. So they began to hit me in my weak spot. They began to talk about you—constantly."

I'd remained mostly quiet until then. I'd guessed what he wanted to tell me, and I'd decided to patiently hear him out—and then show him how wrong he was about us. But his comment about the voices distracted me; I couldn't help myself. "What did they say about me?" I blurted out—and then wished I hadn't. There was no answer that would make me happy.

"They told me that I was making you miserable, that I was a selfish bastard," he said in a low voice. "They told me that I was killing you."

"Jonah—"

"They said that if I cared about your happiness, I would end it all and let you live your life."

"But you've told me that before. I know that's why you tried to hurt yourself. And you admitted that you were wrong."

"I was only partly wrong, actually. I *should* have ended it between us, but not like that."

"No, you were *completely* wrong—"

"I should have broken up with you then. I know it—we both know it. I'm truly sorry that it's taken me so long to do the right thing. But I have to do it while I'm thinking clearly, or I might not have the strength later, especially if I get sick again. April, I have to break up with you now. That's—that's what I came over here to tell you."

At least he'd finally said it, the words that had been hanging between us. I could argue with him now, as I had meant to from the beginning. But somehow, I couldn't find the energy to fight; I felt completely numb.

"I don't want to hear this," I told him finally. "I don't want to hear that you're breaking up with me because you're trying to save me."

"I'm not," he responded sadly. "I'm breaking up with you to save myself."

There was no way that I could argue with that. I felt an angry knot forming in my throat. I wanted to shake him, to scream at him, but I had no idea what to say. He looked absolutely miserable. I'd never seen Jonah so pale before; even his lips were white. The only color in his face was the red rim around his eyes.

"I know how awful that sounds," he continued. "I'm *not* blaming you, April. You've meant everything to me. But I can't keep using you like this, even if you agree to it. I can't get well if I'm always feeling guilty about us, if I feel that I'm wronging you every time I have a setback. And I've learned enough about this illness to know that there are going to be a lot of setbacks, that this is just the beginning of my recovery, and that it might literally take years—if I ever get better at all."

"But you're getting better every day," I insisted. "Most patients don't even admit that they have a problem until after years of therapy."

"I know. But I need to be sure of myself before I can ask anyone to be with me. A few days of clarity are not enough. I don't trust myself yet. And I remember enough of what I've been through, what I've done, to be really scared about my future."

"Jonah, I've waited this long already, a few more months won't make a difference."

"But I can't promise you anything, that's what I'm saying. I can't promise a few months or even a few years. I don't want you to be tied to me while they raise and lower my doses, while I slip in and out of psychotic phases, while I analyze my voices and mess around with sanity. I can't stand the idea of doing that to you. I want you to start the next year fresh, in a new school, with new friends—maybe even a new boy…"

"I don't want to hear that!"

"Okay, okay," he breathed. "Just friends then. You'll make new friends. Maybe you'll actually have time for them, without me hanging around your neck. Tell me honestly—haven't you neglected everything else about your life while you've been taking care of me?"

"Not at all!" I protested. "I got into the art school, didn't I? I couldn't have done that without you!"

He smiled and shook his head. "I nudged you in the right direction. Months ago. The rest you did on your own."

"You just don't get it, do you? I'm *better* when I know that you're behind me."

"Really?" he asked me. "Was I behind you when you gave that talk to our history class? April, I didn't even know about it. My mom heard about your presentation from the principal. Apparently everyone was talking about what you said."

I nodded. "Yeah. Even Cora."

"What?"

"Cora apologized to me afterward. She wanted me to tell you she was sorry."

He was speechless for a moment, his expression alternating between shock and pride. "Unbelievable. You actually got her to apologize! No blackmail, no tricks. Just by being *you*. And yet you still think you need me?"

I took his hand. "Maybe you're right. But I liked it when you needed me."

He took a deep breath and looked away. "I still do. Which is why I have to go now. I think you see that."

I did see it. Although I knew I'd fight him in my mind for months to come, I understood him when he said it. He needed time, and I needed space to breathe a little on my own, without him.

There was only one thing, one pale, weak feeling that was left now, one last emotion that I was sure would never go away.

"I love you," I told him miserably and put my face into my hands because I didn't want to watch him leave.

He was getting ready to go; he was sitting so close to me that I could feel the tension in his body, the sharp, shallow breathing of someone in pain. *It's over now*, I told myself. *In a moment, I'll hear the door slam and he'll be gone.*

And then his arms were around me, and I was folded up against his chest, my face pressed over his heart. I felt his cheek brush against my forehead, and then he bent his head down and kissed me hard. Everything he'd said, my grief, his tearstained face and unhappy eyes, disappeared now beneath his kiss. I wrapped my hands around his neck and pressed my lips to his. *He's taking it all back*, I told myself. *He's changed his mind, we'll work through everything somehow, he'll never let me go…*

And then he did. As I leaned into him, he suddenly pulled back; I felt his arms loosen around me. "I'm really sorry," he murmured. "I shouldn't have done that."

I couldn't answer him; I could barely breathe.

He rose quickly from the sofa and stepped away from me. "I love you, April."

Then he was gone, the door shutting softly behind him, the retreating sound of footsteps blending with the rumble of traffic in the street. I didn't move for minutes after he'd left, frozen in place while I listened for his step, a knock, anything to break the awful silence he'd left behind. It wasn't real to me. I couldn't accept it; I couldn't grasp the thought that there was nothing to look forward to the next day, nothing to wait for or believe in. He had to be coming back. This couldn't be how our story ended.

And then I heard a shuffle on the porch outside, and I sprang out of my chair and ran down the hall to meet him. The knob turned, the door creaked open, and I stepped forward with a cry—and my mother was standing in the entrance. She stared at me for a second, and I saw her take in my disappointment. She dropped her purse onto the ground and gathered me into her arms. "I'm sorry," she said quietly. "I know you were hoping that I was Jonah."

I held onto her for a minute, and she hugged me tightly, whispering sympathy card words about pain and time. I couldn't imagine how she knew what had just happened, but at that moment, it didn't matter to me. It was a relief not to have to explain anything to her. "I don't think he's coming back," I said as she led me into the living room. "I really think that this is it."

"I know," she replied. "I just had lunch with Rachel. She told me that he was coming over here today. So I took the afternoon off. I figured you might need me around after he spoke to you."

Her timid smile hurt me a little. I'd kept her at a distance these last few months. I'd been afraid of her advice, afraid of hearing what everyone had told me already—that I didn't need Jonah, that I'd be better off alone. But maybe my mom could have helped me if I'd let her. All this time, even when she'd seemed like she was against me, she had actually been waiting patiently for a chance to comfort me.

"He said that he needs time to heal without me," I told her. "That his guilt about hurting me was one of the things that kept him from getting well. I tried to argue with him at first, but in the end, I wasn't sure which one of us was right."

She shook her head and sighed. "It's not about being right. It's just what Jonah needs now. And what you need too."

"I don't need anything," I protested. "I just want to be with him."

"I know you do, baby. I wish there was something I could say that would make it easier for you."

There was nothing to say, of course. She could have told me that I was going to be all right, eventually, even if it took months to get over missing him. But there was no point in saying that; she knew that I didn't want to hear it anyway. It was hard to believe then, when I could still feel the pressure of his lips on mine, that one day all of this would be a distant memory—lazy afternoons curled up beside him, his arms around me, our almost perfect interrupted kiss by Quarry Lake. It seemed impossible that one day I'd think of Jonah as just a bittersweet daydream.

"Does he actually expect me to forget him?" I wondered out loud. "Is that really what he wants?"

"I don't think he expects you to forget," my mom answered. "I just think he wants you to give yourself a chance without him. To see what happens. You're starting a whole new chapter soon, and he wants you to be free to really experience it. And then—"

"And then, who knows?" I finished for her.

Who could tell what the next year would bring? Maybe a fresh start would be good for me. Maybe it would be good for both of us. He wasn't ready to come with me yet; we'd agreed on that, at least.

I need to be sure of myself before I can ask anyone to be with me.

"Who knows?" I repeated softly, smiling at my mother's worried, faintly hopeful face. "Maybe in the end, it'll be okay."

And in that moment, I honestly believed it would be. It was too soon to give up hope; I would hold on to that belief for as long as I needed it, the faith that eventually Jonah and I might find each other again. There would be new schools and teachers, new friends and doctors between us for a while. But someday, far off in the future, maybe we could put together a different ending. We'd both be a little older; he'd have learned to trust himself again, and I'd have learned to stand on my own without him. Then maybe we would run into each other one last time, somewhere when we least expected it, in a mall or at a park, some simple place like a corner bus stop. And maybe then Jonah and I would finally finish our first kiss.

ACKNOWLEDGMENTS

I owe so much to my agent, Rena Rossner. We met as university students at Johns Hopkins; I was a senior juggling a new baby and premed studies, she was a freshman majoring in poetry and nonfiction writing. Twenty years later, thousands of miles from my hometown, we found each other again, with the help of a college buddy. Thank you, Morry, for introducing me to the greatest agent and an amazing friend. Without you, Rena, I wouldn't be holding this novel in my hands.

I want to thank my editor, Annette Pollert-Morgan, for her dedication to April's story. Your insight and enthusiasm made the revision process enjoyable and exciting. Thank you to the publishing team at Sourcebooks Fire, especially Elizabeth Boyer and Sabrina Baskey, and Nicole Komasinski for the beautiful cover design.

My three daughters are a constant inspiration and joy. Aviva, thank you for the tireless advice on all things musical, and especially for composing and editing April's lyrics. Miriam, thank you for being my first faithful beta reader and expert consultant on all things teen. Talia, thank you for inspiring the character of Katie. By now you are much older, but Katie's fairy magic and innocent wisdom will always remind me of you.

Thank you to my husband, Eric, for urging me to write, and for waiting patiently while I messed around in my imaginary world. Thank you to my mother and father who encouraged me to daydream and to my sisters who smiled when I communicated with my fictional friends. (For the best "spacey Leah" imitation, please see my sister Tammy.)

And thanks to my readers for the kind support and the lovely emails asking when my next novel is coming out.

ABOUT THE AUTHOR

Leah Scheier is the author of *Secret Letters*, a historical mystery featuring the daughter of the Great Detective. After finishing up her adventures in Victorian England, Leah moved back to modern times, and currently writes about teens in her hometown of Baltimore. During the day she waves around a pink stethoscope and sheets of Smurf stickers; at night she bangs on her battered computer and drinks too much caffeine. You can visit her website at leahscheier.com or say hi to her on Twitter @leahscheier.

AUTHOR`S NOTE

April told her class, "There are no casseroles for schizophrenia." But there is support for families and patients dealing with mental illness. For information, discussion forums, and the latest news, visit www.schizophrenia.com. For advocacy opportunities and locations of schizophrenia anonymous group meetings in your state, visit www.saarda.org.